ZEINA

Nawal El Saadawi is an internationally renowned feminist writer and activist from Egypt. She is the founder and president of the Arab Women's Solidarity Association and co-founder of the Arab Association for Human Rights. Among her numerous roles in public office she has served as Egypt's National Director of Public Health and stood as a candidate in the 2004 Egyptian presidential elections. El Saadawi holds honorary doctorates from the universities of York, Illinois at Chicago, St Andrews and Tromso, and her numerous awards include the Council of Europe North-South Prize, the Women of the Year Award (UK), Sean MacBride Peace Prize (Ireland), and the National Order of Merit (France). She is the author of over fifty novels, short stories and non-fiction works centering on the status of Arab women, which have been translated into more than thirty languages.

'The leading spokeswoman on the status
of women in the Arab world'
The Guardian

'A formidable force in the international
world of literature'
New Humanist

'More than any other woman, El Saadawi
has come to embodythe trials of
Arab feminism'
San Francisco Chronicle

Nawal El Saadawi

Zeina

Translated from Arabic by
Amira Nowaira

SAQI

SAQI BOOKS
26 Westbourne Grove
London W2 5RH
www.saqibooks.com

First published in English in 2011 by Saqi Books
This edition published 2019
First published in Arabic in 2009 by Dar al Saqi

All references to the The Holy Qur'an are from
the translation by M. H Shakir.

Printed and bound by Clays Ltd, Elcograf S.p.A

A full CIP record for this book is available from the British Library.

ISBN 978 0 86356 355 3
eISBN 978 0 86356 449 9

To the girls and boys born on the streets without fathers or mothers, without school, church, or mosque, and without papers carrying the official stamp. To children who survive, become adults, and turn into stars that dispel the darkness, bring forth the light, and transform our world.

HER IMAGE was engraved in my memory, and her features were etched in my brain and in the grooves of my subconscious. Her picture reminded me of myself, looking in the mirror at the age of eight. I walked down the street carrying my school bag, my feet stomping on the ground with the sturdy square heels of my shiny black shoes. I walked steadily and proudly, for I was the daughter of the eminent Mr Zakariah al-Khartiti, whose photograph appeared inside a large square frame in the morning paper on top of his daily column called "Honoring Our Pledge".

Her features at the age of nine had an uncanny resemblance to mine, except for the eyes. Her eyes were large, and their pupils radiated a blue light that verged on nightly blackness. I was hopelessly drawn to them. They broke through the crust of my face and thrust deep into my hidden soul like knives.

She looked much older, as though she had been born a hundred years before me. In fact, she seemed almost ageless. She had no father or mother, and no home or even a bedroom. She had no honor and no virginity that she could possibly fear losing, and possessed nothing worth guarding in this life or in the hereafter.

She was just a girl, like myself and the other girls at school. She was tall and thin, and her body was as sturdy as if it had been made of more than flesh and blood alone. When she walked, her figure was like a spear cutting through the air. With her bare feet, she trod on the pebbles, the stones, and the thorns without feeling any pain, without a single drop of blood.

I wrote my full name on the blackboard. Mageeda Zakariah al-Khartiti. The teacher gazed at me, full of admiration. He told the other girls that I would become a famous writer like my father. The morning papers, the magazines and the silver screen would carry my picture. He told the girls that my grandfather, al-Khartiti Pasha, was a famous nationalist leader. The roots of my illustrious family went back to Saad Zaghloul and Orabi Pasha, and reached back to the great city of Mecca and the Prophet Muhammad.

Every girl had an identifiable father, whose name she wrote next to hers on the blackboard. Each girl was proud of her father, grandfather, uncle, or any well-known male relative.

Except for her. She stood proudly erect in front of the blackboard. The teacher ordered her to write her name. She held the piece of white chalk between her long, pointed fingers and turned toward the blackboard. We saw her straight back, the patch sewn with black thread on her uniform, and the flat sandals she wore. On the blackboard, she scrawled her name with large childish letters: Zeina.

The teacher hit her on the behind with his cane, over the patch sewn on the coarse material of her uniform.

"Write your full name like the other girls," he ordered her.

She held the piece of chalk and wrote: Zeina Bint Zeinat.

She turned to face us, her eyes large and their pupils glowing with a black flame.

"Write the names of your father and grandfather, asshole," he shouted at her.

A blue light shone from the two black orbs. She threw the piece of chalk on the ground, stamped on it with her feet, and walked with her head held high back to her seat in the back row of the classroom.

8

The teacher taught us the basics of language and religion. He said that the girl who carried her mother's name was a child of sin.

He taught us the singular and plural of words. The plural of "word" was "words", "greeting" was "greetings", and "sin" was "sins".

On the walls of the school bathroom, we wrote her name: Zeina Bint Zeinat. But she never read our graffiti, for she did not come to school every day as we did. She came only twice a week, on Tuesdays and Thursdays, to attend Miss Mariam's music lessons. Later, a decision was taken to expel her from school. I never saw her again, except by chance on the street.

Miss Mariam taught us how to play the piano. She held up Zeina Bint Zeinat's fingers, raising them high for all of us to see. She was immensely proud of Zeina's fingers. She said they were created for music and that Zeina's talent was unique. There was no one to match her in class. The tears glinted in the corners of Zeina's eyes, but not a single drop fell. Only the glimmer in the eyes intensified and seemed like tears. But we were proven wrong when we saw her pale, lank face beam with a smile. Light radiated from beneath her dark, chapped complexion as it turned soft and pink.

I peered at Zeina's long, powerful fingers as she played the piano, moving over the keys with the speed of lightning. Her voice rose high, singing the national anthem. My voice, in comparison, was raucous, grating, stifled, suppressed. Next to hers, my fingers seemed short, fat, and gelatinous, like those of my mother, Bodour Hanem, the wife of the eminent Zakariah al-Khartiti. She was also a great professor, occupying an equally eminent position.

During the night, Zeina's image came to me in my dreams. I saw her sitting on the little backless stool, playing the piano without looking at her fingers. Her eyes were riveted to her music book as she turned the pages, one after the other. She had learned the music by heart as though the tune were her own and the words of the song belonged to her. Her fingers moved as though of their own accord.

I didn't understand the meaning of the word "sin", which the teacher pronounced with the tip of his tongue as if he was spitting. For some reason I imagined that musical talent had something to do with it, for how could the child of sin be superior to all of us in music?

Deep down, I envied her. I saw her walk with her upright gait down the street, moving her arms and legs with perfect ease, and dancing with other street children in total freedom. She wasn't afraid of returning home because she had no home to speak of to return to, and she didn't have a mother or a father to scold or slap her on the face for arriving late.

In the dead of the night, before falling asleep, I heard my father and mother quarrelling. I was fifteen then, a student at the secondary school. I recalled the words of my teacher when he said that I would turn out to be a famous writer like my father, Zakariah al-Khartiti.

I saw my father's published framed photograph. He had a bright smile I never saw at home, for he was silent most of the time. After coming home from his work at the newspaper, he went straight to his study, a large room with walls lined with bookshelves. His desk, which was made of carved ebony, stood near the glass window overlooking the Nile. Its top surface was covered with newspapers and magazines. The photograph, hung on the wall inside a gold frame, showed him bowing in front of the president while receiving the Great Merit Award on Art and Literature Day.

My father warned me against going out on the street. He told me that girls from good families didn't play with street children, that there were numerous rapes reported in the papers every day, and that crimes increased with the rise of poverty and unemployment. The young men who graduated from universities could find no jobs and no means of earning a living, let alone finding a wife. Living in total deprivation, they assaulted the girls walking on the streets.

Yet something attracted me to the streets. Inside our home, the walls were painted bright pink, but the air was heavy as though it were filled with invisible smoke which the eye couldn't see and the nose couldn't sniff. I felt it seep softly through my body, saturated with hatred, silence, depression, and an imperceptible sadness.

The windows of our home were always secured with double glazing and curtains, to prevent the street dust from coming through, and to keep out the escalating noise from the loudspeakers hung on minarets, the drumbeats and cheery sounds of weddings, nightclubs and discos, and the sirens of police cars and fire engines.

As a child, I once asked my mother why she married my father. "It was love, Mageeda," she answered. I had no idea then what love between a man and a woman meant. I often scrutinized the faces of my father and mother to detect a look of love in their eyes. But I never succeeded in discovering the presence of a single loving glance in our home, until I grew up and understood things I hadn't known.

My father was mostly silent. If he spoke, it was about his daily column in the paper, the editor, the minister, or the president. He would talk about anti-war demonstrations abroad, the fall of the regime in Iraq, or the problems of poverty in Egypt, the Sudan, or Ethiopia.

Like my father, my mother was also a great personality, perhaps even greater. She was the head of the Literary Criticism Department at the university. She obtained her PhD with flying colors and received the Great Merit Award before my father did. A photograph was hung inside a gold frame in her study, showing her bowing courteously as she received the award from the president of the country on the Art and Literature Day.

When I was fifteen, I realized there was something perplexing about the relationship between my father and mother. At night, I heard them quarrel. Their voices began low, slow, and harsh. But the tone grew higher and was sometimes accompanied by the sound of things crashing on the floor, or the sound of kicking or slapping on the face. My heartbeats would quicken with the rising tempo of the fight. My body would shrink under the covers and I would hold my panting breath lest they should hear it and discover that I wasn't fast asleep.

I carried this heavy burden in my heart year in year out, for twenty-four long years. This was our skeleton in the cupboard that nobody in the whole world knew about. I dared not tell anyone, as though telling would be a sign of disloyalty to my parents.

In front of people, my parents were perfectly happy. They spoke to newspapers and the media about married bliss and about their perfect union based on love and high culture.

I concealed the truth inside me, and it grew and multiplied against my will like a malignant tumor, pressing on the cells of my soul and mind simultaneously. I went to a well-known psychiatrist who was one of my father's schoolmates. I imagined that he would cure me of my depression, but, like my parents, he had two faces that were at variance with one another. He wrote books on brain cells and on neurology and its connections with the mind and the psyche, but at the same time he suffered from depression himself. Sometimes he prescribed drugs for me, while other times he prescribed something different altogether.

I graduated from the Faculty of Arts with a general "Pass" grade because I wasn't fond of literature or writing, and preferred mathematics and figures. I was indifferent to what they called the literary imagination, perhaps out of resentment for my parents, or perhaps for the teacher who predicted that I would become a great writer. Since childhood, I have hated that teacher and wished to prove his predictions wrong. I loved music, dancing, and singing. But my short fingers, like my mother's, were incapable of producing any music. My body, like hers, was also short and stout. Although my father was just as short as my mother, he was thinner and often went to the club to play golf. I saw him walking in the distance, with his diminutive stature, his small triangular head, and his angular chin underneath his full lips, the upper fuller than the lower. Whenever he was engrossed in deep thinking or saw my mother walking past, he would pout his lips in dismay.

In my dream while I lay fast asleep, I saw the image of Zeina Bint Zeinat. This image had never left me since I was a child. I wished I could be in her place, even if they called me the child of sin.

They called her "duckling". She wore high pointed heels and walked through the university corridors to get to her office next to that of the dean. She was a little out of breath as she walked, carrying her short, stout body, swaying slightly over her pointed heels. Her neck was short and fleshy and it upheld a small, square-shaped head surrounded by short black hair. The hair was sparse and shot through with some white that quickly disappeared under the sophisticated hair dye applied with special care. She wore a blue skirt suit, with white collars that looked like the collars worn by little girls before they got married or lost their innocence.

She was in her middle years, just before the menopause. Although she was her husband's junior by nine years, he looked younger by a year or two. This was perhaps because he was a man. Women's lives, in contrast, are often consumed more quickly, for men do not bear children or give birth, and never carry the responsibility of home, children, or ill repute. No part of their bodies carries the stamp of virginity and they don't have to deal with the menopause or senility later in life. Nothing, in fact, detracts from a man's honor or worth except his empty pocket, not even consorting with prostitutes.

Ever since she was a child, Bodour had always been mindful of her reputation. She had the responsibility of upholding the family honor. Her father, Ahmed al-Damhiri, was a general in the armed forces. When the 1952 revolution took place, he was an officer in the army, and although he wasn't among the revolutionary commanders, he had a family connection with one of them. He was later appointed as the director or the secretary of the New Cultural Organization. As an adolescent, he read novels on platonic love. In his mirror, he saw himself as the hero of *Romeo and Juliet*. He wrote love poems to the neighbor's daughter. In his dreams, he imagined himself a well-known poet or novelist. Some of his dreams seeped through to his daughter, Bodour, when she was a child. She read the books she found in her father's library. Her heart beat hard as she read in bed before going to sleep, tempted by the image of Prince Charming, who made love to her until she orgasmed. Her body trembled under the covers with the sinful pleasure. She woke in the morning, her cheeks flushed and her eyes swollen. She took a bath with warm water and soap, cleansing her body of its sinfulness, but her heart remained heavy with vice.

Six months before the revolution, the fires blazed throughout Cairo. Bodour al-Damhiri had already obtained her BA in literature and criticism. Her body trembled with intense pleasure whenever she heard the acronym BA. A pleasure akin to sex overtook her wholly, body and soul together, in one wild moment of ecstasy. Her short stout figure swayed above her pointed heels. She wished she could jump in the air, dance, and sing. Had it not been for the earth's gravity which pulled her down forcefully, she would have flown. But her voice was muffled and she struggled to keep her feet on the ground. Her father saw the tears in her eyes and mistook them for tears of joy for having obtained her degree. Totally ignorant was he of his daughter.

Deep down, Bodour had an overwhelming sense of sadness, especially in moments of joy. It might have been her short, stout body, her narrow, lustreless eyes, her suppressed mind, despite her literature degree, or her soul imprisoned inside the confines of literature.

Her chains were never loosened except during sleep, when her mind, soul and body dozed off, when her parents and everyone else went to sleep, when God shut His wakeful eyes, and when everything and everyone dissolved into darkness. It was then that a secret cell buried in the deep recesses of her mind arose from sleep, yearning for love and for the sinful pleasures of the body.

Before the great fire of Cairo, huge demonstrations had broken out. Strong patriotic feelings passed from the father to his daughter, Bodour. He recited for her the clumsy, artless lines of poetry he used to read out to his colleagues in the army. He sang of martyrdom for the sake of the homeland, provided that neither he nor his own daughter were the martyrs in question. He was as certain of his love for his country as he was that Bodour was his own flesh and blood and not somebody else's. He was confident of the existence of God, the angels, the Devil, and the Day of Judgment.

Since childhood, Bodour had absorbed all his ideas. At school, she sang patriotic songs alongside her schoolmates. At the age of seven, she began to pray five times a day, fast during the month of Ramadan, and chase away the phantom of Prince Charming from her dreams and wakeful moments.

Bodour succeeded in controlling her subconscious mind, which sometimes awoke during her sleep. With the power of her will, she sent it back to dormancy. She surpassed her father in loving God and the homeland, and became a model student with limitless faith in God and the nation. Her convictions ran through her veins and dominated her being from head to toe.

But sleep often won the battle and pulled her down like the earth's gravity. Her whole body succumbed to the coma of sleep, except for the sole of her left foot, which was smooth and white like her mother's. It stayed awake and fully conscious, even while the whole universe slept. In her sleep, Bodour would feel something tickling the sole of that left foot. She would kick it with her right foot, thinking it was the Devil's finger defying God's will, prickling the sole of her foot while she lay unconscious and urging her to commit transgressions.

In the morning, she would wake up and regain control of her conscious mind. She would ask herself why the Devil always stood to the left of people during prayers, urging them to defy God. She would argue with herself that communists were heretics because they always stood on the left side.

A secret pleasure passed from the sole of her foot up through her leg, reaching her thigh, belly, and chest. Her breasts were two small buds that protruded slightly and were immensely painful when the Devil's fingers pressed on them.

During her childhood, she thought of the Devil as a pure spirit without a corporeal presence, the same as God. But after she had grown up, she realized that the Devil possessed a finger, perhaps even a body, along with all the other organs, including the sinful part which he used in challenging God's commandments.

At eleven, she saw the Devil's face for the first time. As a child, she was always afraid of opening her eyes while asleep. When she was a little older, she became more curious and wished to see the features of the Devil: his nose, head, forehead, ears, and mouth. She sometimes felt the Devil's breath on the nape of her neck while she lay prostrate. But she never had the courage to open her eyes to see him.

At the age of eleven, she was stunned to realize that Satan had a moustache and a beard just like elderly men. He looked very much like her paternal and maternal grandfathers, and the old man next door, and the elderly man in the movie "Love Among the Elders", which she had seen in the cinema the year before.

She fell into a state of drowsiness as Satan tickled the sole of her foot. She feigned sleep so as to allow him to continue his flirtatious act. But by keeping this event a closely guarded secret from her parents, she became Satan's partner in sin. She would bury her head in the pillow, stop her breath and pretend to be dead, thus encouraging him with her feigned death to continue, reaching the focal point buried in the folds of the flesh, deep inside the womb of existence. As she lay in a deathly state, a sensation of pleasure that was free from any sense of guilt would pervade her whole being.

One night, Satan didn't come as usual. He remained absent for a long time. Bodour imagined that God had punished him with death. But she heard from her mother and father that he had gone to London for a prostate operation. The word prostate sounded uncannily feminine to her ear, and she had no idea where this feminine-sounding part might be located on Satan's body. She wondered why God should insert a feminine organ in a male body. In any case, Satan never came back from London, having perhaps died there. So Bodour drove him out of her dreams, whether during her sleep or her wakeful moments. At eleven, Satan was gone completely from her memory. He survived, however, in the sole of her left foot, tickling her until she fell asleep and telling her the tale of Clever Hassan and the Ogress. In the morning, when she performed ablution and prayers, Satan no longer stood on her left side. She developed into a chaste young woman who was cleansed of all sinfulness.

Bodour had already obtained her BA degree by the time of the great demonstrations. She was a model young woman whose whole life was consumed by the love of God and the nation. Only her heart felt overburdened, for it still carried the imprint of Satan's finger on her body. What a burden it was for her heart to keep God, the nation, and Satan all in the same space!

On the day of the great demonstrations, she found herself squeezed between the bodies of thousands of women and men, young and old. The masses poured forth from the alleys and the boulevards, from Bulaq, Maadi, and Helwan. They were a mix of workers, government employees, farmers, and school and college students of both sexes. With bare, chapped feet, or wearing slippers, sandals, or shiny leather shoes of the best quality, the crowds marched at a single pace.

Bodour walked along with them, stomping on the ground with her leather shoes, energized by the strength of the thousands, or perhaps the millions, who screamed in one breath, "Down with the king, long live free Egypt". The word "free" stuck in her throat like a pang. Although she was moving with the crowds, she felt herself enchained. In vain, she moved her arms and legs to liberate herself from the chains. She cried out, but her stifled screams dissolved in the general noise. Her tears merged with her sweat, and her dress stuck to her body underneath her blue jumper. Next to her walked Nessim. His tall body was gracefully erect, and he trod strongly and steadily on the ground, his blue eyes looking straight ahead. Not once did he look in her direction, although she kept furtively glancing at him. His profile showed his proud pointed nose and his pursed lips. He wore a grey jumper that was tatty at the elbows and made of coarse wool. The white collar of his shirt was creased and his old shoes dusty. The soles of his shoes had a piece of iron like a horseshoe. In her dreams, his thick frizzy hair brushed her fine, smooth face.

Bodour was hugely attracted to men who were masculine and rough, men who wore their lives on their sleeves for the sake of God and the homeland. These men were very different from her cousin, Ahmed, who was scared of cockroaches, mice, and the frogs leaping in the garden, whose fingers were short and fat like hers and whose build was as short as that of his father and of his uncle, General Ahmed al-Damhiri. He inherited their square-shaped head and the square chin underneath thin lips, the upper thinner than the lower. He pursed his lips whenever he fell into deep thought, a gesture he inherited from his father and his grandfather, Sheikh al-Damhiri, who was the deputy or the vice deputy of the great al-Azhar Mosque.

Bodour met Nessim while in her freshman year at university. From the first moment their eyes met, something trembled deep inside her. He wasn't her colleague in the Faculty of Arts, but he came to university on the days demonstrations were to take place. When she saw him from afar, her heart fluttered wildly against her ribs. Her short figure swayed and swung over her pointed heels. She pressed with her hand on the strap of her bag slung over her shoulder, holding on to it to regain her balance. He often passed her without looking or smiling at her the way the other colleagues did. He sometimes nodded in greeting but continued on his way without looking back. She peered at his straight back, his taut muscles, and his lean body. She admired the way his arms moved in harmony with his legs and the way his tall, spear-like figure cut the air as he walked.

For two years she saw him in her dreams. In the third, when she saw him at one of the meetings, she initiated the conversation. The seat next to him was empty. She smiled at him and sat next to him saying, "Good morning, Nessim." They met again inside the university or in the Orman Garden nearby, and sat on a wooden bench talking and exchanging revolutionary books. Bodour was at heart drawn to the idea of rebellion. She revolted against everything in her life, including her own parents, uncles, and grandparents, perhaps God and Satan as well. Since the age of seven, her fear of God bordered on hatred, but she never had the courage to admit her fantasies or dreams to herself. Ever since her childhood, she had been committing many sinful acts in her sleep.

She studied Nessim's profile as she walked side by side with him during demonstrations. The harsh, acute contours of his face looked as though they were carved out of stone. His nose was so pointed that it seemed to cleave the air, and his tall thin body seemed to be made of something other than flesh. As he walked, he carried his body as though it were weightless.

From the moment the Devil's finger started stroking her, Bodour wished to be free of the weight of her body, the load of plump flesh that she carried each and every day on her arms, chest, belly, legs, and the soles of her feet. She dreamed of a force that would lift this weight off her shoulders. She dreamed of two strong arms reaching down from heaven to crush her body until the flesh dissolved and vanished completely.

After the demonstration ended and the crowds dispersed, she continued walking beside him, wishing she could walk on and on with him until the end of her days. She wanted him to carry her in his arms and march ahead until the moment of death. They walked silently, side by side, through one street after another, until Nessim stopped in front of the basement of a huge building. He stood there for a moment, silent and thoughtful. Then, raising his eyes to her face, he spoke, his voice slightly hoarse and the blue irises of his eyes sparkling with what seemed like choked tears. His words were fitful and broken as he said, "I don't know what I should say, Bodour! But I feel ... I feel you ... I have strong feelings like you ... but you come from a different class, Bodour ... I live here in this basement flat ..."

All this happened many years earlier when Bodour was twenty and was still dreaming of love and revolution. She later obtained her BA from the Faculty of Arts, although she disliked literature and criticism. She only loved and wanted Nessim, dreamed of him and couldn't imagine life without him. She would have preferred a life in the basement flat to her life with her parents in the large fancy villa in Garden City.

Bodour couldn't recall what she told him as they stood in front of his basement room. Did she tell him that she loved him? She might have said it, although her voice was completely silent. The words might have come out of her mouth like warm soundless vapor.

She stood there hesitantly, one hand resting on the cracked wooden door and the other holding on to the strap of the bag slung over her shoulder. She pulled at it as if to keep her balance and resist the earth's gravity which dragged her down.

He was equally hesitant and quiet. The air was also still. Nothing in fact moved except her breath, while he seemed to have stopped breathing completely and stood there transfixed, almost like a statue.

She couldn't remember how long it was they stood there, near the closed door. He didn't produce the key to open the door although it lay there in his pocket. His arm didn't move, and nor did any other part of his body.

What was he waiting for? Did he expect her to turn and head home? Or raise her hand and slap him on the face before going away? In her eyes, he saw an imprisoned tear that neither fell nor disappeared. Were these the suppressed tears of a young woman feeling mortified, having offered herself to a man only to be rejected by him? Was she a young woman reaching out for help from another human being, but receiving only rejection?

He finally took the key from his pocket and opened the door, and she followed him like a sleepwalker. She stood with her back against the wall, hoping its hardness might provide her with support and strength. But its coldness sent a shiver through her overheated body, and an unnameable fear overtook her whole being.

He held her little white hand in his large palm, and she fell into his arms like a ripe fruit dropping from the tree, or Newton's apple pulled down by the force of the earth's gravity.

Bodour was familiar to some extent with the physics of Newton and Einstein, was aware of the theories of relativity and Marxism, and was well read in literature and criticism. Nessim on his part was greatly interested in science and philosophy. He didn't believe in the story of Adam or the apple that Eve tempted him with, unlike Bodour who still held on to what her parents and teachers at school had always told her.

The mattress on the tiled floor was covered with books, papers and pamphlets. Lining the walls were wooden shelves holding books, magazines, and folders. In the corner stood a bamboo chair on which was spread a washed white shirt. A square iron latticed window opened out onto the asphalt street.

Then the room and all its contents disappeared. As he drew her close to his chest and kissed her hair and eyes, time and place vanished completely. The dream which had been visiting her every night came back to her, although the pleasure she experienced in the dream was much more intense than in reality, for the Nessim of her fantasies was more daring, and much more forceful in invading her body. In the dream, his body seemed harder than a spear that cut through the universe to reach the ultimate point. Reality always seemed pale in comparison with the stark beauty of fantasy.

When Bodour came to, she saw the tiled floor and the latticed window with the iron bars. She could hear the sound of Nessim's breath as he lay sound asleep beside her. It was almost like she could hear the sound of her father's snores, and the Adam's apple on his throat was like her father's too. Nessim's muscles were now sagging, passive and unchallenging, like her own muscles and her mother's.

She got dressed in a hurry, slung the bag strap over her shoulder and tiptoed toward the door. But she heard him calling her, "Bodour?"

She turned. He came toward her with his tall, upright gait, the firmness of his muscles restored and his eyes radiating a blue light bordering on blackness. She felt that she was looking into the depths of the sea or the skies at night.

It was not yet dawn. She wanted to throw herself on his chest and cry, for there had always been a vague sadness inside her since childhood. In his arms, grief vanished and was replaced by an overwhelming sense of joy that shook her whole being and removed all the deep-rooted pains and sorrows. But in her head there was a tiny cell, like a little needle, that reminded her of her father, her grandfather, the family honor, God, Satan, and the blazing fires awaiting her after death.

"Bodour?"

"Yes, Nessim."

"Shall we go to the Ma'zoun, the marriage registrar, to get married in the morning?"

"Oh my God!"

Her chest heaved with the quickening of her heartbeats. The word "Ma'zoun" had a terrifying, vague, and elusive ring that had absolutely no connection with love. Could she possibly get married in the morning?

Her father was lying in bed sipping his tea, reading the papers, yawning and stretching his limbs, fully at ease and confident that his innocent, virgin daughter was sleeping in her bed or taking a bath in preparation for going to university.

"Is the Ma'zoun necessary?"

"Of course, Bodour. No marriage is valid without the Ma'zoun ... and then ..."

He didn't finish the sentence. He closed his lips and gave her a protectively paternal look, although she was barely two years his junior. But he felt a hundred years older, for she had never known poverty or hunger and never slept on the pavement. She hadn't worked as a child apprentice at a mechanic's shop or gotten kicked by the master mechanic in the stomach. She had never been beaten up at a police station, and nor had she seen her mother die of grief or bleed with every breath she took, or witnessed her father drown in prison.

"I'm older than you, Bodour, and I know how hard life can be. You're a nice girl and I fear for you if ..."

He stopped at "if" because he wanted to say, "If you became pregnant outside marriage, your father, General Ahmed al-Damhiri, might kill you!" He gave her a sunny smile. The light in his eyes intensified, and he enveloped her in his arms, whispering, "If we could just have a child who is as beautiful as you are!"

She closed her eyes with her head resting on his chest and fell to dreaming. Could she possibly have a boy or a girl who looked like Nessim? A child with the same tall, graceful figure, the sparkling eyes, the lively, rebellious spirit, the defiance and the hardness?

Before the light of dawn appeared, she was shaken out of her reveries by the sounds of police car sirens. Armored vehicles roamed the streets, rifle butts knocked on doors, torch lights fell on the pale, emaciated faces of poor workers and college students who were being pursued by the security police in factories, schools, or universities, because their photographs appeared on the records of the Ministry of the Interior.

Bodour didn't know how she found herself lying in the safety of her own bed. She closed her eyes under the covers as the warmth slowly engulfed her. The latest events infiltrated her dream as she fell asleep. In the dream, she walked with the demonstrators. Beside her were the two gleaming eyes radiating light like two stars in the darkness of the night. Under the covers, her hands felt her body. Within the folds of the flesh, the dream became a palpable reality, and the fantasy turned into a concrete fact she could touch with her own hands. His voice reached her ears like light waves, "If it's a boy, we'll call him Zein, after my father." Bodour whispered, "And if it's a girl, we'll call her Zeina, after my grandmother."

In the dream, she saw her grandmother's ghost coming into her room. She was a graceful woman with sparkling eyes. Bodour called her Nana Zizi. When she was eight years old, her grandmother, who was still alive then, sat next to her bed and told her bedtime stories. She also told her the sad story of her life, and how she had wished to become a famous singer, for she loved singing, dancing and writing poetry. But her father took her out of school at the age of fourteen. They dressed her in a white wedding gown, and after the drumbeats and the festivities, she found herself alone, locked in a bedroom with a strange, rough-looking man who was short and hunch-backed. He wore a thick, black moustache on his upper lip.

While Bodour lay warmly in her bed dreaming of her grandmother, an armored vehicle stopped in front of the splintered wooden door of the basement of the tall building. Five police officers carrying rifles surrounded Nessim and flashed a bright light in his face. The pupils of his eyes blazed with bluish black anger. His tall, lean body seemed as hard as a spear, and his head was held high above his firm, sturdy neck. One of the police officers hit him on the head with the butt of his rifle, while another slapped him on the cheek. He stood upright, nevertheless. Not a single muscle in his face moved, and he didn't bat an eyelid.

One of the police officers grew so angry that he spat in his face and punched him below the ribs, at that point of both pleasure and pain, the source of life and love.

When they dragged him to the armored vehicle outside, his nose and mouth were bleeding, dripping over his white vest which revealed the black hairs covering his chest. The blood streamed to his white Egyptian cotton pants. The smell of cotton merged in his nostrils with the smell of blood, dust and the fertile black soil, where green shrubs grew, carrying spots of white buds. He was eight years old when he sang with the other village children, running all over the green expanse dotted with white buds, "You've come to bring us light, oh Nile cotton, how lovely you are! Come on, girls of the Nile, collect the matchless cotton, God's gift!"

Inside the police vehicle, he sat handcuffed. He saw the image of his grandmother, Zakia, who was tall and proud. Her large cracked hands held an axe and her dark wide eyes could hold the whole universe. One day, she gripped the axe and brought it down on the head of the village mayor. She then lay on the ground and slipped into eternal peace.

The connection between Mageeda, the writer, and Zeina Bint Zeinat had never been severed. Since childhood, something attracted them to each other, despite the vast gulf separating them. With the help of her parents, Mageeda became a columnist at the *Renaissance* magazine. Deep in her heart, however, she hated writing, which she had inherited from her parents, as much as she hated her short body and the large villa in Garden City. The name of her father and grandfather was engraved on a shining brass plate on the external door of the villa: Al-Khartiti Villa. The name al-Khartiti seemed to her like a deformed limb affixed to her name and her body.

Surrounding the huge redbrick house was a large garden, where trees, roses and other flowers grew. An iron fence encircled the garden in which jasmine and bougainvillea trees grew, with their yellow, white, and crimson flowers.

From the outside, the place looked beautifully cheerful. But inside, there was ugliness in every corner, lurking underneath the colorfully embroidered silk tablecloths.

Mageeda went to school every day in a limousine driven by a dark chauffeur. Before she went to bed, a nanny took her to the bathroom and washed her with warm water and scented soap. The nanny would dry her with the large white towel and carry her to her bed, telling her the story of Cinderella and the prince until she fell asleep.

In her dreams, Mageeda saw herself flying like a sparrow in the sky. Her thickset body no longer weighed her down, and her arms moved powerfully and lightly through the air. Her large wings flapped and fluttered, and when the sunrays or the moonbeams fell on them, they assumed an angelic white color. Her fingers were no longer short and chubby, but became long and thin, like Zeina's. They moved more quickly over the piano keys than the speed of light. Miss Mariam held her hand high for all the girls to see. She spoke with a voice that was so loud that it reached everyone: her parents, her uncles, her grandfather, the neighbors in Garden City, the porters sitting in front of buildings, the barber in the square, the chauffeur who drove the car, and her nanny who told her the story of Cinderella before she fell asleep. She told them, "Mageeda's fingers have been created for music. Her talent is unparalleled. There isn't anyone like her in the class."

In the dream, Miss Mariam's voice sounded like a harmonious tune, tickling her ears and sending a titillating sensation from her neck down to her chest. The wave moved to the left breast, just over the heart, and crept stealthily to the belly, then quivered a little when it got to the smooth hairless pubic area. From there it slipped down toward the left thigh and through to the left leg, and thence to the sole of her left foot. It titillated her as it used to do in the past, giving her the well-known but fresh sensation of pleasure together with an overwhelming feeling of guilt.

Mageeda never knew how music, in her childish dreams, turned into a sinful pleasure, a pleasure that was akin to, though still different from, Satan's finger, for although music descended from her ears to the sole of her foot, Satan's finger went up from the foot until it reached the focal point of the universe.

Before she slept, Mageeda told her nanny about Miss Mariam and how she held Zeina's fingers up high for all the girls to see, and how her voice rose high saying: "Zeina's fingers have been created for music. She's a talented girl like no one else."

Mageeda would bury her head in her nanny's bosom, pushing her nose between her breasts, trying to inhale some motherly love.

Nanny would stroke her head and whisper in her ear, "Sleep, Mageeda, God has been kind to you and has given you plenty. Your father is a celebrity and your mother, may God protect her, is a great professor at the university. But Zeina, poor heart, has no father or mother ..."

Nanny's voice would stop, as though choked. She would raise her large dark hand to wipe the tears with the wide sleeves of her long, loose gown.

"Are you crying, Nanny?"

"Not at all, my child."

"Do you have a father and mother yourself, Nanny?"

"Of course, my child, everybody does."

"Except for Zeina Bint Zeinat, Nanny?"

"She had a father, child. He was a real man, a proper man ..."

"But where did he go, Nanny?"

"He went to heaven, child."

"You mean he died?"

"Yes, Mageeda, my child."

"Why did God take him?"

"God always takes the best people."

"But why didn't God take my father and mother then?"

"Stop talking, Mageeda. Not so loud. Sleep my child, may God protect your parents from evils and mishaps."

At eight, Mageeda couldn't understand what her nanny told her, for if God took the best people to heaven, why didn't He take her distinguished father, Zakariah al-Khartiti, and her great mother, Professor Bodour al-Damhiri? And why did Nanny feel disturbed, and why did she pray to God to protect her parents from evils and mishaps?

If death was an evil sent from God, why should the best people die and go to God up in heaven while the evil ones stayed alive?

On the street, she would glimpse Zeina Bint Zeinat playing with other children. They would encircle her, dancing, playing, and singing the folk songs chanted by peasants: "You've come to bring us light, oh Nile cotton, how lovely you are!" "The Sun is up, lovely and bright! Let's go milk the cow!"

She didn't enjoy being driven by the chauffeur, because he took her straight home from school without stopping, not even for a little while that she might see the children dancing and singing on the streets. He told her that they were little fiends, the Devil's children. She didn't know the meaning of the word "fiends" so the chauffeur told her it meant little Devils.

Mageeda couldn't imagine the Devil having children, for she thought of him as childless, like God.

"They're illegitimate bastards! They're little thieves, and you shouldn't be talking to them, miss."

"But Zeina Bint Zeinat was with me at school and she was talented. Miss Mariam said she was the best girl at school ..."

The chauffeur never listened to what Mageeda said. His

sunken eyes would gaze straight ahead of him, fixed on the road. With his dark complexion, he looked like the Garden City porters, although he didn't wear their white galabeyas. Instead, he wore a khaki suit similar to the outfits worn by soldiers. On his head was a khaki cap called a caskette and made of thick material. His large dark fingers firmly holding the wheel looked like Nanny's fingers when she rubbed her head with warm water and soap in the bathroom. They were markedly different from her mother's chubby white fingers.

Mageeda hid her fingers under the covers. She closed her eyes to sleep, but the light of the bedside lamp revealed to her the large room. She could see the delicate pink drawings on the walls, the pink cupboard in the corner, her little desk with her books and notebooks, the color pencils, the big copybook with the pink cover in which she recorded her dreams, and the small table covered with a blue tablecloth on which jasmine flowers were embroidered.

Her nanny sat in her loose dark gown on the colorful Persian rug next to her bed and told her bedtime stories. She had a long muscular neck holding a head wrapped in a white shawl. Her face was pale and lank, and the black pupils of her eyes looked tiny inside the large, reddish eyeballs.

By the time Mageeda turned twenty-five, she was a columnist at the *Renaissance* magazine, which was published every Thursday. Her father proposed "Honoring Our Word" as the title of her column, in keeping with his own column called "Honoring Our Pledge" in the daily newspaper. He was always careful to articulate every letter of the word "pledge", as though fearful that one of the letters might get lost, or the whole word might slip away or vanish into thin air.

Since the age of eight, Mageeda hated writing, for, like her short, stout body, it was imposed on her. She inherited writing from her parents like the five prayers every day, the fasting of the month of Ramadan, and the shape of her fingers and toes. There was no way she could get rid of it.

On top of her desk lay a big fat copybook full of blank pages. It was as fat and white as her own body, and its blank pages eyed her with derision. The scorn continued throughout her childhood, her adolescence and her adulthood. A voice hissed in her ears, speaking in the tones of Satan, or perhaps of God, telling her, "You have no talent, Mageeda. I gave all the talent to Zeina Bint Zeinat because I took away her father and mother."

In his column, her father wrote that God was just and that the head of the state in Egypt wielded his power fairly. If God deprived a child of family or wealth, He might bless him with intelligence, music, or the love of God and the homeland. A poor person might still be morally rich.

Her mother, Bodour, wrote on literary criticism. She gave lectures at the university on literature, poetry, novels, the theater and the cinema. People sent her letters and parcels containing books, magazines, and tapes of music and film. She received taped literary discussions on radio and television every day by mail. Writers, both women and men, sent her gifts in order to curry favor with her, for a single article written in the literary criticism magazine could bring a writer out of the darkness and into the light, and might move an obscure writer from oblivion to the limelight of literary or artistic stardom.

Although Bodour didn't enjoy the same political or journalistic status as her husband, her own literary and artistic position was supreme. She received invitations to attend meetings with the president, ministers, and ambassadors, as well as literary and artistic conferences abroad.

Deep down, Bodour al-Damhiri didn't want to be a literary critic, for she considered the work of a literary critic to be inferior to that of a novelist, poet, playwright, or scriptwriter. She would whisper in the ears of her friend and mate, Safaa al-Dhabi, saying, "Literary criticism is parasitic on real literature and art, like tapeworms living off the human body. Literary critics like us are failed creative writers. We make up for our failure by criticizing the works of others. We are ordinary, mediocre people who have no talent, but we try to reach the limelight by highlighting other people's creative work. We are like shoe polishers, nothing more, Safi!"

She called her friend, Safaa, Safi.

"I tell you Safi, in all honesty, although I never admit it to anyone, that I don't feel any pride or pleasure when I write a critique. In fact, I feel rather humiliated, because I feel I'm shining the shoes of a person who is more talented than myself."

Inside the drawers of her desk, Bodour concealed a large fat folder filled with handwritten papers. On its yellow cover was written *The Stolen Novel*. She had begun writing this novel many years earlier, specifically on a night that passed like a terrifying nightmare or an ephemeral dream of paradise when she had eaten the forbidden fruit.

In her novel, she gave the heroine the name of Badreya instead of Bodour, and called the hero Naim instead of Nessim.

In the dead of night, after both her daughter, Mageeda, and her husband, Zakariah al-Khartiti, had gone to bed, after the house had become empty of servants and the nanny had taken her black leather bag and left, after the loudspeaker of the adjacent mosque, the drumbeats and the cymbals of the neighboring nightclub overlooking the Nile had all become silent, after the police cars, the sirens, and the hooting had stopped, after the screams of the patients at the old al-Qasr al-Ainy Hospital had subsided, after the funerals coming out of the huge wrought-iron front door with bereaved and widowed women wailing and following the procession had ceased, after the universe had gone to sleep and Satan had forgotten his prey, and after God, out of His infinite mercy, had closed His watchful eyes, Bodour would get out of her wide bed where the body of her husband lay and tiptoe barefoot to her study. She switched on the small lamp, extended her short fat hand to the locked drawer and opened it with a key concealed in her clothes. With her white fingers, she brought out the small folder, and her throat felt dry as she looked at the hundreds of pages before her, some of which were filled with words and others still blank. Night in night out, day in day out, one month following another, and one year after the other, there were hundreds, even thousands of pages, which she wrote and rewrote countless times with her own hand and with pain, sweat, and tears. As she read, she felt her throat parched and the blood escaping from her face to her feet. She would pout her full lips as she often did when she read a mediocre novel written by a writer who lacked experience or talent.

Her daughter, Mageeda, was eight years of age then. She lay in bed in her bedroom with her eyes closed except for a thin slit between the eyelids. A faint light filtered through the chink underneath the door. Waves of light moved in the stillness of the dark night, coming from her mother's distant room or perhaps from her father's room on the other side of the hall. The light waves were as imperceptible as the movement of the air or as faint as the gritting sound of a pen on paper. Papers were torn and thrown into the bin, hot air rose from the chest along with the breath, and a deep sigh escaped with the act of inhaling and exhaling.

The light seemed to disappear and give way to silence. But other noises started coming through the wall. Those were the voices of her parents talking loudly in bed, her father's voice rough, hoarse, husky, and her mother's as sharp as the sound of a jingling bell. They fought until they both fell asleep.

In the morning she imagined that that they would break up, that her mother would prepare her bag and leave, or that her father might take his bag and go. But they both stayed. And they didn't pack any bags. Actions only happened in dreams.

At the breakfast table, they would sit together as usual, sipping their tea and coffee, reading the papers, exchanging a few words about events in Egypt or around the world, or reading in complete silence. Mageeda heard nothing but the sound of sipping: her father produced a sharp loud noise as he drank his tea, while her mother sipped hers, producing a femininely delicate sound that was hardly audible.

Badreya was only one of the characters in *The Stolen Novel*, but she lived in Bodour al-Damhiri's world as though she were a woman of flesh and blood. Bodour felt her lying next to her in bed or sitting with her in her study, gazing at her in silence as she read or wrote. They often exchanged words, fought together, and made up exactly as Bodour and her husband, Zakariah al-Khartiti, would. Badreya sometimes crossed out a few sentences she didn't like from the novel, at times even deleting or adding whole chapters. Sometimes she condemned herself to death by firing squad or under the wheels of a train.

Being a specialist in the field of literary criticism, Bodour knew that Badreya, like any character in a novel, was capable of rebelling against the writer, of severing her ties with her creator and of revolting against, and triumphing over, her.

Badreya's steps were more assured and steadier than Bodour's, for she never wore high heels. She was taller and more graceful, more daring in breaking rules and more willing to face death without batting an eyelid.

On that particular day, Badreya made up her mind to get rid of the heavy weight inside her and to become liberated from the painful memories residing within the cells of her brain. She got dressed and went out, choosing a loose, grey gown that hid the feminine curves of her body. It had pleats in the chest, hiding the shape of her breasts and her belly. On her shoulders she slung the strap of her leather bag. In the bag there was an envelope containing a packet of pound notes that she had saved from her daily pocket money or filched from the pockets of her parents.

She was overcome by a vague kind of pleasure whenever she stole a few pounds from her father and mother. They never discovered the theft, especially her father, whose wallet was always bulging with banknotes. He used to conceal his wallet from prying eyes by putting it in the pockets of his expensive suits hanging inside the bedroom cupboard. He had a huge number of suits made of expensive English wool for the winter and of silk for the summer. All his suits had internal and external pockets.

Before placing his wallet in one of the pockets, he would turn furtively around, afraid of being noticed by his wife, the servants, or the nanny, who sometimes cleaned the room, put the freshly ironed clothes inside the drawers, or offered him a cup of coffee. He never noticed the eyes of his daughter, Badreya, perhaps because she always observed him through a chink in the door standing ajar, or perhaps because she wasn't the daughter of his own loins, but a character in a novel that his wife wrote and lost. Because his daughter was honest and chaste, like all the virgins her age, she couldn't possibly steal from her father.

Badreya walked steadily along the asphalt street, stomping on the ground with the square heels of her shoes. On the wall of the building, a clock revealed the time to be 2:45. Her appointment was at 3 o'clock exactly. Another fifteen minutes and she would be transported into a completely different world. A cold shiver ran down her spine despite the end of winter and the heat from the sun. An old man walked in front of her, panting and wiping the sweat away with a large, white handkerchief. He seemed to be murmuring verses from the Qur'an or perhaps talking to himself. A woman in a black scarf dragged a little girl producing muffled sobs behind her.

She stopped in front of the tall building to catch her breath, and raised her eyes to the sign posted on the ninth floor. She brought out a tissue from her handbag and wiped her face and eyes. A hefty, dark-skinned porter led her to the lift, giving her an artificial smile. She handed him a pound, and a wide grin revealed his large white teeth for a second and then vanished.

The apartment door stood open, like the doors of clinics, undertakers' offices, barbers' and butchers' shops, brokers, lawyers, foreign agents, private businesses, political party offices, businessmen, charity organizations dubbed non-governmental organizations, human rights' and women's rights associations, all inviting and enticing their victims to enter.

On the door hung a shining brass plate carrying the doctor's name and title, and opening times and prices. At the entrance stood a small reception office, behind which a man in a white coat sat. He noted down her name in a huge ledger, took a pile of pound notes from her, and gave her a number. She stared at him for a long time as she stood there, then sat in the waiting room, perusing the faces present. They were all women with pale, distraught faces, sitting silently, dejectedly, weighed down by worries and fears of the unknown. One of them had a white shawl wrapped around her head and sat murmuring sacred verses. A young woman with long black hair and wearing a miniskirt glanced at her quickly and turned away. Her face was heavily made up and her thick eyelashes blinked incessantly.

The hour struck four. The male nurse led her toward a small door at the end of a long corridor. She felt that death lurked there, concealing itself behind the white coat.

Since childhood, Badreya hated doctors, although she didn't cry as Bodour did when the doctor gave her an injection. She would only grit her teeth and swallow her pain.

She climbed onto the long shiny metal table, which stood next to a smaller table covered with a large number of sharp tools, such as scalpels, knives, needles, and steel rods. A huge pail full of congealed blood and little pieces of red meat stood on the tiled floor.

Before he could tie her open legs to the two iron poles, she jumped up, shook off the shivering and trembling, got dressed quickly, and ran out into the street. She didn't take back the money she had paid to the male nurse and she never looked behind her ...

Bodour came to the end of the first chapter of her novel.

Bodour asked herself, "Did Badreya have more courage and motherly tenderness than myself?"

At night, Bodour cried for her stolen novel. She lost it in her sleep, together with the daughter she had carried in her womb. She lost her in a time and a place that she wasn't fully conscious of. She lost her in the dream.

In her sleep, she roamed the streets, alleys, and pavements, stopping at church and mosque doors, looking for her. Sometimes she tripped over a bundle covered with a soft pink woollen blanket. She would recognize the color and the smell, and would see the small, white fingers like hers, and the little face looking as bright and soft as a petal. Her complexion was similar to her own. The blood stains had dried on the face but the tears hadn't, and the closed eyelids were wet with drops of rain.

If the baby hadn't opened her eyelids at that moment, nothing might have happened. Bodour might not have known that she was her child. And neither would she have known whether she had been pregnant with her in her wakefulness or sleep. She wouldn't have got up from her warm bed in the middle of the night and roamed the streets searching for her, tearing her hair, striking her face, or stabbing herself with a knife in the chest.

But the baby's closed, swollen eyelids suddenly opened, realizing perhaps that her mother was going to leave her for good. The mother might have also realized at this point in time that she was leaving her child forever, that she would be tearing out her own liver, wrapping it, dripping with blood, in a soft, woollen blanket to protect it from the cold and the dust and the stones of the street. She rubbed her palms clean on the ground and tore out her liver from her chest, depositing it on the street and following the dark, endlessly long road.

A mysterious force often woke Bodour in the middle of the night. She would feel a sharp pointed finger stabbing her shoulder blade, a foot kicking her in the belly, a razor blade moving over her wrist, or a fist rising high and falling to give her a powerful slap. She would get up from her sleep, her eyes wide open, imagining it was her husband, Zakariah al-Khartiti, who was slapping her, or Badreya rising from the heap of pages near the bed to punch her hard. Bodour wanted to raise her hand to deal an equally powerful blow, but her white hand was too heavy to lift. Her short, fat arms were glued to her sides, her heart incarcerated within the cage of her ribs, and her liver removed through the long gash on her right side. Since that long, deep cut had been made in her body, Bodour had lost the ability to resist. She had been more courageous as a child. At school, if one of her mates hit her, she returned the punch just as powerfully, if not more so. She walked among the girls with her head held high, and joined demonstrations, shouting against the government and occupation. Next to her walked Nessim, with his erect, graceful body and his large eyes reflecting the sunlight. His eyes changed color with the change of the light, turning dark blue during the night and light blue during the day.

In the dream, Badreya said to Bodour, "You will have a child with the same eyes. You will look into these eyes and possess the universe."

If Bodour hadn't opened her eyes and seen the dark blue pupils, she might have lived happily like other women. She might have built a happy home with Zakariah al-Khartiti. She might have become satisfied with her distinguished status at the university, her great critical works, her husband's daily column in the *Sphinx* newspaper, and her daughter, Mageeda, who wrote for the *Renaissance* magazine. She might have revelled in the invitation cards coming to her through the mail, and the books and works sent to her by upcoming writers, both men and women, pleading for a word, a reference, a gesture.

Bodour concealed the depths of her sorrows in the layers of her chubby face. Her secret was buried deep inside her. She feigned a bright smile, and every now and then gave a resounding laugh at nothing in particular. Her laugh came long and sharp, almost like a suppressed sob.

Cattle experts have noted that if the mother cow gets the chance to look into the eyes of her newborn calf before it is taken away, she will suffer from chronic depression. They therefore recommend placing thick blindfolds on her eyes to stop her seeing her calf after she has given birth to it, to prevent her from meeting its eyes even once. This single look stays with the mother until the moment she dies. If this happened to cows, couldn't it happen to a renowned critic like Bodour? Or to the heroine of a literary novel like Badreya?

At night, Badreya touched her belly under the covers. She could feel the little heartbeats, the kicks of the tiny feet against the walls of her womb. She pressed with her hands to stop the sound and wrapped her fingers around the little neck to strangle it, wishing it were dead but at the same time hoping it might live to see the light of day. She was torn between two wills: God's and Satan's. God wished it dead because it was a bastard child, while Satan wanted it as lively and radiant as a star in the firmament.

Bodour walked in the dark alleyways, dragged by Badreya like a cow being driven by a farmer. Her eyes didn't see the road ahead of her, because she was either blindfolded or fast asleep. Or because she had left her destiny in the hands of Badreya, who urged her to rebel. Since childhood, she pushed her to go out on the streets, to play truant from school, to join demonstrations and to shout against God and the nation, against her father, mother and grandfather, against teachers, both male and female. It was Badreya who drove her to enter the basement room, to fall in love with Nessim. It was Badreya who wanted to have his child, a child that would inherit his gracefulness and his proud walk, a child that would become heir to his unwavering eyes, which turned dark blue at night and light blue in the daylight. She imagined him a different man called Naim, who was her first love before she got her period. It was Badreya who opened her eyelids to see the eyes before they disappeared into the darkness. She saw them for a split second, but she never stopped looking for them afterwards. After the whole universe had gone to sleep, she got dressed and went out, walking along the streets, looking into the eyes of little children, trying to find those pupils. A girl might be sleeping soundly on the pavement, her eyes closed, her little feet charred, her dark complexion burnt by the heat of the sun and dotted with white and yellow spots as well as scars and bruises. Her lips would be open a little, like a baby's mouth during sleep, smiling to her mother or her unknown father in the dream. She would open her eyes to find Badreya sitting next to her, handing her a loaf of bread fresh from the oven or a piece of cake before she got up and left. But these were not the same pupils, not the same eyes, and this was not the same glance engraved in the cells and grooves of the brain. It was not Zeina, daughter of Naim.

The girl didn't reach out to touch her, for she realized that she wasn't her mother. She was an unknown woman, a woman perhaps belonging to a charity organization that helped street children or looked after people suffering from tuberculosis, leprosy, or AIDS. She might have been one of the women on the Childhood and Motherhood Council, or an employee at one of the political parties or at a human rights organization.

The girl was too proud to extend her hand. She didn't want the charity or pity of anyone, and didn't crave a piece of bread or cake. What she wanted was to go to school and university like the other girls from good families. She wanted to have dignity, pride, a birth certificate, BA and PhD degrees.

Badreya came back home totally exhausted, her head bent, looking almost like Bodour after marriage. Zakariah al-Khartiti was not her Prince Charming. He asked her father for her hand in marriage. This was the period after the revolution and the overthrow of the king. In the seats of power sat little kings wearing military uniforms, like her father, Captain al-Damhiri. His sister was married to the cousin of one of the revolutionary leaders. Al-Damhiri removed the military uniform and dressed in an elegant civilian suit. He was given a lavish office in the Foundation or Committee of Culture, Literature, Art, and the Press. Like other military personalities, he accumulated a number of posts and sat on several higher committees. One person might supervise a number of authorities, councils and committees. The name of any committee was always appended by the words "Permanent Higher". Each one of the military personalities held a yellow rosary in his hand and went to Friday prayers to sit behind the first or second row. He imagined God to be always on his side in every step he took and that his "permanent higher" committee was inspired by God and was as permanent and everlasting as God Himself.

Zakariah al-Khartiti was a young upcoming journalist. He

had written a few articles in praise of the king, which he deleted from his memory after the revolution and started writing about the glory of the new regime. He later switched to writing about Arab Islamic socialism, which he contended was a very different kettle of fish from the socialism of Karl Marx, the "Jewish atheist".

He pressed with his pen on the words "Jewish atheist", because one of these two epithets was enough to ruin the reputation of any human being, living or dead.

In the morning, while the young Zakariah al-Khartiti was sipping his coffee, he looked at the photographs published on the first page of the newspaper. His dreams didn't go so far as to imagine himself among the great writers on the front page. He turned the pages with his lean fingers, his narrow, sunken eyes, and looked at the faces on the second page. He saw the face of the great writer, al-Damhiri, who had turned from a military man to a great thinker, with opinions on literature, art, and culture. His photographs appeared inside a square frame on top of an item of news concerning him, an article he wrote or a clumsy poem he composed on political or amorous themes.

One day, as he was reading the paper, he saw the picture of a girl with a chubby moon face and smooth, long hair falling about her shoulders. She had the sleepy eyes of a female dreaming of love. Her plump, white hands rested on the desk, and between her fingers was a small pencil resembling an eyebrow pencil. The caption underneath the picture read: "Young Critic, Bodour al-Damhiri".

The wound deep inside her womb had healed and she had banished his image from her memory: the face, the tall gait, the eyes, and the room with the tiled floor. According to the medical report, he had died of natural causes in prison. But he wasn't the only one who died as a result of being beaten up in prison, shot by a stray bullet during demonstrations, or chased by a police squadron while trying to run away in the middle of the night.

How many were they? How many trampled on the picture of the king, railed against British imperialism, raised their voices for a free, dignified Egypt and paved the way for the revolution? But as soon as the men in military uniforms were seated at the helm, they rewrote history. They became the heroes, while all the past martyrs were sent into oblivion, their blood congealing on the streets and in jails and detention camps, completely lost to the collective memory of the nation and banished from the textbooks of the national curriculum.

Bodour's wedding was a lavish affair, attended by the great dignitaries of the state and the distinguished names in the realm of literature, art, and the media. Zakariah al-Khartiti walked pompously in his groom's suit, while Bodour wore a wedding dress made of white lace, her large bosom squeezed into a silk brassiere. Her chest heaved and fell with the strong, escalating beats of the tamborines. She panted as she sat staring at the profile of her bridegroom, with his triangular head, his eyes sunken underneath his large forehead, and his large aquiline nose. His black hair was thinning in the middle and his small feet were concealed by a pair of shiny pointed black shoes. His triangular chin looked almost like an acute angle.

Her friend, Safaa al-Dhabi, held her little white hands in hers. Her fingers trembled and her palm was moist with sweat.

"Courage, Bodour!"

"May God help me, Safi!"

"Yes, God is great!"

The drumbeats sounded and the music played. A wedding song celebrating the bride and groom was sung. "Oh beautiful bride, fall in the arms of your lovely groom ..."

The words "fall in" sounded in Bodour's ears as "fallen". She let out a sigh, a smile, and a little short nervous laugh, which sounded like a stifled sob. Safi gave her a side glance, suppressing her laughter.

In the bedroom, before he took off her wedding gown, he whispered in her ear the words "I love you". But she knew he was lying. She began to breathe more calmly and the beats within her chest slowed as Badreya's voice came to her from below the pillow while she lay underneath him. A lie for a lie, and an eye for an eye, Bodour, as God has said.

Bodour believed in the Holy Books, while Badreya, like her friend Naim, believed that the future of humanity lay in science and art, that the universe has been evolving over millions of years, and that Adam wasn't created out of clay.

Miss Mariam carried on looking for Zeina Bint Zeinat after she stopped coming to school. The image of her walking tall among the girls and sitting on the backless piano stool, her back straight and her thin, long fingers moving with the speed of light over the keys, was engraved in her memory. Her eyes were two blue volcanic stones, two dark blue flames that changed with the movement of the earth around the sun and with her mounting anger at one of the girls. When Miss Mariam smiled at her, she had a bright childish smile like the sunlight in the morning dispelling the night's darkness. Miss Mariam lived in a two-bedroom apartment on a narrow street off Tahrir Road. Her Muslim mother, Fatima, had married the Christian Mikhail without an official marriage contract. Both Shari'a and civil law forbade the union of a Muslim woman and a non-Muslim man. Fatima ran away from her family in Upper Egypt and Mikhail ran away from his in al-Beheira province. They met in Cairo during one of the anti-government demonstrations.

Miss Mariam became a music teacher. Before he emigrated abroad, Mikhail had been an oud (lute) musician in a band. Her mother, Fatima, was shot dead by her Upper Egyptian father.

On a cold, dark night, as Miss Mariam was walking along Nile Street, she saw a little girl lying on a long wooden bench inside a wooden shack, where street children slept in their ash-colored galabeyas. A huge cat with green eyes gleaming in the darkness lay near them, surrounded by her six little newborn kittens, clinging to her for warmth. She licked the dirt and blood from their little bodies.

Miss Mariam wore black leather shoes with thick, square heels. She stomped hard on the ground, one foot after the other, the sound ringing in the stillness of the night. On hearing the sound, the mother cat started to her feet. She encircled her six little kittens, her green eyes burning, and bared her teeth, ready to defend them. Like street children, street cats were always engaged in fights: against stray dogs, gangsters, drug traffickers, unemployed and unhopeful young people, farmers who had deserted their poor, barren land, workers laid off by bankrupt factories, prostitutes with nothing left for them to sell but their bodies, and wives living on the streets after their husbands had pronounced the words "You're divorced" three times.

Zeina Bint Zeinat was unique in that she was fortified against molestation and rape. No man could touch her, even when she was fast asleep. Her long pointed fingers would stick like nails into the neck of any man, and her strong, sharp teeth would cut into any part of his flesh like knives and would tear it out.

During the day, she sat with other girls on the wooden benches or on the stone or iron fences along the Nile. She recited aloud to them a song she had written in her dream, which she knew by heart along with the music and the rhythm. She tapped with her toes, or with her fingers that were as hard as nails, on the wooden bench, on the iron fence, or on the asphalt of the street. She trod on rocks and digested stones, tapping the rhythm and singing along with the girls who danced in their tattered galabeyas and stomped with their little chapped feet on the ground. The clouds in their eyes vanished, revealing their true color: dark blue or green, like those of newborn kittens. Zeina Bint Zeinat watched over them like a mother, even though she was only a year or two older than they were. She looked as though she was a hundred years older, as though she hadn't been born a baby but had grown tall inside the womb and come out into the world as a fully formed girl. She was so strong that whenever the world dealt her a blow, she retaliated with equally strong blows. But the child inside her survived and sang until the very end. Her heart beat hard within her chest whenever Miss Mariam or one of the girls on the street or at school smiled at her, and when she stood on stage.

She had no friend at school except Mageeda al-Khartiti, who sometimes invited her to her large house in Garden City. There they played together in the big garden around the house. They also played the piano together in the large lounge, although Mageeda's plump fingers were extraordinarily slow. She was as short as her father, and when she walked she swayed like a duckling, very much like her mother.

A large room built of red brick stood in the back garden. On its walls grew little bougainvillea shrubs that reached the roof with their various colors: purple, white, yellow, and crimson red. The inside walls of the room were lined with bookshelves up to the ceiling. In the corner, next to the window, stood a large desk. On it there were many items: a big electric lamp, piles of papers, clippings from magazines and newspapers, and handwritten articles by Zakariah al-Khartiti. He sometimes came to this room in search of peace and quiet, when he wished to be away from the house and his wife, Bodour, and her friends with their high-pitched voices, especially her bosom friend, Safaa al-Dhabi. These two were inseparable, whether at university or at home. Bodour would read her critical articles aloud to Safaa before they were published. They would argue for hours on end until night-time. Safaa would then take her handbag and leave.

But before she left, Bodour would call out to her, "Forgot to tell you, Safi ..."

"Yes, Bodour?"

They would stand and talk on the marble staircase, laughing every now and then. Zakariah al-Khartiti could recognize his wife's laugh from among a thousand, a soft elongated laugh that trailed into an intermittent gasp which sounded like suppressed sobs. He couldn't bear that laugh and often slapped her on the face in bed to stop her laughing. And if she cried, he slapped her, for her tears were identical to her laughter as he lay on top of her. She never raised her hand to slap him back. She'd look down and suppress the tears or the laughter, stifling the urge to raise her hand and bring it down on his face. She wouldn't slap him or hit him, and she wouldn't tell him what she thought of him. If he told her that he loved her, her lips might open to produce the stifled words buried deep inside her, but only a stream of voiceless hot air would come out.

Her husband never slapped her while her father was still alive. He only married her because she was the daughter of the great al-Damhiri, whose photograph appeared next to those of the eminent personalities of the state and whose image flashed on television screens. He travelled around in a stretch limousine driven by a dark-skinned man in a soldier's uniform. He lived in a villa overlooking the Nile, with a study lined with books on literature, art, politics, history, philosophy, and religion. With a single line, he could transform an unknown, upcoming journalist into a great writer or an editor-in-chief.

In the large garden surrounding the house, Mageeda played hide-and-seek with Zeina Bint Zeinat. Mageeda would hide behind a tree, underneath a car parked in the garage, or in the storeroom behind the big wooden or cardboard boxes, where her mother stored the books and novels she received by post. She usually stacked them on the floor next to her desk, along with the newspapers and magazines she had finished reading. When Nanny cleaned the room, she'd carry the books and novels, still in the packages carrying name, address and postage stamps, in a huge black plastic bag, and would take them across the great hall, down the marble staircase to the garden. She would pass along the stone pathways in between the flower basins, arriving at the long corridor standing between the iron fence and the trees. She would follow the pathway round the house until she reached the back garden, sometimes stopping briefly to catch her breath or to peep inside the master's room. She would glimpse him through the glass window sitting at his desk, reading in the light of an electric lamp, writing his daily column, or just staring into emptiness with his eyes fixed upward as though waiting for inspiration from heaven.

Mageeda didn't hide in her father's room. Only once did she enter that room while her father was engrossed in writing. He raised his head from the paper and shouted angrily, "Get out of here! Never come in here again. Nobody should enter this room, is that clear?"

"Yes, Dad."

Zeina Bint Zeinat was capable of finding and catching Mageeda in any hiding place in the garden. Her large eyes sparkled with a blue, green, or red flame, reflecting the colors of the flowers. They revealed to her all the hiding places as though they could emit light rays. Her body was light and agile. She was like a white butterfly in her Egyptian cotton dress running among the trees. Her mother Zeinat used to buy three meters of cotton from the al-Mahallah al-Kubra outlet on Tahrir Street for her. Miss Mariam paid for the material, the black leather shoes, and the white ribbon in her frizzy hair that stood like black wires.

A girl with this kind of hair was the object of people's scorn, for girls from good families had long smooth hair falling softly down their backs. Their hair submitted easily to the movement of the gentle breeze and the fingers of their husbands after marriage.

Zeina Bint Zeinat had no family. Her father died while

she was still in the womb. She inherited from him the tough, stubborn "gene", the upright gait and the robust head. She inherited the hair which stood like iron spikes protecting the head from blows, and her large pupils which had the black and blue colors of earth and sea. The pupils of her eyes rolled in their spheres like the earth around the sun, and were surrounded by the clear white color of the waves underneath the sunlight or the mountaintops rising high beyond the sea.

Through the wall of the womb she heard her mother shouting against injustice and hailing freedom. She heard the irregular whimpers and suppressed sobs, the sound of the whip lashing in the air and falling on living flesh, dripping with blood. Rifle butts kicked him below the stomach, between the firm thighs, on the tip of the male organ they call "the rod" in prison. The prison warden, with his narrow sunken eyes, glanced at the prisoner's penis. His eyes were filled with envy and admiration, since envy and admiration often went hand in hand. The prison warden's was tiny, thin and curved, with hardly any blood flowing through it. The little blood that flowed there was yellowish, anaemic, and full of the fear of God and of his superiors. If it had an erection, it would totter and reel, hesitating between going forward and refraining. It stayed shrunk in the marital bed and never had any action except when stimulated by a young jailed prostitute. He lied to his wife that he went to see a doctor about his sexual incompetence. He crept from her bed at night to visit prostitutes after swallowing the blue Viagra pill.

Admiration and envy were directed at the prisoner's proud head. Even when crushed under blows, it remained erect, looking up to the sky, challenging both the sky and the superiors. At night, the prison warden dreamed of striking the prisoner's neck with his sword, removing the proud head and installing it on his own wobbly neck. But this was an impossible dream, for the prisoner's head could never replace the jailer's.

Mageeda and Zeina Bint Zeinat played hide-and-seek in the large garden. Whenever Mageeda disappeared, Zeina managed to find her and to take hold of her arm, pulling her and screaming with joy "Got you, Mageeda!"

Roles changed during the course of the game, for Mageeda would become the hunter, and Zeina Bint Zeinat would hide. When Mageeda untied the blindfolds covering her eyes, she would look around for Zeina. She would look behind the boxes in the storeroom and underneath the cars parked in the garage. She would inspect the holes in the ground between the trees and the flower basins.

But Mageeda never managed even once to catch Zeina Bint Zeinat, for the latter was born and bred on the streets. She was experienced in hiding from the eyes of deities and Devils. Satan's watchful eyes couldn't find her and God's sleepless eyes dozed off when Zeina Bint Zeinat disappeared in the darkness.

Only once did Satan's eyes glimpse her as she ran between the flower basins. He reached out with his long, firm arms, which were as hard as steel, and caught her by the hand. He pulled her into the back room in the garden. In one instant, as she ran and sprinted among the flowers like a white butterfly and the air lifted the hem of her white dress, baring her legs, Satan's eyes fell on the soft thighs exposed to the wind. His eyes moved upward from the legs to the smooth body, until they rested on the soft pubic area where no hair yet grew.

Zeina Bint Zeinat was nine then, a schoolgirl. Miss Mariam held her fingers high for all the other girls to see, saying, "These fingers are created for music. Zeina Bint Zeinat will become a great musician one day!"

Ashamed of her short, stout body, Mageeda shrank in her chair. Her plump fingers couldn't move smoothly or quickly over the keys of the piano. Her neck, like her short plump body, sagged under the weight of her head when she walked.

Mageeda's little heart was filled with a combination of admiration and envy. Although Zeina was Mageeda's senior by one year only, she seemed to be a hundred years older, for she seemed to have known life and death, God and Satan, and was no longer scared of them.

Mageeda's heart, in contrast, was filled with fear, for she was terrified of the everlasting fires of hell after death, and of her father's fist when it rose high and fell on her face or her mother's. She suffered the blow, like her mother, without uttering a word or shedding a tear. She couldn't lift her hand high and bring it down on his face, for her hands were plump and slow like her mother's. She'd look down in shame, as her mother did as she walked.

On that Friday, Bodour went to visit her only friend, Safi, accompanied by her daughter, Mageeda. Safi lived alone in a small apartment on al-Agouza Street. In her early youth, Safi was married to a Marxist university colleague. She abandoned God and the Prophet for the sake of love. Her husband vowed undying loyalty and fidelity. But he broke his vows to her, for she caught him with the young housemaid in her apartment. He told her that men were polygamous by nature and that change was a constant and unchanging natural principle. Infidelity for him was the residue of feudalism and private property. A wife didn't own her husband because human beings were free, and freedom was the highest ethical value, only paralleled by love. After her divorce, Safi got married to a man who believed in God and the Prophet, a man who held a yellow rosary in his hand. On his forehead was the dark prayer mark gained from frequently lying prostrate with his forehead touching the ground in obedience to God. When he vowed love and fidelity, Safi gave up Karl Marx and Friedrich Engels. She wore a scarf round her head to hide her hair. She was married to him according to God's law and following the Prophet's example. Two years later, as she was walking along a street at the other end of town, she read the name of her husband on one of the houses. The exact name was engraved on a brass plate nailed to the door.

She hesitated for a moment. Before ringing the bell, she told herself that full names were identical in many records, including election lists and police registers. An innocent man could be detained because he had the same name as a criminal, or a dead man might even rise from his grave to cast his vote for the president.

She rang the bell three times before the door was opened. At the door stood her husband, in the flesh and with the dark prayer mark on his forehead. He wore white pyjamas adorned with pink flowers. His trousers were loose and unbuttoned and his penis peeped through the opening. She couldn't mistake it. Her nostrils were still filled with his odor from the night before. She raised her hand high in the air and was about to bring it down on his cheek when a little girl appeared from behind him, pulling at his hand and yelling "Dad!" He pushed the girl inside and said to her, as he lifted his face toward the sky, "You believe in God and the Prophet, Safi. God's law gives me the right to marry another woman. The law of the land gives me the same right. Go to court if you wish!"

It was Friday when Zakariah al-Khartiti left the villa in Garden City and headed to the mosque on the adjacent street. Mosques proliferated on streets, pavements, and alleys. Tiny mosques sometimes sprouted inside houses, in courtyards, or in entrances. A little minaret might emerge from a wall, and a loudspeaker might be attached by nails to it to turn the structure into a mosque for men to go for Friday prayers and listen to the imam's sermon.

It was a warm spring morning. The warmth of the sun seeped through the body after the chill of winter. Zakariah al-Khartiti had abandoned the heavy woollen suits and the scarves around the neck. He wore instead a silk suit over an open shirt without a tie. The soft breeze tickled his short, fat neck and moved to his hairy chest whose little black hairs grew thinner year after year.

After reaching the age of sixty, the black hairs on Zakariah al-Khartiti's chest and head became interspersed with white hairs. He had a large bald spot in the middle of his head which gleamed gold in the brightness of spring. His narrow, sunken eyes had a sly look about them. Whenever his eyes fell on the column of his newspaper colleague, he'd turn his face away.

No street or alley was devoid of a newspaper kiosk or a pavement covered with magazines and newspapers, especially the distinguished daily *Sphinx*, which was everywhere. It was displayed in kiosks at the corners of streets and squares, and spread on the pavements near mosques, churches, schools, law courts, nightclubs, theaters, and cinemas. On its front page the picture of the president loomed large. Laid out on the street around the paper were charms, the Qur'an, rosaries, censers, Ramadan fasting schedules, prayer times, photographs of candidates for parliament, the consultative council, presidential elections, or village and city councils. There were also pictures of theater, cinema, and television stars. All the photographs were placed side by side: the photographs of the Great Imam with his turban, beard and moustache, and the rising star, Zizi, who took the torch of dancing and singing from her mother, Zozo.

Zakariah al-Khartiti moved the beads of the rosary with his short, lean fingers. He felt relaxed after finishing writing his daily column and after his wife and daughter had gone out. He was particularly relieved to see the back of his wife. Her observant eyes, like God's, knew his infidelities before they even happened. She detected them before they even became an idea in his brain cells or a passing shiver down the hidden member beneath his belly, when his eyes fell on the thighs of a little girl jumping on the street or an adolescent girl wearing a miniskirt.

After prayers, Zakariah al-Khartiti was relieved of the weight of his conscience. He used to visit Mecca on an annual basis to wash clean his numerous sins. In the mosque he whispered to the man squatting next to him, "Good God, brother! God shows His mercy to human beings. Man by nature is sinful, but God is merciful nonetheless. If it hadn't been for prayers, fasting, and pilgrimage, we wouldn't have been able to bear the weight of our guilt, we would have died of a guilty conscience!"

"Very true, brother! God forgives all sins except the sin of worshipping other gods besides Him. Even adultery may be forgiven as long as we worship Him alone."

"But this adultery subject is controversial. We haven't been introduced, brother, have we?"

"I'm one of God's worshippers, a small employee at the government archives. And you, sir?"

"I'm Zakariah al-Khartiti."

"What do you do?"

Zakariah al-Khartiti felt a pang in his throat. He had imagined that everybody knew who he was. He thought everyone read his daily column in the paper, saw his picture inside the square frame on the pages of magazines, or recognized his face on television screens during interviews and discussions.

"Don't you read the papers, brother?"

"Not really, sir. I used to read them when I was younger and I believed every word they published. As I grew older, I came to realize that they were all liars, beginning with our own president to the American, British, and French presidents. Even my son lies to me, and so do my wife and daughter. But my wife is the greatest liar of all. She covered her head with a scarf and is pretending to be a saint. All the women have put on scarves to cheat us, sir, or what do you think?"

"What?"

"What do you mean by 'what'?"

"It means there are people who fear God and the fires of hell, doesn't it?"

"Right or what?"

"What!"

A laugh escaped the two at the same moment. It sounded like a jarring note in the middle of the murmurs of holy verses in the mosque. It rang shamefully inappropriate as the heads were bent in holy fear and the foreheads touched the floor in total submission.

"Tell me, sir, does God really exist?"

"Of course, sir. May He forgive us for all our trespasses!"

"My son is an intelligent boy and he has read many books. He tells me that the science of the cosmos proves that God doesn't exist!"

"Your son is an ignoramus, a half-literate human being. Lower your voice so that no one hears you. Concentrate on prayers, for God exists, no doubt. Let your son read my daily column in the daily *Sphinx* so that he can unite science with religion."

"Do you write in newspapers, sir? Are you a journalist?"

"Yes, sir!"

"Then you are a liar as well?"

Another laugh escaped, this time not from the lips of Zakariah al-Khartiti. He pouted his lips, got up slowly and rubbed his back. He left the mosque, walking slowly, his thin legs curved a little and his back arched somewhat. He tottered as he walked, vacillating between misery and joy, between virtue and vice, between religious belief and science. He was no different from the words of his column, swinging like a pendulum between the government and the opposition, between sincerity and lies. His column had the title "Honoring Our Pledge". He borrowed some of his terms from Karl Marx and others from the verses of the Holy Books, quoting freely from the Qur'an, the Bible and the president's speeches. His readers were puzzled about what he was trying to say. Was he for the war or against it? For peace or against it? For faith or for apostasy? Bodour, his wife, called him the mercury man, while her friend, Safi, described him as the mirage that ignorant eyes mistook for water.

As Zakariah al-Khartiti walked along, the movement of his legs produced a titillating sensation that ran through his veins, invigorated by the warm sun and the soft breeze coming through the opening of his shirt onto his chest and belly, and tickling the lower part of his abdomen containing the hidden body part. With the movement of the thighs as he walked, and the friction of flesh, the hidden body part began to feel some ecstasy, to tremble with some pleasure or the promise of pleasure which his wife could not give him. The reason, perhaps, was that her clitoris had been cut off in childhood. Since the day she was born, she had been repressed and oppressed. She was oppressed by her military father, who became miraculously metamorphosed into a great writer overnight. Or perhaps because she was in love with another man, a fact he realized from their wedding day, and even earlier, when he saw her framed photograph. Her sleepy, downcast eyes radiated an elusive femininity, and revealed a whorish glance that hid behind the veil of literature, art, culture, and dramatic and cinematic criticism.

Zakariah al-Khartiti often forgot his numerous transgressions, which he wiped clean by going on pilgrimage, praying and fasting. He married Bodour without love and without sincerity, a marriage of convenience. From the moment he saw her father's picture in the paper alongside top government officials, and from the moment her father became head of the great cultural and literary establishment concerned with art and journalism, his subconscious mind told him to pay heed, for this was his last and only chance to achieve his dreams in journalism.

From the first moment Bodour saw him, her subconscious mind told her to watch out, for he was an opportunist, an upstart who was using the chance to arrive at the top before any of his peers. She realized that he was the product of the school of the revolution, like the other young people of his generation. It was a lost generation that fell between a corrupt monarchical system and a republic that was even more corrupt, between Karl Marx and the Prophet Muhammad, between British imperialism covering itself with fig leaves and American imperialism shamelessly flaunting its nakedness, between women wearing headscarves and others parading in miniskirts. Between these were the young women who hid their hair with scarves but wore extra-tight jeans revealing their bellies.

Zakariah al-Khartiti gazed at women's legs as he walked down the street. His narrow, deep-set eyes would move up the long slender legs until they got to the plump thighs. Girls stomped with the heels of their shoes on the ground like wild mares. When a girl's round buttocks moved, his finger reached out in his imagination to the deep cleavage between them, each buttock hard and round like a rubber ball. From the back, one couldn't tell a girl from a boy. In his adolescence, he used to desire males with their firm, tiger-like haunches. A senior teacher once took him to the lavatory and violated his virginity. He later did the same to a younger orphan boy with no father or mother.

Zakariah al-Khartiti banished these old, deeply buried memories from his mind. He moved his head with the rhythm of the dance music on the radio or television. He felt relieved because he had just finished writing his daily column. It was a heavy load that weighed down on his mind until he finished writing the last page. He had a whole day without his wife and daughter. Whenever his wife was away from the house, a secret ecstasy overtook him and the invisible chains fell from his mind and body. During her brief absence, the house became his own.

He would extend his arms and legs until the discs of his spine creaked. He would bring out the small green notebook from the secret drawer at the bottom of the desk. This was where he kept his old secrets: secret pamphlets detailing political actions, his secret sexual activities, pictures of prostitutes, love letters sent to him by women or written by him but never sent, lines of love poetry, decent expressions, vulgar expressions by street children that he found exciting and sexually arousing. Vulgarity was essential for him to reach sexual arousal. But his wife was decent, like all women from good families. If he whispered a vulgar word in her ear during lovemaking, she'd pout her lips in disgust and a cold chill would run down her body, from top to toe. If he pressed on her with all his might, or if he pricked her with a knife in the sole of her feet or the folds of her flesh, not a cell in her body would move and neither would she bat a single eyelid.

He glimpsed her as she entered the garden door. He was examining his face in the mirror, arranging the little hairs sprouting in the bald spot on his head. He looked with disgust at his triangular chin. He had been trying to call an old mistress. The phone rang for a long time. He dialled other numbers, but to no avail. He couldn't find any of them, so he wondered to himself in dismay, have they all found husbands or lovers? Or have they all gone on a pilgrimage to wash their sins? Or have they become infected with the HIV virus as a punishment from God?

He moved his head toward the window and looked up at the sky. He watched her come through the door as though heaven had answered his prayers. She came into the garden with her tall erect gait, looking more like a young woman than a little girl of nine. Because she had no parents, Nanny Zeinat took her on and treated her like a daughter. Miss Mariam paid her expenses and predicted a rosy future for her in music and singing. His daughter, Mageeda, looked after her like a sister, and his wife, Bodour, was as kind to her as she was to orphans and illegitimate children. As he opened the door for her, her cheerful voice came to him like the chirping of a bird.

"Is Mageeda here, Uncle?"

"Yes, sweetie. Do come in."

It was Friday. Through the loudspeakers came the noise of cheers, prayers, and the pronouncements of "There is no god but Allah" repeated a thousand times. The deafening sounds filtered through the various layers of earth and sky, audible to the gods, the angels and the demons, as well as to the living creatures on earth. Even cats reiterated it. They listened to the sounds without understanding the meaning of the words. Like street children, however, the cats picked up the rhythm and repeated it, thinking it was a lullaby a mother sang to her child at bedtime, a poem recited by little girls at school, or the cadence of a dance performed by children on the pavement or on stage.

Zeina Bint Zeinat went into the large study whose walls were lined with bookshelves. She gasped with childish wonder, "So many books, Uncle!"

"Yes, sweetie."

"You read them all?"

"Of course, sweetie!"

On top of the elegant desk stood a plate on which the statement "God guides whom He wills and leaves astray whom He wills" was engraved in an Islamic calligraphic style.

It was Zakariah al-Khartiti's motto in life. Guidance came from God and so did transgression. But transgression held a much greater fascination for him than obedience. Sinful joys flowed through his body as warmly as the blood in his veins. The blood accumulated beneath his belly and crept underneath the pubic hair toward the Devil's gland and the center of temptation.

Zeina Bint Zeinat walked around the room, tall and graceful, looking at the paintings, vases, and antiques. In the corner of the room sat Zakariah al-Khartiti on a sofa made of soft luxurious leather. He held the statuette of Nefertiti's head.

"Come, sweetie, have a look at this statue!"

"Oh! How lovely! Who's this woman?"

"Queen Nefertiti."

"Was she a real queen?"

"Of course! Do you like the statue?"

"Very much, Uncle"

"Take it, then, it's a gift from me to you!"

She wrapped her long, slender fingers around the statuette and held it firmly. Zakariah al-Khartiti cast a furtive glance at her profile. She held up her nose proudly and her little unformed breasts with their tiny nipples throbbed underneath the white dress. As his finger reached out to touch them, the blood boiled in his veins with the power of an electric shock running through his entire being. He started, panting heavily as if possessed by a mighty force.

She leapt off the sofa, dashing the statuette to the floor. Her fingers clutched the doorknob to open it, but the door was locked and Zakariah al-Khartiti had the key in his pocket. Unlike girls from good families, she had training in self-defense gained from living on the streets. She had lost her virginity long ago, when her mother left her on the pavement. Though only nine, she wasn't afraid of thieves or highway robbers. He was fifty-one years her senior, a man whose male urges had suddenly erupted. According to the words of a holy man, when men were in the grip of erotic urges, they lost two thirds of their minds. A battle therefore broke out in the study, a conflict between a man bereft of two thirds of his mind and a little girl whose mind was much bigger than her years. He tore off her white dress and her petticoat made of Egyptian cotton. He removed her little white panties and pulled one leg away from the other, forcing his male organ between her thighs. But he couldn't enter her. His erect phallus couldn't find its way through the folds of her flesh.

The route inside was completely blocked, as though there was no aperture there and no vagina. She wasn't like other females.

He couldn't imagine that a young girl could have such strength or those muscles. In his experience, even after resistance and fighting, women gave in in the end. Strong young women often stopped the fight and lay powerlessly underneath him. A student might weep and plead with him to let her go, but her tears only increased his appetite for rape. Deep down, he was a schoolboy that had been raped himself. The pleasure of sex became therefore connected in his mind and body with violence and the desire to take revenge on the senior teacher who had violated his virginity, on his father who had caned him, and on the university guards who had chased him during demonstrations and beat him with batons. But he sang defiantly along with the others, "You can beat us but you cannot break us!" He also sang the love songs of deprivation, abandonment, and unrequited love. Love was connected in his mind with pain, and sex was inseparable from violence and cruelty. The more cruelly a woman treated him, the more head over heels in love with her he became. He only cared for the women who deserted him and made him suffer, women who fought with him and beat him up so hard that he moaned like a child in front of them, a child being disciplined by his cruel parents, or a worshipper being punished by God Almighty.

In the long fight that ensued, he imagined that she would relent and give in, deprived of her will and overpowered by her feminine weakness. Throughout his life Zakariah al-Khartiti knew only one type of femininity. He was only familiar with women raised in submissiveness. If these women withheld themselves, it was only part of the game. A woman's tears were also a part of the game, even if she left him or thrashed him with a leather belt until he whinged. It was all a childish game.

But Zeina Bint Zeinat had no home and never played games.

She grew up on the streets and the sidewalks like a tree of cactus figs with prickly skin. If you held the figs in your hand against their will, they'd cut your skin with their thorns until you bled. With teeth as hard as nails, she dug into the flesh of his shoulder, neck, belly, and into the tip of his penis, which she tore off. Blood ran profusely onto the decorative patterns of the Persian rug on the floor of the study.

For a few moments, Zakariah al-Khartiti was completely unconscious. He lay on the floor moaning in a suppressed voice that turned, in seconds, to a sound like snoring.

Zeina Bint Zeinat reached out with her slender, pointed fingers and drew the key from his pocket as he lay prostrate. She tiptoed to the door, turned the key twice in its lock, and crept outside noiselessly, locking the door behind her. Zakariah al-Khartiti became a prisoner in his own study until his wife came home at the end of the day.

Zakariah al-Khartiti lay in bed for three days, nursing his wounds with iodine and cotton. On the fourth day, his sexual desires returned. He stretched his hand across the wide bed to touch the back of his wife, Bodour, who was fast asleep. The sound of her snoring was muted, because even during her sleep she tried to suppress it, fearing that her husband might hear it. Women from good families didn't snore. Women with perfect femininity had soft breaths that produced no sound.

He shook her softly by the shoulder saying, "Bodour, sweetheart, are you sleeping?"

"I am sleeping, Zakariah!"

"And can you talk in your sleep, Bodour?"

"Yes, Zakariah!"

Bodour didn't open her eyes. She knew his voice when he softened and wished to empty the contents of his gland inside her. It was one of his prerogatives, according to the marriage contract. She should be ready for him whenever he pleased.

He would wake her from her sleep and pet her a little on the sole of her left foot with his finger. Over the years he had long training in discovering the sites of pain and pleasure, the spots of ecstasy and love. He massaged her childhood memories and tried to awaken her lust during sleep or death, pulling her gently by the hair to wake her, or hitting her softly on the cheek. If her coldness upset him, he'd slap her on the face or whip her with his belt on her belly and thighs.

She never hit him back. He dreamed that she might slap him on the face or whip him so hard with the leather belt that his skin would graze, in the hope that she might awaken the desires that had lain dormant within him since childhood. But all this happened only in his dreams. He didn't have the courage to tell her, "Hit me, sweetheart, hit me. Graze my skin and take me ..."

What would she think of him then? A man who had lost his manhood? A male without a shred of masculinity, who craved to be beaten up like a woman?

That night, he lay oscillating between dream and reality. His mind was almost absent and the Devilish gland was swollen and full to the brim. He could not triumph over a nine-year-old girl. She tore his flesh with her teeth and locked him in the room. Deep in his heart he was overcome with a sense of humiliation and the desire for revenge. He could wreak revenge only on his wife, or on his daughter, Mageeda, by beating her up either for no reason at all or for a triviality. He had to vent his anger, to avenge himself on all the men who had beaten him up and all the women who had rejected him, starting with the head of the state, the minister, or the editor-in-chief who wouldn't smile at him. His body shook with rage, for he was also angry with himself for the meanness of spirit that led him to utter obscenities, to embezzle, steal, rape young girls, and sneak from his marriage bed to brothels. He told himself that the human spirit was abject and longed for sinfulness, for man was sinful by nature. What, otherwise, was the function of penitence and forgiveness? God, in fact, guides whom He wills and leaves astray whom He wills.

With these words of God, he tried to alleviate the weight of his guilt, but to no avail, no avail ...

Deep in his heart, he wished to whip himself with the leather belt. He wanted to wake up his wife so that she might take the belt and beat him. He screamed aloud as she lay next to him, "Please beat me up, Bodour, beat me up so that I may desire you! Hurt me so that my soul may heal and mend!"

But Bodour only heard his gasps, because he was fast asleep. He moaned softly and the sound of snoring merged with that of moaning. The sound stopped momentarily as he turned from one side to another, or moved his head from left to right.

He handed her the leather belt one night and asked her to beat him. Bodour was speechless, unable to lift her hand with the belt to beat him. Something held her back, something deeply ingrained in her soul that was akin to fear, shame, or the sense of what was proper for a woman to do. No, a woman could not raise her eyes to meet those of her husband, just as a slave could not raise his eyes to meet those of his master. By the same token, a husband had the right to hit his wife, just as the master had the right to hit his slave. A woman had no such right. This was prohibited by religious and secular laws, by social customs, and by family ethics. Bodour took the belt and beat the wall really hard as though it were her husband, father, uncle, grandfather, Satan, or God. She hoped the wall might crumble and fall. She wanted to hear its moans and to trample it with her own feet.

But the wall stayed in place. Bodour was so angry that she started hitting herself with the belt, hitting her own body, her arms, legs, and thighs, from the tip of her head to the sole of her feet. She hit herself so hard that she finally fell on the floor, moaning like a wounded animal.

In bed, Mageeda trembled. Through the wall she heard the slaps and the smacks. She had no idea who was hitting whom. Was it her father hitting her mother, or the opposite? Since childhood, she had heard them quarrel at night. The fights continued year in year out, for twenty-four long years. In the morning, everything was back to normal. They drank tea, read the papers, exchanged smiles or glances of love or blame. But a word, a gesture, or a furtive glance sometimes escaped, carrying the full weight of their enmity and hate.

Bodour looked at his photograph framed above his daily column. His name, Zakariah al-Khartiti, was written in large font. He looked at her photograph on the cover of a literary criticism magazine. Beneath it was written "great literary critic and university professor". News of them appeared in the section dedicated to the social elite. The press followed their every move with the same avidity it pursued movie stars, the celebrities of the world of art, literature, and politics, party leaders, and the presidents of supreme councils and societies. Bodour pouted her lips as her eyes moved over the names that she knew either slightly or well. Zakariah al-Khartiti also pouted his lips, the upper much fuller than the lower. He was a little man with a small triangular head. He held his pointed, triangular chin in his hand and stroked it gently as he read his column from start to finish, beginning with the title "Honoring Our Pledge" until the last word and the signature. He reread it, stroking his chin or the hairs that grew on his chest underneath his silk pyjamas. He might reach down to touch his pubic hair through the opening of his trousers, or he might fiddle with his ears or nose. It was a habit that his wife found disgusting, revealing as it did his humble origins, for his family had no claim to cultivation. The king had awarded his grandfather the title of pasha for no obvious reason. In the old corrupt days, the king used to award pimps titles, for they took him to the prostitutes in bars and brothels.

The king also offered titles to the barbers who shaved the chin of the sultan, his grandfather. He didn't only award the titles of bek and pasha, but he also offered large plots of land as well as posts in government or parliament. The awardees would appear in the papers along with statesmen inaugurating charity projects for the sake of God. This continued until the revolution, when the throne was pulled away from underneath the plump royal buttocks and was occupied by their lean republican counterparts. They strived to acquire and accumulate property under the name of purification, purity, and socialism.

Al-Khartiti senior had dreamed of being a great writer like Taha Hussein, with his books widespread in libraries, universities, and homes, something along the lines of Taha Hussein's book on pre-Islamic literature or poetry or whatever it was, for al-Khartiti never read that book. He only heard about it through the conversations of the men sitting in the barber's shop, their eyes gleaming with admiration whenever the name of Taha Hussein was mentioned.

"A great man!"

"The bravest in the land!"

"They accused him of apostasy."

"Ignorant cowards!"

"This is a marvellous book!"

"Do you think he's really an apostate?"

"Never! Taha Hussein is a believer, no doubt, a man who studied at al-Azhar!"

"The Grand Sheikh of al-Azhar is the biggest apostate of all!"

"But this can't be!"

"He delivered his sermon every Friday in the mosque praying to God to save the king! What a hypocrite!"

"Malicious lies and hypocrisy are worse than apostasy."

"You're right there."

When Zakariah al-Khartiti was at primary school, he heard

his classmates saying that his father, al-Khartiti senior, had published a book similar to Taha Hussein's. His picture appeared in the papers together with the cover of the book entitled *Taha Hussein: Leader of Thought in Egypt.*

Successive generations of young critics learned this easy trick. They would use the name of a celebrity in the titles of their books to attract attention. In their books they would write some critical articles about the famous personality, filling pages on a writer they probably hardly read.

Unwittingly, al-Khartiti senior made the ultimate blunder, for his book on Taha Hussein was banned. The authorities, including al-Azhar, confiscated it, and the newspapers wrote that al-Khartiti's book supported Taha Hussein's atheistic ideas.

The father used to take his son, Zakariah, to the barber's shop, the café, and the club, in order to train him from this early age to sit with adults and listen to their conversations about politics, literature, and philosophy. The son inherited his father's childish dream of becoming a great thinker or writer, of having his framed photograph in the papers along with other celebrities.

On the day of the investigation, the father took his son to the court hearing. He wanted his son to witness his greatness, to see him surrounded by lights and cameras. Journalists chased him in front of the court, each carrying a pen with which he noted whatever words he uttered. Even before the words came out of his mouth they were picked up by the tip of the journalists' pens, as though by a magnet picking up bits and pieces of precious metal. Al-Khartiti senior strutted among them like a peacock, holding his head high and casting furtive glances at his son, Zakariah. He would bide his time to give journalists ample chance to congregate around him and give his son the opportunity to witness the whole scene. He wanted the story to become engraved in his son's mind, so that he would later pass it on to his own son, and the great episode would thus be recorded in the annals of history.

Zakariah walked holding his father's hand. He held his small triangular head high and his ears picked a few scattered words hanging in the air.

"My dear sir, your book is wonderful, but I have a question. Are you with Taha Hussein or against him?"

"But if you read the book, sir, you would know the answer! It seems you haven't read the book, like all journalists."

"I swear to God I read it from cover to cover, but I couldn't figure out where you stood exactly."

A journalist shoved his colleague and took his place in front of al-Khartiti. He promptly asked him, "Do you believe that the court will give a verdict of innocence, sir? The book is great and filled with faith. I haven't read a single word of atheism in it."

"Thank you, sir."

"Do you think Taha Hussein is a believer or an atheist, may God forbid?"

"Please go read my book and you will know."

Al-Khartiti senior purposely answered the journalist with a loud, harsh voice. He wanted his son to witness his authoritative tone and his ability to rebuke the journalists. But his father, like other great writers, lost interest in the limelight. Although the lights of fame pursued him, he shunned them and preferred to wear dark glasses to prevent people from discovering his identity.

Al-Khartiti senior wore dark glasses that looked like Taha Hussein's. But unlike Taha Hussein, who was tall and upright, he was short and diminutive.

The cross-examination continued for a long time inside the closed room at court. In the end, the prosecutor asked the great writer, "Do you believe in God, sir?"

"Is this question a part of the legal investigation? I don't have any legal background, but I know that this is a question that only God can ask us on the Day of Judgment."

"This is a perfectly legal question, sir. Our country is a state based on Islam, God's great religion. Please answer the question with a yes or a no."

"Would you repeat the question, please?"

"Do you believe in God?"

"What exactly do you mean by God?"

The father glanced at his son, sitting, all ears, in the corner of the room and trying to catch every single word and syllable, his small body shaking in his chair whenever the prosecutor shouted at his father. He had never heard anybody raise their voice to his father, for there was no power higher than his. But the prosecutor's voice rose higher than his father's, especially when he received elusive answers. Al-Khartiti senior tried to avoid giving straightforward answers, for he did not wish to be defeated in front of his son. So he sometimes raised his voice and shouted with an arrogant, authoritative voice at the prosecutor.

He wanted to embarrass him by asking him, "What exactly do you mean by God?", to uncover his ignorance, to implicate him in a vague answer, and to prove to his son that he was capable of confrontation and challenge.

The prosecutor thought for a moment, during which time al-Khartiti regained his composure and authority. He turned his head toward his son, smiling proudly, assuring him that his father always won in the end. No one could vanquish him, not even the law or the government.

The prosecutor lifted his head and shouted angrily, "You are the defendant here, sir. You have no right to ask questions. You just have to answer with a yes or a no. Do you believe in God?"

Al-Khartiti senior looked down in silence, a muscle twitching underneath his left eye. Since childhood, this muscle had twitched every time his father or a teacher at school shouted at him.

With downcast eyes, Al-Khartiti senior gave the one-word answer that the prosecutor had demanded. "Yes," he said.

On the way home, the father walked in silence with his head lowered. He didn't exchange a single word with his son. When his wife opened the door to them, she asked him, "What did you do?"

He exploded angrily at her, venting his pent-up rage at the prosecutor and all those who had upset him since the moment he was born. He shook his hand in her face, his finger almost gouging her eyes, "Can't you wait a little, woman, until I've caught my breath?"

She left him standing in the lounge and went into her room, closing the door behind her. He sat in a chair, panting a little, although he was never short of breath, even after climbing ten floors. It was as if he had suddenly aged, his face turning long and pale and ashen. His son sat in the corner of the lounge looking at him but trying to avoid meeting his eyes. Al-Khartiti senior sat silently with his shoulders hunched forward. His hair was thinning and the shiny bald spot on his head gleamed in the light. He looked the spitting image of his father in the photograph hung on the wall with a black ribbon around it.

"Get me a glass of water, son."

As he sipped the water, he looked at his son with narrow, sunken eyes. A reluctant tear floated in the corner of one, neither falling nor evaporating. He looked into the eyes of his son and swallowed the tear with the sip of water and spoke in the voice of a wounded lion.

"During the investigation Taha Hussein retracted and declared that he was a believer. Your father, son, is not more courageous than Taha Hussein."

Zakariah reiterated his father's statement whenever his wife accused him of cowardice. Her critical eye would scrutinize him whenever he disclaimed or changed his earlier views under the pressure of his editor-in-chief, the minister, or someone higher up. He would retract, adopt their opinions and use them in his daily column. He would imbue the words of the president with an aura of sanctity or of profound philosophy. He would present them as inspirational ideas that no thinker or philosopher had ever come upon before.

Bodour would go over his column with her critical eye, pulling a long face. He would pull a longer face and respond to her critical attitude by being more harshly critical.

"Your husband isn't more courageous than Taha Hussein, but what about your own courage, ma'am?"

"I've never pretended to be brave, Zakariah. I've been a coward all my life."

To herself she would add, the strongest evidence of my cowardice is the fact that I married you.

She was always asking herself why she married Zakariah al-Khartiti. His name was derived from a word meaning "rhinoceros". He had a pear-shaped head and his eyes were narrow and sunken like those of rats.

She struck her chest with her hands, asking herself why she married that man.

She remembered that she was going through a bad patch. Her psychiatrist prescribed sleeping pills, tranquilizers, and anti-depressants, but all to no avail.

The psychiatrist asked her about her childhood. "Anything bad happen to you when you were a child, Bodour?"

"Nothing at all, doctor. I had a happy childhood."

She lay on the couch in the psychiatrist's room and he kindly patted her white hands.

"Try to remember, Bodour!"

An unwilling tear sparkled in the corner of her eye, brought on by his one kind gesture. She wanted to reach out to touch his hand, to lay her head on his chest and cry. He looked sharply at her, the look of a serious psychiatrist who wouldn't allow his patients to fall in love with him, particularly the type of women who were ready to fall in love with him as soon as he patted them tenderly. They were women deprived of love and tenderness, women who were akin to the thirsty soil yearning for a drop of rain.

"Try to remember any important incident from your childhood."

"A painful incident, doctor?"

"Yes."

"Like what?"

"A rape, for example?"

"Never happened."

The psychiatrist's ears detected the secret quiver in her voice, the extraordinary speed of the response, and the denial, the red flush spreading over her face and the imperceptible tremor of her white fingers, a tremor that was only apparent to the trained eye.

"Was he a stranger or a member of the family?"

"What do you mean, doctor?"

"Do you mean you don't remember?"

"Remember what?"

"How old were you, Bodour?"

The doctor kept on, asking different questions. He was trained to use this method to extract information from his patients. It was similar to police cross-examinations that aimed at extorting confessions from prisoners. The psychiatrist gave her an injection of some light sedative or handed her a glass of Omar El-Khayyam wine or some scotch diluted with water. He stroked her with his tender hands, smiled at her with his bottle-green eyes, and whispered in her ear, "Close your eyes, Bodour. Try to get some sleep."

"Sleep?"

"I mean relax a little, Dr Bodour. Let your mind go a bit and let your memories loose."

Bodour closed her eyes and her tense muscles relaxed. The leather belt surrounding her mind loosened and the crust of the brain melted under the impact of the flow of hot blood whose chemistry changed with the soft waves of the drug. The heart was unburdened and a dreamy smile appeared on her face, followed by a frown, which in turn disappeared. Her face relaxed as she surrendered to the warm current.

She whispered, "They stole her from me, doctor!"

"Who is she?"

"The novel, doctor ..."

"Are you a critic or a novelist?"

"All my life I've hated criticism and never wanted to be a critic. Literary criticism is a parasitic profession and the critics are parasites, living on other creatures like tapeworms. They live off talented, self-sufficient writers. As critics, we have an inferiority complex because we are all failed writers, compensating for our failure by criticizing the work of others. Literary criticism is like shoe-shining, for we shine the shoes of others ..."

"Is this the reason why you wrote a novel?"

"Yes, I had to prove to the world that I could write a novel, that I was a great writer and not a worthless critic."

"I would love to read the novel, Bodour. Bring it along next time."

"I don't have the novel, doctor."

"Where is it then?"

"Thieves ..."

"What thieves?"

"Those who stole it."

"Stole what?"

"The baby, doctor."

"What?"

"I mean the baby novel ..."

The doctor was at a loss concerning Bodour's case, for he

couldn't get to the source of her pain, and was unable to decide whether it resided in her mind or her body. Her conscious mind was in control of her past memories and stopped them from surfacing. Her unconscious mind was a chain of accumulated fears, one layered on top of another, one generation after another, starting from her mother and going back thousands of years to her ancestral grandmothers and the vilification of Eve and the original sin.

"Yes, doctor, I'm a coward. How can I be more courageous than Taha Hussein? The strongest evidence of my cowardice is the fact that I married."

"All women say that, Bodour! They always have regrets, and regret is a dangerous thing, for it causes depression. Your husband is a great man, a celebrity. I read his column every morning. Zakariah al-Khartiti's column is the best in the paper."

She looked at him sceptically. Hypocrisy had become the hallmark of the age. It was an epidemic that infected all, including doctors. There was no remedy for it except a revolution or a volcano erupting from the earth.

Her short, stout body trembled on the couch. Deep in her heart, she yearned for the revolution. She longed to be nineteen once again, joining demonstrations, shouting, "Down with injustice and long live freedom". At her side walked Nessim, tall and graceful, his eyes gleaming. He held her in his arms, whispering in her ear, "We'll have a baby who will change the world."

Bodour didn't read her husband's column, and she didn't listen when he told her of his glories either, or of the fan letters he received from male and female readers, from ministers, and even from the president himself. The president congratulated him on his column when he met him once during Friday prayers. He stood in the second row, right behind the president. He heard the president reading verses from the Qur'an, heard his breath as he kneeled before God, and the creaking of his bones as his forehead

74

touched the floor. He was exultant as he told the story to his wife, as though the president had awarded him an honorary medal or a great prize.

At the breakfast table, he never tired of looking at his photograph above his column. He would steal a glance at the column of his colleague, Mahmoud al-Feqqi. He'd follow his wife's eyes as she read the column. Bodour stopped for a while at al-Feqqi's column, reading it from beginning to end.

Her husband said sarcastically, "You seem to be a great fan of his column!"

"The truth is, his column is truly excellent."

"Better than mine?"

"I haven't read yours yet, Zakariah."

"You read his before mine?"

"Yes, Zakariah!"

"You mean his column is better than mine?"

She looked at him out of the corner of her eye. He seemed draped in the yellow color of jealousy, and his voice rang in her ears as if saying, "My phallus is better than his". Columns, rods, and pillars were often used interchangeably with the word "penis" or "phallus".

"What are you laughing at, Bodour?"

"I'm not laughing at anything, Zakariah!"

"I know what you're laughing at. I know you consider me mediocre and you've never liked my writing. From the day we got married, I've never seen an admiring look in your eyes for what I write. All your life, you've admired al-Feqqi's column, and he has always admired you. You should have married him. I don't understand why you married me!"

"And you! Why did you marry me?"

"A mistake, my dear! Youth and inexperience!"

"Yes, that's right! A mistake, Zakariah!"

"A life-long mistake!"

This was their conversation year in year out, each admitting that their marriage was a huge mistake, but neither trying to fix it.

On the table in front of them stood the tea and coffee pots, for Bodour drank tea in the morning while her husband drank coffee. He took the coffee with skimmed milk and ate fat-free cottage cheese, tomatoes, cucumbers, watercress, and olive oil. They were now older and their cholesterol levels and blood pressure were higher. Zakariah played golf at the club with his journalist friends, while Bodour walked in the club with her friend, Safi, or with her daughter, Mageeda. Two or three times a week she walked around the golf course for forty minutes.

Sometimes a university colleague would join her. At other times, after finishing his game of golf, Mahmoud al-Feqqi would join her on her stroll and exchange talk and news about politics, literature, criticism, art, and culture.

Bodour sipped her tea and bit into a piece of toasted bread with white cheese blended with olive oil. She held the small, sharp knife to cut a slice of tomato. The knife glinted in the sun. Bodour looked at him, her white fingers trembling. Since she had gone to see the shrink, the tremor in her hand and her fears had increased. Would the knife creep and cut her own hand? Or would it cut her husband's hand holding the paper? Or the other hand holding the white coffee?

The knife was moving as if of its own accord. Bodour might have been sleeping and dreaming and not sitting at the breakfast table. Since she had started writing her novel, the lines between reality and dream had become confused. The novel could have been the source of the ghosts chasing her, the voices she heard as she sat writing in her room, the shadows that moved over the walls, assuming human and non-human shapes. The knife rushed across the table and cut through the paper, through the frame of the photograph on top of the column. It penetrated the silk pyjamas and cut into her husband's chest. Red blood flowed on the white pyjamas and the tablecloth. But Zakariah continued reading his column, never stopping, never taking his eyes off that picture. Hugely frustrated, the knife turned toward Bodour's white hands. She felt its smooth, sharp edge move over her wrist, slowly cutting into her flesh, making a deep groove in it.

Bodour realized that it was Badreya holding the knife, for Badreya had the courage to commit murder without being found out by the police. She could conceal herself between the pages of the novel, or escape people's eyes like a phantom or a moving shadow on the walls. Bodour's husband peered at her as she cut the cheese with the knife, her fingers trembling, her face pale, her eyes downcast. She didn't raise her eyes to him, fearing that the meeting of their eyes might tell him what was going on inside her mind. He might take the knife and plunge it into her chest before she did. She saw the buried desire in his eyes. In their hearts, the desire for murder was just as strong as that for sex. Her psychiatrist told her that human beings hadn't evolved a great deal beyond the animal stage, as far as sex was concerned. The instinct for destruction and death went hand in hand with sexual lust. When a man desired a woman, he'd tell her that he loved her to death, and she would say that she'd die for him.

Her psychiatrist assured her that she loved her husband to death, and to the desire to kill him or kill herself. Those who committed suicide did so because they loved themselves to death.

While walking with her friend in the club, Safi said to her, "Your shrink needs a shrink to cure him of his neuroses, for most men are sick. They suffer from schizophrenia, especially those from the upper, educated classes. A man marries a colleague from the same educated class, a marriage of convenience, pure and simple, so that she might appear with him at parties and events. At night, he creeps out of her bed to the housemaid in the kitchen or the secretary in the office. He only lusts after low-born younger women. Such a woman would regard him as a great man, a rare, unparalleled genius, a god or a demi-god, as his mother saw him, for his mother regarded him as a paragon of beauty, even if he was as ugly as sin. From his childhood she would fill his ears with statements such as, 'You're smarter than all your mates. You're unique, you are!'"

Safi, wrapping her head in a white scarf, pursed her lips and swallowed her bitter saliva. She was a Marxist until she left her Marxist husband. After marrying her Islamist husband, she wore the veil and published a book on women's rights under Islam. Following her divorce from him, she married a liberal writer who asked her to take off the veil and stop ranting about religion. This was when she took off the scarf, wore an elegant turban sprinkled with pearls and published a book on literary criticism. But that husband abandoned her for a university student, with whom he lived without an official or an unofficial marriage contract. She discovered the relationship by chance, and her husband confessed to her that he was in love with the girl and she with him. He was free and so was the girl. Safi didn't understand this kind of neo-freedom and decided to break it off.

"You're much stronger than I am, Safi. Each and every day I dream of leaving Zakariah, but I don't have the courage to do it."

"You're scared of loneliness, Bodour, aren't you?"

"Don't you feel lonely, Safi?"

"Loneliness is much nicer than a hateful companion. Like you, I feared loneliness and accepted humiliation. I was a prisoner to that fear until I came to know loneliness and found it to be beautiful and inspiring. We are born in fear and live and die in fear."

"Aren't you at all afraid, Safi?"

"Afraid of what?"

"Of death, for example?"

"Death, like loneliness, is an illusion, for we don't feel death when we die. The dying person feels nothing. Imagine, Bodour, that we spend our whole life in fear of something we cannot feel?"

"Do you believe in life after death?"

"I used to believe in it, but I am now free from this illusion as well."

"And believing in God, Safi?"

"I was a firm believer in God, Bodour, before I studied religion. I wanted to study religion in a profound manner, as a way of strengthening my faith. But the opposite, in fact, happened. The more I learned about God the less I believed."

Bodour trembled as she walked beside her friend, Safi. Her eyes quivered and she raised them to the sky, fearing that God might shower curses on Safi. She feared that her friend might collapse on the ground, suffering from complete paralysis, or that her heretical tongue might become paralyzed.

"I used to believe, Bodour, in God's three Holy Books, as the Qur'an instructs us. I gave religious talks at conferences and on the radio. I published articles on faith, piety, and the women's veil. But something kept me awake at night. I used to get up in the middle of the night to perform ablution and prayers. I continued kneeling and praying. I kept my voice low in order not to wake my husband as I whispered the plea, 'Oh God, forgive me for all my trespasses', which I repeated countless times. I moved the rosary beads with my trembling fingers. I thought I was suffering from fever. But I was infected with doubt, and continued to be so until I delved deeper into the study of religions. The deeper I went, the less trembling I suffered from and the less faith I had. We inherit faith from our families, Bodour. Faith infiltrates the cells of our brains and our bodies from birth till death. You can't get rid of it except through studying science, knowledge, and religion itself. This is a route fraught with perils. I'm opening my heart to you, Bodour, because you are my life-long friend. Please keep this a secret, or they might kill me. We live in a religious state that doesn't allow freedom of thought, despite the incessant babble about freedom. The free, however, don't talk about freedom. They live it. People who lack freedom, in contrast, talk about it all the time."

With her head bent, Bodour listened to her friend. A shudder ran through her whole being and surges of hot blood gushed up to her head then down to the soles of her feet. Something resembling Satan's fingers of her childhood was working on the soles of her feet, tickling her left foot, for Satan always stood on the left side as people around her, at home and outside of the home, had often confirmed.

"My husband used to tell me that religion was essential for ethics. Without religion, no ethical sense could exist. But I discovered that there was no connection between religion and ethics. My husband was an ultra pious man, but every day he lied to me. He'd tell me that he was going to a meeting or a conference, to see a minister or a deputy, but would go instead to see the other woman in her home or in the brothel. He said that a husband had the right to marry four women, in addition to the women slaves and the concubines. He was a member of the group which held the banner that 'Islam is the Solution' and called for the application of Shari'a law and the suspension of the constitution. He was a colleague of Ahmed al-Damhiri, the Islamist prince."

Bodour shuddered to hear the name of Ahmed al-Damhiri, her cousin. His father was a sheikh who occupied the position of deputy or vice-deputy of al-Azhar. He inherited his father's turban and his small square-shaped head, as well as his square chin underneath the thin lips, the upper thinner than the lower, which he pursed when he was engrossed in deep thought. Ahmed al-Damhiri became one of the neo-leaders and was addressed with the title of emir, or prince. A number of unemployed youngsters with university degrees and frustrated hopes surrounded him. As their prince, he led them into the fold of religion. He was small and thin, and his fingers were short, supple, and girl-like. His voice was soft and his body flabby. He was scared of cockroaches and rats. Deep down, he had little self-esteem, but he compensated for this sense of inferiority by being extremely vain and grandiose. He puffed out his chest and walked with his head held high. On his forehead was the dark mark of prayers, as big as a peanut. His thick black beard grew profusely down to his chest. His gown was snow-white and so was his turban. He greeted youngsters with a slight tilt of his head accompanied by a faint smile.

"My cousin, Ahmed al-Damhiri, has become a dangerous man, Safi. He was a spoiled child who got everything he wished for, whether by entreaty or cunning, by softness or violence. Ahmed al-Damhiri would kill to get what he wanted, and now he wants ..."

Bodour stopped before finishing her sentence.

"Ahmed al-Damhiri wants Zeina Bint Zeinat."

"How did you know?"

"Everybody knows the story. Zeina Bint Zeinat has become a famous star and many men are after her. But nobody really deserves her. She's truly talented. She's her mother's daughter, Nanny Zeinat, who suckled and nursed her!"

Safi looked Bodour hard in the eye, but Bodour turned away from her gaze. She glimpsed Zakariah al-Khartiti playing golf, bending his small, thin body in order to hit the ball, which flew for a short distance in the air then fell. He walked proudly toward it, holding his nose high like his colleague, Mahmoud al-Feqqi, and other great writers. Behind him ran a little boy dragging a cart laden with golf equipment. Beside him walked Mahmoud al-Feqqi, tall and graceful, with wide, self-confident steps that were similar to his words on paper. But his back was more handsome than his face, and his eyes were dull and lustreless, the pupils small and colorless.

Bodour was never attracted to Mahmoud al-Feqqi. But when

she saw him from the back, she would be overcome by memories, as though she was a different woman, a woman who was not Bodour but perhaps Badreya. Badreya was nineteen when she joined the great demonstrations. Next to her walked Nessim, with his graceful, erect bearing. His large eyes radiating a bluish black lustre that was similar to the color of the night or the sea reflecting the rays of the sun.

"Zakariah al-Khartiti is jealous of Mahmoud al-Feqqi. He believes I'm in love with him."

"But you're in love with your shrink ..."

"He's in love with me. It's a one-sided love, Safi!"

"But the opposite is true, Bodour!"

The conversation drifted to love and men. Safi had more experience in this area than her friend, for she had known a greater number of men: colleagues, friends, and lovers. She told Bodour, "I'm looking for the man who deserves me. But such a man is not born yet, and perhaps never will be!"

She laughed, tossing her head back. Her thick black hair was cropped short after she had gotten rid of the veil and the turban along with the husbands. She was slightly taller and less plump than Bodour. Her stride was also longer. She stared at things steadily and hard. Her lips were thin, and she would often wet her lower lip with the tip of her tongue as she talked.

"As a matter of fact, men don't attract me. In my adolescence, I was in love with a woman. Now, at this advanced stage of my life, my adolescence is coming back to me. To be frank with you, Bodour, I'm attracted to women. I sometimes catch myself feeling hopelessly in love with a woman. One day, I dreamt of embracing Zeina Bint Zeinat. Imagine!"

"An innocent embrace, to be sure, a sisterly or a motherly embrace!"

"There's no innocent embrace, Bodour!"

Safi laughed aloud, a laugh that the golfers almost heard.

Bodour joined in her laughter, which eased the burden on her heart a little, the mysterious load of vague childhood fears.

"Yes, Bodour, laugh as much as you can, for life isn't eternal. We only live once and must therefore live to the full. Let me tell you a joke about the stupidity of men ..."

Safi laughed heartily before she embarked on telling the joke, her head tossing in the air along with her short, cropped hair.

"There was this man who was bent on marrying a young woman who was a one hundred per cent virgin, a woman who hadn't known any man in her entire life. Every time he planned to propose to a woman, he'd subject her to a test. He would ask her, as he dropped his trousers and uncovered his penis, "What is this, little girl?" The girl naturally said it was a penis. So the man would pull up his trousers and leave, telling himself that he couldn't possibly marry a girl who knew about men. He repeated the test with every young woman he proposed to, but they all naturally failed the test. After several years of tests, one young woman passed, for when he uncovered his penis and asked her what it was, she told him it was a whistle.

The man was over the moon and congratulated himself on finding a woman who had never seen a man's penis before. "Eureka, Eureka!" he said to himself.

After thirty years of marriage and a dozen children, as they sat one starry evening on the balcony, it occurred to him to ask her a question. Pointing at his penis, he said, 'But how is it, darling, that you didn't know that this was a penis?' His wife burst out, saying loudly, 'Do you call that a penis? A penis is as long as my arm here.'"

Bodour and Safi burst out laughing. They laughed so hard and so long that the tears poured from their eyes. Each wiped her eyes with aromatic tissue, as Safi said, "That's men's stupidity for you, dear. Shall we go to the theater this evening to hear Zeina Bint Zeinat sing? She's singing a new song tonight for the first time. You know, she writes her lyrics and her music herself. A truly talented artist! Umm Kulthum used the lyrics and music of others, but Zeina Bint Zeinat is a musician and a poet, and has a lovely voice to boot. I wish I had a daughter like her!"

"I too wish I had a daughter like her!"

"You have your Mageeda, may God protect her, a great writer. Her articles in the *Renaissance* magazine are widely read."

Safi stressed "widely read", for she didn't like the writing of Mageeda al-Khartiti. She imitated her father's style of writing and her mother's literary criticism.

"Mageeda is her father's daughter, Safi. She looks exactly like him when he was young. I sometimes feel she is his daughter and not mine. I wish I had a daughter who took after me."

Badreya whispered to the pages of the novel "I wish I had a daughter who looked like Nessim."

In the dead of night, Bodour embraced her pen. A conversation took place involving her, Badreya, and Nessim, as well as the other characters of the novel. But the conversation sometimes came to a halt, the pen ran dry and the light emanating from his bluish dark eyes was extinguished. His tall, lean body was as hard as a spear, and his head towered high above a rock-solid neck. They hit him on the head with the butt of a rifle and slapped him on the face. But he still stood tall, unflinching. He didn't bat an eyelid and not a single muscle twitched in his face. As they dragged him to the armored vehicle parked outside the basement flat, blood trickled down from his nose and mouth, flowing onto the white vest that revealed the black hairs of his chest and his ribs, gradually coloring it red. Redness tumbled down to his white Egyptian cotton trousers. The smell of cotton filled his nostrils along with the odors of blood, dust, and the black clay of the earth, where little green shrubs sprouted, carrying white buds. He was a child of eight when he sang along with the other village children, running all over the green expanse sparkling with white buds, "You've come to bring us light, oh Nile cotton, how lovely you are! Come on, girls of the Nile, collect the matchless cotton, God's gift!"

On the pavement, the children sang that song. Zeina Bint Zeinat played the tune for them, tapping on the asphalt with her long, slender fingers. It wasn't the same old tune, and nor was it the cotton song about the little white buds dotting the green expanse. Green spaces had shrunk, and the shrubs and the buds had withered. Children's faces had also shrivelled, for they no longer had land, homes, or families. They walked miles in the darkness of the night with their bare little feet. Born on the asphalt of the streets, they survived by scavenging the rubbish heaps alongside the stray cats and dogs. The passengers of lavish cars, locking the doors and drawing the curtains, peered at them with contempt and tried to keep them at bay. They closed their windows for fear of contracting diseases, and felt their pockets to make sure their wallets were still there.

The children would stomp with their chapped feet on the ground, encircling Zeina Bint Zeinat as though she were their mother. They would sing along with her and dance to the rhythm of her music. Passers-by would stop to see the spectacle, a complete band of children who exchanged roles and crude instruments: drums, tamborines, flutes, and lutes. Their voices would rise with the rising crescendo of the music, their cracked heels kicking the ground. The singing would turn into cheers produced by thousands of voices saying, "Down with injustice, long live freedom". Human bodies blocked the streets, for there were laid-off workers of shut-down factories, unemployed and unhopeful university graduates, widows, divorced women, bereaved mothers, government employees with heads bent low, oppressed housewives, housemaids, shoe-polishers, and nannies.

Nanny Zeinat marched with the demonstrators. Tall and slender in her gabardine gown and white rubber shoes, she joined the housemaids walking in the last lines of the demonstration. But the protestors were dispersed by the water hoses, the tear gas, and the loudspeakers shouting above the din of bullets. Some bodies fell. Some blood flowed. Armored vehicles moved over the blood, snatching a number of young people. Smoke and dust filled the sky.

Nanny Zeinat continued walking until the night descended. They took her son and he never came back. She had no idea who took him from her, the police or God. She raised her eyes to heaven, entreating God concealed behind black clouds, "Oh God! Did you take him or did the government?"

She trembled, fearing God's punishment. Faith returned to her with a shudder. The dust filled her nostrils and mouth. He was her only son and her only hope, the apple of her eye and her life. He was tall and graceful, and his stride was long and steady. Light shone in his large eyes as he looked into hers and smiled, "The revolution is definitely coming, Mother! Look, the whole population is rebelling, even the kids on the streets, the cats and the dogs."

Nanny Zeinat hadn't been able to sleep at night since her son's disappearance. Wearing her gown and her rubber shoes, she would go out in the darkness to look for him, her eyes searching earth and sky, raking the rubbish bins and the boxes thrown randomly on the streets. She might rest awhile on a broken wooden bench on the Nile front and follow a column of ants or beetles marching toward a rubbish heap. She'd stare at children competing with little kittens over a crust of bread, their buttocks bare. A small child limped as he raced a limping dog. He had lost his leg when he was run over by a speeding car in the dark.

Nanny Zeinat came back to her room in the basement and filled a black plastic bag with leftovers of food. The basement was the dumping ground for all the rubbish abandoned by the residents of the building. This was where they disposed of unwanted items: old clothes, food leftovers, broken chairs, tattered mattresses smelling of urine, and old worn blankets that had become wafer-thin.

Nanny Zeinat filled the black plastic bag after wiping the dust off the bread crusts and wrapped the pieces of meat in an old newspaper carrying, she saw, the picture of the president, the minister, or a columnist above his column. The eyes were effaced by the dust and mud, or perforated by a fish bone or the remains of a rib bone.

With her hand, she wiped the dust and the mud off the newspaper and used it to wrap a crust of bread, a piece of meat or cake, the remnants of feast cakes, a slice of cheese, a few green or black olives, some pickled lemons, or half a cucumber.

Nanny Zeinat went out at night carrying the black bag. She sat on the wooden bench, surrounded by children, cats and dogs. She opened her bag on the pavement, her eyes staring at them as they devoured the food, their eyes gleaming with happiness. Their happiness reminded her of the sparkle in her son's eyes when she placed in front of him a glass of milk or an egg fried in butter.

On her way back through the darkness to her room, she tripped over a small, swaddled object. It wasn't a child, or a dog or a cat run over and killed by a speeding car, which she often found on the road or the pavement. She bent down and picked up the object with her long, slender fingers. She shook it several times to make sure it was already dead, to carry it in her arms away from the road, to place it on the side of the pavement or to dig a hole for it between the asphalt of the street and the earth along the bank of the Nile.

The swaddled object was warm. Hot blood ran in its veins, and Nanny Zeinat felt the warmth as she carried it in her arms. Its pulse throbbed against her breasts. She trembled and stopped in her tracks. Uncovering the face, she was struck by the large eyes radiating light. Uncovering the legs held firmly together, she couldn't find the little phallus of her son. Instead, there was the feminine slit. She raised her eyes to God, saying, "It's all the same, God. A girl is like a boy. I thank you, God, for everything, both good and bad."

Her image had never left my memory since childhood: her erect bearing, her head held high, her large sparkling pupils, and her long, slender fingers moving with the speed of lightning over the keys of the piano. I wished I was like her, even if they called me the child of sin.

On the walls of the school toilets we wrote her name in chalk: Zeina Bint Zeinat.

She wrote it on the blackboard in front of us without a trace of shame, as though she were proud of her mother, Zeinat. We were all ashamed of saying the names of our mothers aloud. We couldn't write them in our copybooks, let alone on the blackboard. My mother was not a housemaid like her mother, for she was a distinguished professor and her name was Bodour al-Damhiri, the wife of the great writer, Zakariah al-Khartiti. I wrote his name next to mine on the blackboard: Mageeda Zakariah al-Khartiti.

I told the girls that my father wrote a long column in the paper and owned a large farm in al-Mansoura. The girls looked at me admiringly. The principal and the teachers, both men and women, flattered me, except for Miss Mariam.

She taught us music. She held up the fingers of Zeina Bint Zeinat for all the girls to see.

"Look, girls, at these fingers! They've been created for music. She's talented and unique, born to be a musician."

But the word "music" had a bad reputation. We heard a

teacher say, "Music, like dancing and singing, is the work of the Devil. Singing is the job of whores and prostitutes, and not of girls from good families. If you fall asleep to the tunes of music and not to the sound of the recitation of the Qur'an, you'll be thrown into hell, where you'll burn forever."

A shiver ran through my body as I sat in class. A shudder overtook me from the tip of my head to the soles of my feet. Underneath my uniform I felt a line of urine trickling down to my left foot, soaking my socks and seeping into my black leather shoe. I pressed my thighs hard together to prevent the stench from escaping to the classroom and the girls.

At night, ghosts chased me. God appeared to me in the shape of a gigantic man with a face all covered with hair, a moustache and beard, his eyes blazing red, his voice assailing me like a rod piercing my right ear. God always came from the right side, unlike Satan, who came from the left.

When I was eight years of age, I confused God with Satan, for both appeared to me in the shape of a man with a hairy face, with a moustache and beard. His blazing eyes threatened me with punishment and his long, pointed finger almost pierced my eyes. I pushed him away from me as I lay fast asleep, but he wouldn't go away. His long, strong finger remained pointed at me like a long and pointed iron pole, then descended from my eye to my neck, choking me. I opened my mouth to scream, but no voice came out. His finger descended from my neck to my breasts, and he thrust his sharp fingernail into my right breast if he was God and into the left breast if he was Satan. My breasts were two little nascent blossoms, each with a round black nipple. The finger pressed so hard that I screamed. The man placed his large palm over my mouth to stop the sound, then the finger descended to my belly and then to the smooth, hairless pubic area underneath. It slid over it and went into the folds of the flesh to get to the hidden heart of things.

At the age of seven, my father taught me to pray. So I sat between God's hands asking for forgiveness, because I thought I was the sinful party, not God or Satan. My father used to say that our dreams revealed our sinful desires, so he asked me to pray before going to bed. One night he heard me talk in my sleep. I was trying with all my might to repulse the finger chasing me. I screamed at the intruder and levelled at him the foulest insults I had heard from the children on the streets.

When I was nineteen, I went to see a psychiatrist, an old schoolmate of my father's. I told him about my dreams but didn't utter a word about God or Satan until he drugged me. I lay on the couch, drifting between consciousness and oblivion.

I heard the psychiatrist say, "Tell me all, Mageeda. Don't be afraid!"

"I am afraid, doctor!"

"Afraid of what?"

"Of God."

"Why do you fear Him, Mageeda?"

Her tongue loosened a little and her voice began to come out, sounding hoarse, stifled, quivering.

"I insult Him in my sleep."

"What do you say to Him, Mageeda?"

"Horrible insults, like those of street children."

"Such as?"

"Like 'son of a ...'"

Her voice stopped before she uttered the word. Her scared eyes widened as she tried to avoid looking in the direction of the doctor.

"Speak, Mageeda. Don't be afraid!"

"I'm scared of being thrown into the fires, doctor."

"Which fires, Mageeda?"

"Hell fires."

The psychiatrist looked at her with compassion. Though

nineteen, she looked like a child, with her short, plump body lying on the couch, her fair, smooth complexion, and her tender, white fingers.

When he reached out for her hands, her five fingers clutched his finger like a newborn baby holding its mother's finger.

She held his finger in her hand and her five fingers were like pincers grasping it.

"Listen, Mageeda. There's no such a thing as hell fires."

Her eyes widened and the eyelids opened to reveal two small black pupils moving erratically. The whiteness intensified.

The psychiatrist understood the meaning of the movement. When the pupils of the eyes hid underneath the eyelids, fear was at its most intense and a human being turned into a little mouse.

"Don't worry, Mageeda. I'm here with you!"

Her little hands were ice-cold. He stroked them with his large, warm palms, whispering tenderly in her ears, "Don't be afraid, Mageeda. I'm with you!"

He talked to her like a mother speaking to her child.

She laid her head on his chest, feeling it was her mother's. She wrapped her arms around him, half naked, "I'm in love with you, doctor. Take me in your arms, doctor."

Mageeda opened her eyes. Waking up, she could hardly distinguish the real from the unreal. The day before, she had walked in her father's funeral procession, but in the morning she saw him eating his breakfast and drinking his white coffee, her mother sitting in front of him drinking her tea. They each buried their faces in the paper, saying nothing. Silence hung heavily over the house like death.

"Good morning, Mum!"

"Good morning, Mageeda!"

"Good morning, Dad!"

"Good morning, Mageeda!"

Then silence returned, heavier than before. Mageeda got

dressed, opened the door, and slammed it shut behind her.

On the couch in front of the psychiatrist, she took off her clothes and lay naked. She reached out to him, wishing to die in his arms, wanting to experience the height of pleasure before dying.

The psychiatrist encircled her with his arms, stroking her soft hair and shoulders. His hand descended to her naked breast, which throbbed beneath his hands.

He said to himself, having sex with patients isn't really one of the principles of psychiatry, but it may be a method of treatment.

It was also a method he liked, for this female body exploding with desire was like the thirsty soil yearning for a drop of water. It wasn't like his wife's body, which was a cold, frigid mass, unmoved by anything, even if he were to prick her with a needle or to plunge a red-hot rod into her belly.

After Mageeda was gone, his conscience began to prick him, chastising him for what he had done. He saw himself roasting in hell, for he had a firm belief since childhood that God was wrathful and revengeful, and would not forgive his numerous trespasses, his most serious offence being his doubt as to His existence. He was torn between doubt and faith.

Increasing numbers of people were returning to the fold of religion, and religious currents were on the rise everywhere, in the West as much as in the East, among Muslims, Christians, Jews, Buddhists, Hindus, and all other religions, each religion more violently orthodox than the next. Sectarian wars carrying the banner of a deity were breaking out everywhere, each deity more bloodthirsty than the next. He tried to get rid of his faith, but to no avail. During the Great Feast, he left for his village, where his parents invited him to celebrate the occasion. As he was driving his light blue Mercedes along the Agricultural Road, it occurred to him that God might punish him for his doubts by killing him in a collision with a huge truck. Worse than death was the fear of becoming maimed, of losing an arm, a leg, or an eye.

He had been studying the relationship between religion and psychological disorders. The deeper he delved in his exploration of religion, the more convinced he became that religion was dangerous. He couldn't get rid of the thought of a vindictive God, for there was no one more implacable than He was. If he published his findings in a book, his name would certainly appear on the death list produced by the emir's group, as well as another anonymous group working underground. In the past, the village was peaceful and had one mosque. The man calling for prayers had a sweet, melodious voice that tickled the ears. Now the village was full of mosques, one in every alley, every corner, and every pathway. Every minaret had a huge loudspeaker blaring out the calls to prayer five times a day. The noises were thunderous and the alleys were filled with young men wearing thick, black beards reaching down to their chests. All the females, old and young, wore scarves on their heads, while sheiks wore turbans and little boys wore caps. The thought occurred to him that God might not be interested at all in clothes, or might not even see them in the first place. And if God saw them, where was the problem? He asked himself why he was so obsessed with people's clothes and why he persisted in gazing at women's bodies.

He stopped the car briefly in front of al-Khartiti's house, which stood in the middle of a huge farm. Zakariah al-Khartiti was his schoolmate. While passing through the square where his primary school stood, he saw the picture of Zakariah al-Khartiti pasted on the wall. It was the same photograph that appeared at the top of his daily column in the morning paper. It announced a lecture by him entitled "Science and Faith" on the occasion of the Feast.

He drove his car to his grandfather's old house on Station Street. Next to the house was a new mosque with a minaret and a loudspeaker. At the end of the street stood the pub and the house of the gypsy singer, Khadouga. He used to visit her with his teenage friends to empty the Devilish secretions inside her plump body, each of them waiting for his turn in the hall, reading verses of the Qur'an or staring at the picture of a naked woman on the cover of a magazine. There was also the hashish, the opium, the drug injections and all the substances that obliterated minds and aroused desires, the local food restaurants of *kushari*, beef burgers, and shin stew, as well as all the other mouth-watering meals.

Then he went to the mosque for feast day prayers. He kneeled and prayed together with the other worshippers, his forehead touching the straw mat on the floor, the dust and the fleas filling his nostrils. He banished the Devil standing to his left who told him that God wasn't fooled by his prayers. He told him that God punished him for his doubts by making his favorite Zamalek Club lose the last match. The Devil knew he was a devoted fan of the Zamalek Club. So he chased the Devil away as if he were a fly, saying, "Shut up, Satan. God can't be so empty-headed as to punish a club for one person who has doubts!"

On his way back from the village, the psychiatrist realized that he was ill and in need of a psychiatrist himself to help him overcome the schism between his mind and heart, for his mind didn't believe, while his heart did. There was no hope of a cure for him, doomed as he was to suffer from this split personality from childhood.

Bodour crept out of bed in the darkness of the night and left her husband who lay snoring. His open mouth slanted toward the left side. His face looked toward the ceiling and his eyes were half closed. He seemed to be looking at her as she crept out of bed and tiptoed with her little white feet. Her movement was as slow as a duckling and she swayed from one foot to another, hesitating between going forward and stopping. There were three men at least in her life. There was Mahmoud al-Feqqi and his column, which she considered to be outstanding, although his own column was far more popular and was even read by the president himself. The second man was the psychiatrist, his schoolmate, who wasn't bright at all, had a low IQ, and chased girls. The third man was the secret of her life. She told nobody about him, least of all herself. Perhaps she told her friend, Safi, and Nanny Zeinat. Whenever these two women put their heads together there was always trouble.

Zakariah al-Khartiti tossed and turned in his sleep. He changed from the prostrate position to the supine, burying his head in the pillow. His snoring turned to whimpering. In his ears, he could hear his father's voice saying that women were the Devil's allies and that cleanliness was a godly trait, while dirt was a womanly trait. He quoted the words of the ancient poet, Ibn al-Muqaffaʾ, who said, "Prevent them from looking by keeping them secluded, because this is better for you than living in a state of doubt. If you can, try to stop them knowing others."

But how could you, Zakariah al-Khartiti, prevent your wife from knowing others? As a distinguished professor, she went out on a daily basis to the university. She taught male students, and her professor colleagues, including the columnist Mahmoud al-Feqqi, looked at her with Devilish eyes. And she lay on the couch in front of the psychiatrist, who used the couch to cure himself of sexual starvation. He made love to all the women he fancied. God permitted him to have sex after he had obtained his PhD in psychiatry. He imagined himself a prophet, God's messenger to cure the suffering women on earth. He locked up his wife at home, and when she went out of the house, she wore the veil. He was jealous of other men's eyes. She swore on the Holy Book in front of him that she wouldn't know any other man either during his lifetime or after his death, and would never get married again. He behaved as though he were a prophet sent and protected by God, as though it were he that was referred to in Verse 53 in al-Ahzab (The Clans): "Nor is it right for you that ye should annoy Allah's Messenger, or that ye should marry his widows after him at any time."

Zakariah al-Khartiti tossed in bed, turning from the supine to the prostrate position, with half an eye looking toward the ceiling. God was looking at him with angry, blazing red eyes through the chink.

A voice shook his body as it thundered, "Oh son of Khartiti! Your great-grandfather was a mechanic's apprentice who was kicked by his master in the belly if he couldn't fix an iron nut. I gave you and your father countless gifts. I fixed the nut in your wobbly brain so that you could become a great writer and have your own daily column in the great *Sphinx* newspaper. Can't you stop these doubts about my existence, you fool? What a beast man is!"

His wife Bodour sat at the desk in her room. In front of her were papers, and in her hand was a pen. The light of an electric lamp revealed her plump, round face. With her eyes half closed, she seemed to be either absent-minded or sound asleep. The characters of her novel appeared to her like shadows moving over the walls, shapes peering through apertures in the black cloud, a speck of light in pitch darkness. She waited for the inspiration from God that would make her pen move energetically on paper as it had in the past. But the pen stood still in her hand and refused to move. Her brain cells had ground to a halt. From the day she married Zakariah al-Khartiti, her head stopped working. The nuts and bolts of her brain had rusted. Her husband's eyes watched her day and night. Even as he slept, he followed her, spied on her dreams, rummaged in the papers inside her desk, stole the parts of her novel he wanted, especially the secret parts breaking taboos. He collected them in a secret drawer in his desk in a black folder on which he wrote, "The deeper the secrets, the more horrifying they are."

Bodour dozed off sitting at her desk. She was suddenly alerted by the sound of footsteps. She knew the sound of his footsteps as he walked from the bedroom to the bathroom, a movement that was etched in her brain. Year in year out, for twenty or thirty years, and perhaps even longer, since she shared his bed, she had known the sound of the balcony door opened by the force of the wind when he went out to stretch his limbs, and the sound of running water when he went into the bathroom. When he went into the shower, she felt a chill move through her veins, from the top of her head to the soles of her feet. She became aware of the rising crescendo of her heartbeats and the currents of blood rising to her head. Her fingers and toes were ice-cold, and her ears were filled with the sound of water splashing in the bathroom and the squeaking of the tap as he closed it. Then silence. There was silence as he dried himself with the large white towel. As he opened the door she smelled the shampoo mingled with the smell of shaving cream, the Eau Sauvage cologne imported from Paris. She knew he had a rendezvous with a new girl. She was probably an intern at the newspaper, or an upcoming writer in love with the limelight, who moved from one great writer to a greater writer until she got her own column and her framed picture. In the picture her long hair would fall down to her shoulders, her lips would be slightly open showing her small sharp teeth, and her eyelids would be half closed in a lethargic, seductive femininity.

At eight years of age, she saw her mother crying in silence, disappearing into her room, burying her face in the pillow, wiping the tears with the corner of the white sheet. Her mother stopped talking to her father completely. She looked at him scornfully as he kneeled in prayer, reciting verses of the Qur'an, for his ears were listening to the voice of the Devil standing on his left side and his eyes were straying after girls' legs. His mind was preoccupied with election results, although his name never made it to the final list. With other men, he suffered from a sense of low self-esteem, which he compensated for through his successful conquests of women.

Bodour was an eight-year-old pupil. It was Friday, the day off school. Her father went out to pray at the mosque and her mother went to visit her mother in Heliopolis. She stayed at home doing her homework or looking out of the window, watching the children frolicking on the street or gathering around a man with a monkey. He played the flute, his cheeks puffed up and his eyes bulging. The monkey danced to the tune, its red backside gleaming in the sun. The boys and girls laughed, dancing with the monkey and clapping.

Her father forbade her from going out on the street. He told her that street children were born of sin. They were the Devil's children, especially the lame boy who looked like a little monkey. His narrow eyes were sunken in his cone-shaped face, which was long and bony. His complexion was dark and dotted with white spots, the effect of malnutrition or anaemia. His small ears were red, and there was a hole in each earlobe from which a tin earring shaped like a star dangled. The lame boy danced with the monkey and laughed with the children, his laughter resounding in the air. Some light seeped into his narrow eyes and they sparkled with a smile that was akin to a withheld tear.

The boy was her age. Her mother was kind to him and often gave him a coin, half a loaf of cheese, a feast cake, or an old pair of trousers that belonged to her husband.

On that Friday, she was through with her homework and the call for noon prayers was blaring from the nearby mosque. The sun was bright on that early spring day after the coldness of winter, and the clouds had disappeared. She wanted to go outside for a breath of fresh air and to visit her friend next door before her father came back from the mosque, for he wouldn't allow her to visit her friend. She was only allowed to go to and from school, without stopping or going anywhere else. She often heard her father say, "A girl's honor is like a match. It can only light once. Do you hear me?"

Before going out, she thought of walking a little in the garden, which was a large dusty expanse full of withering flowers. Her mother put all the objects that were no longer needed in what she called the "junk" room in the backyard. Lizards and beetles ran freely in it, as well as evil spirits, including the Devil himself. Her father called it the "rats' room" and he threatened to put her there as punishment for her disobedience.

The old wooden door of the room was never completely closed. As she walked through the backyard, she saw the door standing ajar. Her curiosity led her to approach cautiously, fearing that a rat, a lizard, or an evil spirit might leap in her face. Unlike her mother, she didn't believe in the existence of spirits, ghosts, or phantoms. Her science teacher told her to think with her mind, and that spirits and ghosts did not exist. She repeated to the teacher what she had heard her father say: "But God in the Qur'an says that spirits and demons exist."

"Who told you that?"

"My father, miss!"

"Your father doesn't understand God's words. You have to understand His words with your own mind, and not your father's or mother's."

Bodour gathered her courage and looked through the chink left by the door standing ajar. The windowless room was pitch dark. She might have gone on her way without seeing anything. But she heard a bizarre sound like that of a child panting. Her eyes froze as she looked through the small opening. She saw the lower half of her father's body completely naked. His white gown was lifted to his shoulders and his penis looked colossal. It was like nothing she had seen in her entire life, for she frequently glimpsed boys' penises on the streets as they walked with their bare buttocks and feet. Their small penises, however, were limp little pieces of flesh dangling from between their thighs. Her mother called them "sparrows". She saw a larger penis in her dreams, dangling from behind a cloud of smoke, resembling the Devil's finger, moving stealthily from the small nipple to the hairless pubic area, then descending to the folds of the flesh before reaching the site of pleasure and pain deep inside.

At eight years of age, she had little experience. Her father's phallus seemed enormous in her eyes, much larger than the one dangling from the sky. It was engorged and extended downward toward the body of the boy, whose buttocks looked like the monkey's. She only discovered the boy's presence after noticing her father's phallus, as though he were an extension of it. The little boy lay on the floor, face down, his head raised a little toward the partially open door and the thin ray of light coming through. His bare lame leg was raised like a barrier separating her from her father, his hand buried under his chin, and his fingers clutching at something hidden underneath his belly. His small ears were red, and from each lobe a tin earring dangled.

At first glance, she thought they were a single body. But she soon realized that they were two: her father's body and that of the lame street boy who was eight years old like herself. The two bodies merged in one huge mass, like the kangaroo carrying its child on its back or underneath its belly.

Bodour forced her eyes open. She found herself sitting at her desk holding her pen, a blank page in front of her. Her mind was equally blank and still. Since she'd got married, she'd been incapable of writing. She might have written the novel that her husband later stole. While she was fast asleep he searched her drawers and stole her secret notebook, her old love letters, the chapter she wrote about that scene, which she could not write again. Years passed and the scene was lost from her memory. She forgot the expression on the boy's face at that moment. She forgot the incident itself, imagining that it never happened. Many other incidents also seemed to her like figments of her imagination. A black cloud of smoke floated over her eyes. Satan's finger hid behind the cloud, and so did God's face, which disappeared behind a column of smoke. But she saw him through the chink of the door standing ajar, her own father in the flesh, kneeling as though praying to God, tilting backward, his right palm like a camel's foot resting on the ground, his left hand cramped, frozen over the boy's neck. Smoke gathered over Bodour's memories as she closed her eyes. Her fancies seemed real, and reality seemed fanciful. Her white fingers holding the pen could not hold the truth, which trickled through them like water. She tried hard to recall the scene, but it was as elusive as mercury, perhaps because the past was dead and gone, or perhaps because the pain was too much to bear.

Bodour rubbed her eyes to force herself to wake up. She remembered her father as he half sat up and half kneeled. His long beard was stuck to his chest and his round face blazing red. He was gazing up at the ceiling, his muscles twitching with pain, pleasure, and relaxation. It was as though the doctor had just removed kidney stones, or extracted a painful tooth from his jaw, or removed a malignant tumor from his testicle or prostate. She had heard the word prostate before when she was a child, and thought that prostate was a feminine organ placed in a male body. Ecstasy was evident in her father's eyes, the ecstasy she herself had never known in her entire life. It was the ecstasy that the flesh craved in the same way that the earth scorched by the sun yearned for a drop of water. Pleasure and pain merged in excitement, relaxation, sorrow, and happiness. Then consummation came as the finale, as death, as the end of worshipping a vindictive, vengeful god who burned with fire, and another god who was merciful and forgiving, who forgave everything except worshipping other gods besides himself. Both were the same.

Tears fell from her eyes and she could see nothing. Her father's face disappeared behind a dark grey cloud of tears which bordered on blackness. Her body shivered as she remembered her father's shiver as he snatched his pleasure, wanting and rejecting it at the same time. He was like her husband, Zakariah al-Khartiti, who loved her and hated her at the same time. She suffered from a split personality as well, for she wanted and rejected him, loved and hated him. She loved writing and hated it at the same time. She started writing with fervor and excitement, but as soon as the pen touched the blank page, the miscarriage happened. The words died under the nib. The hero and heroine of the novel would die, as though everything was a dream or a fancy.

Her psychiatrist told her, "Contradiction is an essential characteristic of life, for there is no life without death. The laws of nature are based on contradiction, and so are heaven's laws. And if God had a split personality, Bodour, is it possible for human beings to be otherwise? I only love the woman who hurts me and deserts me. I love her after I lose her. This is the reason why prostitutes and unfaithful women triumph over us men, while virtuous women and faithful women suffer in their love for us."

Bodour tried in vain to forget the face of the lame boy, which was dark and pale and almost bloodless. His eyes were wide open and his eyelashes were wet with frozen tears. The whites of the eyes were bulging. Underneath the clouds was a horrified look that was as frozen as tears.

Before Bodour became conscious again and before she came to grips with what she had seen, her childish mind realized the undisclosed secret lodging in the hearts of her father, mother, grandfather, uncle, aunt, neighbors, and all the adults in her parents' families and at school. It was the secret she understood after she had grown up. It was the secret that resided within the thighs, the part that became erect and as large as a donkey's phallus.

Bodour felt drops of cold water falling on her head like rain coming from the sky. Profuse sweat covered her as she stood looking through the slightly open door. Cold winds blew, removing her clothes and her whole body. She trembled as she saw the frozen tears in the eyes of the lame boy. She felt it could have been herself who was lying on her belly underneath the huge phallus and the kangaroo-like body. She remembered her mother when she went into the room with her father. Through the wall she heard moaning sounds, like a little girl crying with pain. There was also the repulsive smell, for he didn't brush his teeth every morning. And neither did he shower after sex. He moved from her mother to other women without having washed. He took the Prophet as his role model in this respect only. The perfume and the stench were the same in her nose. Good and evil, God and Satan, love and hate, pleasure and pain, life and death all became the same to her.

Bodour stared at her daughter Mageeda, who was eight years old. But she drove the memory out of her mind. She remembered that she was her age. But she didn't tell her daughter the secret, and it stayed buried within her, locked inside an iron cage under the ribs. She didn't have the courage or the daring to open it without splitting her heart in two or tearing her liver out of her body with the knife.

Mageeda al-Khartiti threw a huge party to celebrate her twenty-fourth birthday. Among the guests was Zeina Bint Zeinat, who was only a year older, although she looked older by a hundred years. She was tall and erect, and her long slender fingers moved with the speed of lightning over the keys of the piano. Everybody looked at her with admiration and envy: men, women, and children. Zeina Bint Zeinat was a star in the world of show business, and she had her own band of little boys and girls drawn from the narrow streets and alleys. Their little dark fingers played the lute or banged the drums and tamborines. Their pale cheeks were puffed while playing the flutes as they chanted the cotton and wheat song, their own national anthem: "Oh God, bless the wheat tonight, may it grow ...", "You've come to bring us light, oh Nile cotton, how lovely you are!", and "I love you my land with all my heart ..."

Their eyes gleamed, the black clouds cleared and the frozen tears melted. The dark pupils twinkled like stars in the sky and the little feet kicked the earth to the beat of the music. They danced, sang, and played music. Their feet and legs were bigger and their bones sturdier. Their wounds and bruises had healed, and their limping, rickets, and heartache had disappeared. Zeina Bint Zeinat led the children on the piano. She had known the tune since childhood and dreamed of it at night. The lyrics came to her during her sleep, for her mind was as active during sleep as when she was up and about. She saw the sparkle in the eyes of her mother, Zeinat, and in the eyes of Miss Mariam and her schoolmates. Her friend, Mageeda, looked at her with narrow eyes filled with envy and admiration. It was an ambivalent look that harbored love and hate at the same time. In front of the girls, she defended her, but on the toilet walls she wrote her name: Zeina Bint Zeinat. Like her father, Zakariah al-Khartiti, she remained impartial in her column in the *Renaissance* magazine. She repeated his maxim: "The middle ground is the best." So she stood half-way between left and right, between praise and censure. In the jargon of literary criticism, she kept a balanced, objective view. She stayed neutral and uninvolved in partisan politics, always raising the banner of independence and freedom.

Ahmed al-Damhiri, her mother's cousin, came to attend her

birthday party. He had acquired the title of Eminent Sheikh by raising the slogan "Islam is the solution". His aides in the underground group called him the emir. His voice rang out on popular radio channels but was low during secret meetings. His small head was square-shaped, and at the beginning of his career he wore no beard. But then he grew a thick black beard. His forehead used to be smooth and soft before a black mark started appearing there. His short, white fingers, which looked like those of his father, grandfather, and uncle, held the rosary by day and the wine glass at night. With these very fingers he stroked the bodies of prostitutes before dawn. In the dark, he was afraid of demons, cockroaches, beetles, and rats, but his courage returned with the daylight. He wore a turban or a cap on his head. He was usually dressed in a loose white gown, but in formal meetings with ministers, ambassadors, and party leaders he wore a suit made of English wool. The yellow rosary never left his hand. Its soft beads moved along with the soft murmurs of the holy verses, the sayings of the Prophet and the other messengers, and the words of holy men and ancient sages. He was in the habit of repeating God's name and wiping his head with his little fat palm.

His eyes fell on her as she sang and danced. They caught sight of her graceful, slender body and her long, slender legs that ended in taut thighs resembling those of a tiger. In her there was a touch of overwhelming masculinity merged with soft femininity. Her breasts, which were as firm as rubber, moved underneath the white cotton dress with the rhythm and cadence of the music. She was like a wild, unruly mare that no one could possess. She moved her arms and legs freely in the air, jumping, bending like a soft blossoming twig. Her voice rose high without barriers or restrictions from earth or sky, and her large blue-black pupils gave forth a dark bluish flame that was unafraid of hell fires.

The seat next to him was occupied by Safaa al-Dhabi, the friend of his cousin Bodour. She stared at him because he looked like her former Islamist husband. She could almost read his thoughts. She even detected the quiver in his fingers that held the rosary. Her eyes pierced through him like the edge of a razor, shaving off his beard and his moustache and removing his pubic hair to see what lay underneath. She had extensive experience of men. They came in all shapes and views and attitudes. They flaunted rightist or leftist slogans, engaged in cock fights on radio and television, went to the mosque without performing ablution first, stood behind the president or the minister in the second, third, fourth, or even first row. They would hear their knees creaking during prayers, or their stomachs rumbling with envy and admiration. A fart might escape, producing a soft sound like stifled snoring during sleep or of bare feet tiptoeing at night.

Safaa al-Dhabi's mind travelled back in time and recalled her former husband, who said to her, "I admire your writing, Safi!" Like Bodour, he used to call her "Safi". Like the other women writers, and critics of her colleagues, she was proud of her intellect. So if a man praised her lips or breasts, she would look daggers at him.

"I'm not a piece of flesh, sir. I'm a thinking human being and a writer. Have you read my book on literary criticism? Don't you read my articles in the paper?"

Safi let out a resounding laugh and her short, fat body shook. She started wearing the white scarf around her head to repulse men's eyes. She had vowed everlasting fidelity to her husband, and he swore by the Qur'an that he wouldn't touch another woman.

Safaa al-Dhabi was preparing to write a critical book on the theater or the cinema. But her husband said to her, "Write about women's rights in Islam! What's the point of criticism? It's all nonsense, Safi! We don't have any theaters, cinemas, literature, or culture in our country. It's all copied from the West. Art in our country is nothing but pornography and lewdness. Write on Islam, Safi, for Islam will solve all our problems."

Safi prepared to write the book and collected the necessary references and materials. She created the table of contents and wrote the chapter headings. She gave the book the title *Women in Islam*, which she wrote in large font on the cover of a green folder. She spent hours working on her papers, staying up late at night sitting at her desk until she was overcome by sleep. She then closed her folder, stretched her limbs, and walked to her bedroom, where the wide bed which she shared with her husband stood. Before getting into bed, she would take a shower in order to wash away the dust and the exhaustion.

She had an apartment on the ninth floor on al-Agouza Street. The water supply was often cut off at certain times of the day and night, because the lower floors used all the water before it could find its way to the higher floors. So an electric pump was installed to push the water up. But the electric power was sometimes cut off during the night. The air was filled with dust and smoke, and a black cloud covered the sky. Lidless rubbish bins stood in front of apartment doors, and cats and cockroaches played hide-and-seek there. The water pipes and sewage pipes sometimes burst at the same time. Car wheels were submerged in the water and the traffic came to a halt.

On the front door of the building there was a large plate with the words "Piety and Faith Building" in large font. Even buildings had convictions. The owner of the building was a man who had a money investment company as well as an Islamic bank. His photograph appeared in the papers, with his beard, moustache, rosary, and the prayer mark on the forehead. He appeared in pictures shaking the hands of ministers, ambassadors, eminent writers who had their own columns in government papers, and university professors, including Safaa al-Dhabi and her ex-husband. Both of them had no other income than their monthly salaries, payments for lectures delivered in oil states, royalties on books and articles written about Islam, textbooks sold to university students, and private coaching in religion, jurisprudence, and Islamic law. At the bank, or perhaps at an Islamic investment company, they had accounts running into thousands. Even money had religious persuasions. Safaa al-Dhabi objected to usury but she accepted interest under the guise of money investment.

From the window of her apartment on the ninth floor, Safaa al-Dhabi looked up toward the sky, but her nostrils were assailed by the smell of sewage wafting from the street, and her ears were deafened by the blaring noise of loudspeakers. So she closed the double-glazed window the whole day, in an attempt to stop the flies and the calls to prayer from coming through. At night, she also closed it to stop mosquitoes and little flying gnats. She sometimes opened the window for a bit of fresh air, but the air was non-existent and the smell of sewage and accumulating rubbish was unbearable. Although she covered herself with the blanket from head to toe, she was still attacked by mosquitoes and gnats. A black cockroach ran underneath her head. She sprang to her feet, holding a slipper in hand to hit it. But it was more agile and won the battle by disappearing into a chink in the wall, leaving her panting, sweating, and cursing life. She lay next to her husband, looking enviously at him, for he slept soundly, undisturbed by anything. Should the war break out or the building shake, he would not budge.

From a distance, a sound like the cheering of demonstrators came to her. People were going out on protests: laid-off workers, unemployed youngsters with university degrees, women in black gowns and slippers, street children, beggars of both sexes, handicapped people, and people maimed in war or peace.

From a distance, she could hear the rumbling, which was faint at first but grew louder with the break of dawn. The city seemed like a huge black animal that was waking up lazily, slowly, with withering eyes peering through the black cloud, or like a devout woman veiling herself from head to toe. The maid came to clean the house. She would hang the clothes on the line and beat the carpet on the balcony railing, the dust dispersing on the lower floors. The street began to wake up: grocers, hairdressers, pharmacies, plumbers, cafés, and restaurants on the Nile front and under the bridges, police stations, pubs, courts, schools, educational institutions, and mosques. Safaa al-Dhabi put the kettle on while her husband smiled in his sleep, for he no longer smiled at her. He turned his back to her and fell fast asleep. He was short and stout, and she liked men who were tall and graceful. His face was plump, and she liked lean faces. His voice was extremely masculine, and before marriage he told her, "I like your writing, Professor."

He stressed the "f" while pronouncing "Professor". He thought everything about her was beautiful, even her round nose. He told her that her unique nose set her apart from other women. He saw all her faults as marks of distinction. The difference in opinion between them was natural and healthy. It was in keeping with the democratic spirit of Islam.

"I believe in pluralism, Safi, for differences enrich life. If God wanted to create all humanity as one faction, He would have easily done that. But He created people to be different. Islam is based on reason, Safi!"

He read out an article he had written for the *Islamic Newspaper*. At the start of the article he wrote, "In the name of God, the Merciful, and Most Compassionate, Islam is distinguished from other religions by its reliance on reason and intellect. It is true that veiling is the duty of a Muslim woman to ward off temptations, but menstruation is not evil or unclean. A woman can hold the Qur'an in her hand and read during menstruation. As for marrying a person who had nursed from the same mother's milk, it isn't forbidden, because it is not logical. If a child nurses from the breast of a woman, he should not be prevented from marrying a girl who nursed from the same breast.

How can we stop them marrying if their hearts are set on it?"

She dozed off while he was reading. His mind was filled with nothing but menstruation, childbirth, and breastfeeding. He grew angry when he noticed her falling asleep.

"Naturally you don't like my writings. These are the same writings that you liked before we got married."

"Do you mean you like what I write? You used to like them before we got married, and you used to say, 'I like your writing, Professor', stressing the 'f'."

"What do you mean I stressed the 'f'? How dare you?"

"How dare YOU?"

There was havoc after her husband's article was published. Ahmed al-Damhiri was hugely upset.

"This is heretical talk. This man is objecting to God's words in the Qur'an. If there is a clear text, we cannot improvise or innovate. There is a text saying that menstruation is evil, that men should not go near women until they are purified of this evil ..."

Ahmed al-Damhiri didn't know the verse concerning menstruation by heart, but he was certain that that the word "evil" was mentioned in the Holy Book. In addition, there was a saying by the Prophet (may peace be upon him) which forbade the marriage between children who suckled together, which he did not recall verbatim, but the gist was clear.

Next to her sat Ahmed al-Damhiri, his eyes following Zeina Bint Zeinat and her every move.

"This girl was a child only yesterday. Today she's a woman, a luscious female. Girls grow at the speed of lightning, and their breasts grow almost overnight."

He closed his eyes, imagining her in his arms, seeing her underneath him in bed. He would have her, no doubt, for he never desired a woman but had her in the end. God had made slave girls and concubines lawful for all men, and for him as an emir, no doubt!

The emir had a mysterious power, which he called the power of God. He used to meet the officials of the government in secret, and oppose its policies in the papers, pretending to be its enemy. He received money and arms from abroad, and hired fighters for God from everywhere. He had assistants in government offices, schools, universities, unions, courts, and ministries. He had eyes in all establishments, even the police and the security apparatus, and in nightclubs and brothels.

One of the emir's men filed a suit against both Safi and her husband. She had made a statement supporting her husband's view that menstruation was not an evil visited on women, and that Islam in essence respected them. Menstrual blood was similar to other types of human blood. As such it was sacred. Without women, there would have been no humanity. The legal charges directed at both of them were the following:

Contempt for the word of God.
Straying from the Islamic faith.
Denying the accepted axioms of religion.
Profanity.

Intellectual men and women were split in two, for while some, led by Ahmed al-Damhiri, sanctioned the charges, others, led by Bodour and her daughter Mageeda, attacked them. The whole thing ended when the case was shelved, which meant a state of neither acquittal nor conviction. The case remained unresolved, stashed in one of the drawers. It would stay there until the government saw fit to reopen it and bring it back into the light.

Contradictory currents and views often coexisted in the same family. The pious father would have an atheist son, and the Muslim mother's womb would bring forth a Marxist daughter. A brother would be on the side of the government, while his sister would be on that of the opposition. But blood was always thinker than water, and families were united during funerals and weddings. They exchanged kisses and hugs, then returned to the arena of conflict and dealt blows to one another, above the belt as well as below it.

It was natural for Ahmed al-Damhiri to attend the birthday of his cousin's daughter, Mageeda Zakariah al-Khartiti. Bodour's image had been in his dreams throughout adolescence. Her daughter, Mageeda, was a rising writer with her own column in the *Renaissance* magazine. He wished to show her the righteous path of Islam. Her father had a permanent column in the *Sphinx* newspaper, and he swayed between science and religious faith. Ahmed al-Damhiri wanted him to become an asset to Islam, for religion needed the protection and support of worldly power, such as the power of money, arms, and the media.

Ahmed al-Damhiri taught political sociology at the American University, for he spoke English and French, and travelled to Paris, Washington, and London to attend religious conferences. He swam like a fish in seas and oceans, and established a company specializing in publishing religious books, manufacturing censers, rosaries, and charms. It supplied arms and audio-visual transmission and reception equipment, and exported salted fish, sardines, and pickles, in addition to translating the Qur'an to the various languages of the world.

"Hello, Ahmed. Lovely to have you at the party!"

"Lovely to see you, dear cousin Bodour!"

"Hello, Uncle Ahmed."

"A very happy birthday to you, Mageeda, and many happy returns!"

"Thank you, Uncle."

"I follow all your writings. Bravo, Mageeda. But I wish one day you would write more on Islam and religious matters. The hereafter is more permanent than this world, Mageeda!"

His eyes followed the movements of Zeina Bint Zeinat. She

played the piano, sitting on the backless stool with her back upright. He saw her profile, her hair raised high like a crown on her head, her complexion tanned by the sun, her long, graceful fingers speeding like fingers of light over the keys of the piano. All the eyes in the hall gazed at her, and the voices were drowned by the music.

"Is Zeina your friend from long ago, Mageeda?"

"From my school days, Uncle."

"Try to advise her, Mageeda, to go back to God!"

"My friend Zeina is a decent young woman, Uncle. Her life is given completely to art, music and sing—"

"All these things are forbidden, Mageeda."

"Why forbidden, Uncle?"

Safaa al-Dhabi turned to them, chipping in, angrily whispering, "Why forbidden, Mr Ahmed? Beautiful art is a gift from God, for God is beautiful and He loves everything that is beautiful. Isn't that right, sir?"

"Can we stop talking now please and listen to Zeina?"

It was Bodour's voice. Sitting in the chair behind her friend Safi, she was worried that the jolly atmosphere might be ruined. She didn't want her cousin, Ahmed al-Damhiri, to create bad vibes, for she knew him well from childhood. He wouldn't keep quiet until all eyes were on him. He expected Bodour to introduce him to her guests. He expected them to look at him with awe when they realized that he was present. But he had to sit like all the other guests, a nonentity, in spite of being an emir, a star who was recognized everywhere, a god or a demi-god in the eyes of his followers.

He fidgeted in his chair, wavering between staying and leaving. But he changed his mind once Zeina Bint Zeinat started to sing, her voice producing a mysterious electric charge inside his body. His whole being quivered, wiping out old sorrows. His lustreless eyes began to gleam. Zeina stood in front of the piano facing the audience in the large hall sitting in rows, their eyes fixed on her. She saw the face of her mother, Zeinat, sitting in the last row next to the servants and cooks. Her eyes twinkled with tears. She left her place on stage and went to her, passing through the rows with her head held high, as she used to do between the rows of girls at school twenty, thirty or a hundred years earlier. The past seemed to have happened only yesterday. She embraced her mother and walked back with her between the rows, climbing with her the few steps leading to the platform. She bowed with natural pride in front of the audience and said, "I dedicate this song to my precious mother, Zeinat. She's more precious to me than the earth and sky, than this world and the hereafter."

Bodour al-Damhiri looked down, swallowing her tears in silence.

Ahmed al-Damhiri fidgeted in his chair. "This girl is blasphemous, what does she mean by better than the earth and sky? There is nothing better than the hereafter, you infidel!"

The words passed through his head, but he said absolutely nothing. The hall became totally silent, then the band began to play. The children were now young men and women, having climbed high in the world of music and art together with Zeina Bint Zeinat. Miss Mariam had trained them, day in day out, month in month out, until Miss Mariam's band became famous all over the country. Miss Mariam sat next to Mageeda al-Khartiti. Her face lit up when Zeina Bint Zeinat pointed at her and took her to climb the platform with her. She introduced her to the audience, standing between her and her mother Zeinat.

"Miss Mariam is my second mother, for she was the one who taught me to love music and singing. She trained us and took us from the street to the world of art. We called our band the 'Mariam Band' and we had no place except the streets, with their dust, women, men and children, with their demonstrations and cheers, 'Down with injustice, and long live freedom'. The streets inspired our tunes and music and rhythms. We drew music from the streets, from the pavements, and the dust, from people's warm breaths on earth and not from the coldness of the sky."

When she spoke, her voice sounded melodious. Her large pupils sparkled and her warm voice touched the hearts of the audience, transforming sorrows to innocent joy. The simple words came as naturally out of her chest as her breath. Everything around her seemed natural, though a little peculiar.

Ahmed al-Damhiri trembled in his chair. "This woman is not a simpleton. She is dangerous, for she plays with words. What does she mean by the coldness of the sky? This is heretical talk."

This was how he spoke to himself.

The hands in the hall clapped, and the sound of applause drowned out all other noises. Some of Ahmed al-Damhiri's aides were sitting in the back rows or standing in the aisles, for the emir never went out without armed guards in plain civilian clothes: white gowns or khaki suits. Inside the pockets of each of them was a silent gun. Although their heads moved in every direction, their eyes remained set on him, for they saw nobody but him, even when the hall was full of people. They heard only his voice, even when other voices rose high or the music played and the singing began. They saw him tremble in his chair and mutter under his breath. His muffled voice might have been lost in the sound of clapping, but they were trained to read his lips, and their muscles moved in unison with them. Then there was silence, and Zeina Bint Zeinat went back to playing and singing.

Something about music charms people, animals, and other creatures. Horses and donkeys dance to the tune of music, birds chirp in the morning, and crickets sing at night with the croaking of frogs. Snakes also relax and refrain from biting when they hear the sound of the flute. Psychiatry uses music to cure the mad and the deranged. Music turns tigers and hyenas in the jungle into tame and docile creatures.

However, not all types of music, singing, or dancing can do that. Zeina Bint Zeinat lived through music. She heard the melody in her sleep, wrote it down when the sun shone in the morning, sang it with the nightingale, and danced to its rhythm as she ran toward her mother, Zeinat. Zeina never imitated other writers or poets, for her lyrics were inspired by her own experiences in life. In her childhood, she learned what adults did not know. She understood the secrets lurking in girls' eyes. As a child, she saw men's naked flesh. Now she was beyond pain and rape, because no man could ever destroy her. She had no father, elder brother, uncle, grandfather, lover, or husband. Only music was her love. She loved those who loved music and loathed those who hated it, even if they were kings or princes.

She held her head high on stage, and under the lights she seemed like the goddess Venus, Isis, Nefertiti or the Virgin Mary. Or perhaps she didn't resemble any of them, for she was a calibre all her own. From her tattered gowns to her proud head, her steady walk, and her pupils radiating a unique light, she had the power to charm, to make the hearts throb and to lead minds to enquire, "But who is she? Why did God give her these self-confident eyes when all the other women's eyes radiate humbleness and timidity?"

Her charm lay in the two daring pupils that had the power to delve deep and uncover all that was concealed, in the steady, unflinching stare, and in the amazing lustre of the eyes of a girl who was always amazed and curious, and yet remained beyond astonishment. She graduated from the school of the streets and knew the pinnacles of sorrow and of joy. That was why she was no longer afraid of heights or depths. No man ever possessed her and never could. Even music didn't possess her, but she possessed it and was therefore free from poverty, fear, and bondage.

Zeina Bint Zeinat became a phenomenon in the world of music, poetry, and singing. At the end of the party, when journalists asked her about her dream in life, her face beamed like a child and, in a singing voice, she recited the words of the first poem she wrote as a child:

I dream of building my mother a house
Made of red brick,
Not of mud,
A house she owns,
A house no one can take away from her.
It has a ceiling to protect her from summer's heat
And winter's cold,
A bathroom with running water
And an electric lamp.

At night, she appeared to Ahmed al-Damhiri in his dreams. During the day, he saw her in the distance as he walked. It might not have been her, but another girl who looked like her, with her tall, graceful build and her head held high. He wanted to hold her head in his hands and smash it, break the insolent eyes, and tame the unruly shrew in bed. He wanted her to lie beneath him so that he could penetrate her with his iron rod and gouge her eyes with his finger. He wanted to make her moan endlessly underneath him, pleading for forgiveness like a worshipper praying to God for His mercy.

Since his childhood, Ahmed al-Damhiri had dreamed of greatness, a myth nurtured by a prophecy his mother had:

"God came to me in my sleep, son, and told me that I was carrying a boy in my womb, a boy who was destined to become a king or a prince, and would ride a white horse and fly ... fly ... fly ..."

His eyes moved to the sky to follow his mother's voice, which urged him to fly. In the dream, he grew wings with which he flew over houses and seas, and over the heads of men. No man's head towered above him.

His father took him to the mosque. He prayed and kneeled down like his father, thanking God that he was created male and not female. If he was stung by a bee, his father would scold him, "You're a man, you shouldn't cry like a woman!"

When his schoolmates beat him up, he hid in his room and cried. He trembled with fear whenever he saw a cockroach, a rat, or a lizard. He was small and short and felt inferior whenever he walked in the company of men. But with women, he was filled with vanity and walked confidently with the steps of a commander. He saw himself as a leader carried by the cheering crowds.

One day his schoolmates took him into the toilets and removed his trousers and pants. With a ruler, they measured the length of his phallus in millimetres. They hit him on the nape of the neck, telling him scornfully, "This is just a whistle!"

On the walls of the toilet, they wrote in chalk: Ahmed al-Damhiri has a whistle.

Safaa al-Dhabi lay on the couch, her eyes rolling, her lips quivering, her facial muscles twitching as though an electric current had gone through her head.

The psychiatrist sat beside her. He injected her intravenously with a tranquilizer, stroked her shoulders with soft, tender hands, and whispered in her ears with motherly kindness, "The crisis is over, Safi. A small nervous breakdown, nothing to worry about!"

The psychiatrist's laugh sounded metallic in the closed, half-lit room. The silk, transparent curtains on the window gave the place a dreamlike atmosphere that was half-way between night and day, sleep and wakefulness, consciousness and unconsciousness.

Safaa al-Dhabi opened her eyes and heard the echo of the

dry, unfeeling metallic laugh. It reminded her of the sound of typing on a computer placed on a wooden or copper board. For a moment she mistook it for the laughter of her Marxist or Islamist husband. She often confused the two, and the other men in her life, who seemed to have the same laugh.

She spoke in a hoarse angry voice. "What are you laughing at, man?"

"I'm happy you got through the crisis, thank God for that!"

"What crisis?"

She was astonished to see the doctor in his white coat while she lay on the couch drenched in sweat, and next to her on the floor was a large pail smelling of vomit. Her head was heavy and her tongue heavier. Her limbs felt as though they were filled with sacks of sand and she could hardly move them.

"What happened, doctor?"

"A slight nervous breakdown, which is now over, thank God!"

"Please, doctor, stop repeating this phrase."

"Which phrase?"

"Thank God!"

"Oh my God! You don't want to thank God?"

"Thank Him for what exactly?"

"That He saved you from death."

"You were the one who saved me, doctor, and not He!"

"So, have you already forgotten God, Safi? Only half an hour ago, you said absolutely nothing except 'please God, please God'!"

"True, that was half an hour ago, but what time do you make it now?"

"Half past six."

"Morning or evening?"

She closed her eyes and fell into oblivion. With the tips of his fingers, he opened her eyelids, felt her pulse and wiped her forehead with a piece of cotton cloth soaked in pure alcohol.

"It's six o'clock in the evening, Safaa."

Her eyes opened, revealing two black, terrified pupils. The whites of the eyes were reddish and yellow. She raised her bosom, preparing to get up.

"Oh my God! I had an important appointment at five."

"The most important thing now is your health, there's nothing more important!"

"Money is more important than health, doctor, and the money is gone now!"

"Health brings money, Safi!"

"And money brings health. My money's gone, doctor. How can I pay you? How can I pay the rent? The food, cabs and cigarettes?"

"You're a university professor and you have a good salary."

"That was in the past, doctor, before the days of democracy and the blessed open-door policy ..."

"Are you then an advocate of iron curtains and dictatorship, Safi?"

"All my money, doctor, is lost in that cursed Islamic bank. They're all thieves, those who advocate Islam and open-door policies. They're no better than their socialist predecessors."

"An educated university professor like you, how could you put your money in one of these money investment companies?"

"They told me that usury was forbidden but that the interests of the money investment companies were permissible. And it was true, God blessed the money and I used to take twenty per cent interest. But it is all gone, the money and the interest, everything!"

Safaa al-Dhabi struck her cheeks and wailed like a woman at a funeral. She wept without tears, a dry, truncated, intermittent whimper. She closed her eyes and opened them again, swaying between drowsiness and wakefulness. But when she was conscious again, she went on with her broken talk about past and present.

"The greatest catastrophe in life, doctor, is to lose your money, your life's work in one instant. I've never had a nervous breakdown before, never, never, never. I've been through a lot of hardships in this horrible life of mine, but never had a nervous breakdown before. When I discovered that my husband was betraying me, I told him to go to hell, and never looked back."

"Which husband was that, Safi? The Marxist or the Islamist?"

"Can't really remember which one, doctor, for they were similar in every way. Secrecy was their established practise, both in politics and in sexual affairs. In their infidelity, lies, and evasiveness, they were identical. They were also similar in their concealment of corruption and their use of pompous words in the service of God or Karl Marx. But the Marxist was more cautious than the Islamist, because Marxists are used to secrecy and underground activities, while the Islamists are stupid and transparent. My Marxist husband was so cautious that he lived with me for nine long years and cheated on me every day without my knowledge. This continued until a friend of mine phoned me and told me that my husband had a flat on Ramsis Street. I took the address from her, grabbed a cab, and climbed the stairs to the third floor because there was no lift in the building. I was out of breath standing in front of the door. I rang the bell and it was like I said, 'Open Sesame', because the door opened and there he was right in front of me, my Marxist husband in the flesh. How could I mistake him? I've lived with him for nine years. He was wearing colorful silk pyjamas and his face turned as pale as death. Behind him stood a child aged three or four, I'm not sure, perhaps even five. The child shook his father's hand, asking 'Who's this woman, Dad?'

"Another woman might have had a nervous breakdown, but not me! I stared him straight in the eye and said, 'Are you a man of principles, you? How could you do that?'

"Do you know what he said, doctor?"

"What did he say to you, Safi?"

"He said, 'How dare you spy on me? Aren't you ashamed of yourself, respectable university professor that you are?' So I chucked him out of my life like a shoe, doctor. No nervous breakdown or anything of the sort. But nine years, of course, is no laughing matter, doctor. At times I woke up in the middle of the night and reached out across the large bed to find it empty. I had insomnia for two years and couldn't sleep without sleeping pills. When I did sleep I was attacked by nightmares, doctor!"

"What kind of nightmares?"

"I saw myself holding a knife and going out on the street, sleepwalking. I looked for a cab but couldn't find one, so I walked and walked until I got to Ramsis Street. I climbed the stairs to the third floor, for there was no lift in the building, and rang the bell. He opened the door dressed in his colorful silk pyjamas, his trousers and pants unbuttoned. I dug the knife into his stomach, into his member which he used to betray me. I cut it to pieces and wrapped it in a newspaper and went back home inhaling the fresh air of the Nile."

Safaa al-Dhabi closed her eyes, looking extremely exhausted. The psychiatrist held her hand in his and whispered in her ear, "You're a great woman, Safi, a professor with a mind. Any woman with a mind cannot find the man who deserves her. All the men are made of tinsel. They're all sick liars and hypocrites. I'm one of them. You're a great professor with a name, publications, and a position. Money will come and go, and men will come and go like everything else. Nothing stays except your mind, work, writing and health."

"But my money, doctor? My life's work? My heart is broken over my money, I'm hurting. Please, doctor, hold my hand, I want to get up and stand on my own feet."

The psychiatrist helped her get up. She tottered a little and was on the point of falling when he caught her in his arms.

She found herself burying her face in his chest and crying. She sobbed as she encircled him with her arms. But her legs gave way and she fell on the couch, dragging him with her. Her semi-conscious body quivered and something inside her trembled, a deeply buried desire stirring, an overwhelming pleasure that she had never felt before. It was the sensation that no man could give her. She wanted so much to experience this pleasure, but her mind was semi-conscious and her feverish lips moved over his chest, neck and lips. But his lips were cold, neutral, without any warmth. He neither encouraged nor repulsed her, but left himself in her arms, his body underneath hers. He let her unbutton his trousers and allowed her to take him the way a man takes a woman.

Before she left the clinic, he held her hand in his and gave her a kiss of gratitude on the cheek.

"Thank you, Safi."

"For what, doctor?"

"I don't know!"

"On the contrary, I thank you, doctor!"

"For what, Safi?"

"For the first time in my life, I feel relaxed as if ... as if ... I had been carrying a heavy load, I don't know why. But the load is gone and my body feels as light as a feather. I feel I have the strength to move mountains."

Bodour al-Damhiri looked for her novel in all the drawers of her desk. It was lost before it was finished, evaporating in the air as if it had never existed. Nobody knew where it was except her husband, Zakariah al-Khartiti. He stared at her enviously when she wrote, for he was jealous of her mind and the words she put down on the page. She never read what she wrote to him, and never asked him for his opinion. Her self-confidence, he felt, bordered on arrogance. He wanted to break this arrogance. He pouted his lips whenever he read one of her articles in the magazine and volunteered his opinion: "Your article, Bodour, would have been better if ..."

She didn't even lift her eyes from her papers, paying no attention to what he said.

"Can't you hear me, Bodour?"

"I can, Zakariah!"

"Don't you want to hear my opinion on your article?"

"I know your opinion."

"What do you mean you know my opinion?"

"I know all your ideas, Zakariah! I've known them for the past hundred years. Since the day we got married, I've been listening to your opinions, every day I've been hearing them. Only an ass can mistake them, and I'm not one!"

He read out his column to her more than once, each time asking her for her opinion. But she would involuntarily doze off while he read. Repetitiveness was boring and it underlined the bankruptcy of his mind, even when it was a feature of one of the books of God. This last statement was not hers, but Badreya's, the heroine of her stolen novel. Her husband no doubt stole it, for he called Badreya a woman lacking in reason and faith because she was making anti-religious statements. The miracle of God's three books was really beyond her deficient reason.

"Badreya is an imaginary character in a novel, Zakariah! You treat her as though she were flesh and blood!"

He pouted his lips and the large Havana cigar shook as it stayed unlit or partially lit between them in the manner of the editor-in-chief, or of Mahmoud al-Feqqi or the other columnists. As soon as a journalist had his own daily column, he would start appearing with the cigar between his lips, which he pouted if he did not like other columns. He didn't in fact like any column except his own, and neither did he like any photograph except his. He would gaze at it admiringly while fiddling with his ear or nose, or scratching the hair on his chest, underneath his belly or in his armpits.

Zakariah al-Khartiti's gait as he walked was in the manner of other great writers. Like them, he leaned more heavily on the left than on the right, as though he was suffering from a slight limp. It was casual, nonchalant, coquettish. He raised his left shoulder, as well as his left buttock, a little higher than his right. He walked with the unlit cigar in his mouth, his eyes riveted on the ceiling and totally lost in deep thought. But in the presence of the president or the minister, he would walk straight, get rid of the cigar in his mouth, and remove the frown on his face and the lost look in his eyes. He would stand upright, all his five senses in total readiness: seeing, hearing, smelling, touching, and tasting. Even the sixth sense would become equally alert, in addition to the seventh sense, which was owned only by those people who were close to the corridors of power, money, and arms. This latter sense was born out of the sense of smell, for the great writer sometimes smelled death coming to take the life of the editor-in-chief and leaving his chair empty.

Zakariah al-Khartiti was getting ready to write his daily column about the Feast. He sat for a long time holding the pen in hand, rummaging around in his brain for an idea, and browsing through the newspapers lying in front of him. He was looking for a phrase or an idea written in another column that he might lift. He would change it and edit it in such a way as to make it totally different from the original.

What could Zakariah al-Khartiti possibly write concerning the Feast?

The Feast was a happy time in his childhood, for, like other children, he enjoyed the sight of the slaughter of the sheep. He woke up at dawn to the sound of the butcher calling out "Butcher, butcher".

He ran to open the door for him. The man held a large knife in his hand, his gown all stained with blood. He rolled his sleeves, recited the Islamic testimony, then struck the neck with the knife. The poor sheep's eyes, filled with terror and sadness, would protrude. Frozen tears covered its eyes as it kicked a little and bled profusely from its slashed neck. The head rolled away from the body as though in a dancing ritual. Children cheered happily, wore their new clothes and shoes, ate the grilled liver of the sheep, went to the swings, hit sparrows with their slings, and walked behind the lame orphan boy shouting and taunting him, "Here's the idiot, the idiot, the idiot."

The lame boy tripped as he ran away to escape them. He fell on the ground and they laughed and shouted happily, "The bull is down, out with the knife!"

Zakariah al-Khartiti was engrossed in writing, "My dear readers, what lovely days those were! The Feast then was a real feast. It was a time of plenty and the children were genuinely happy."

When he read out the column to his wife, Bodour, who was engrossed in her novel, pouted her lips in dismay, saying to herself, this nonsense could only be written by a primary school child, an unfeeling, heartless dimwit without any tenderness or humanity.

Since her childhood, Bodour had hated feasts, particularly the Great Feast when sheep were slaughtered. She would continue to see the sad eyes of the slaughtered animal pursuing her in her sleep. She saw them in the mirror in the morning, before she went to school or went to bed. She saw them in the eyes of Zeina Bint Zeinat when people told her she was the product of sin, and when verses from the Bible, the Qur'an, and the Torah were recited on the radio. She saw those eyes when the sheikh said that the three books were revelations from heaven to Christians, Muslims, and Jews. As followers of heavenly religions, they would all go to heaven after death, if they believed in Muhammad and the Qur'an, and admitted that Jesus, Mary's son, was not crucified or killed by a human hand, but was lifted to heaven by the command of God.

Ever since her childhood, she had been assailed by profound doubts. But her fears kept her faith intact. In her adolescence, she started to read. Nessim asked her, "Did you read the Qur'an, the Bible, and the Torah? How could you believe in books you haven't read? Have you read Karl Marx and Friedrich Engels? Have you read Aba Dhar al-Ghafari, al-Ghazali, Avicenna or Averroes? Or Rab'aa al-Adaweyah, Ibn Khaldoun, al-Roumi or Omar al-Khayyam's poetry?"

Nessim laughed as he said, "Al-Khayyam's poetry is much more delicious than Omar al-Khayyam red wine."

Bodour tasted wine for the first time when she was nineteen years old. It was also the first time she read al-Khayyam's poetry, written a thousand years earlier.

She stopped at four lines of poetry that lit a dark corner of her mind:

Tell me, God, what human being has not disobeyed you?
Tell me, God, what would be the point of life without sin?
If you punished me, God, by sending me evil things in return for the evil I committed,
What would be the difference between us?

These four lines struck her, and she began to ask God many questions. Why did you create me, oh God, as a woman with a hymen and a womb that can carry the seed of sin, and make the male body free?

When Bodour read the first few pages of the Torah, she

wondered if those were the true words of God when they sounded so hard to believe?

Opening the Torah she read:

> And the LORD God caused a deep sleep to fall upon the man, and he slept; and He took one of his ribs, and closed up the place with flesh instead thereof. And the rib, which the LORD God had taken from the man, made He a woman, and brought her unto the man. And the man said: "This is now bone of my bones, and flesh of my flesh; she shall be called Woman, because she was taken out of Man."
>
> Now the serpent was more subtle than any beast of the field which the LORD God had made. And he said unto the woman: "Yea, hath God said: 'Ye shall not eat of any tree of the garden'?" And the woman said unto the serpent: "Of the fruit of the trees of the garden we may eat; but of the fruit of the tree which is in the midst of the garden, God hath said: 'Ye shall not eat of it, neither shall ye touch it, lest ye die.'" And the serpent said unto the woman: "Ye shall not surely die; for God doth know that in the day ye eat thereof, then your eyes shall be opened, and ye shall be as God, knowing good and evil."
>
> [...]
>
> And He said: [...] "Hast thou eaten of the tree, whereof I commanded thee that thou shouldest not eat?" And the man said: "The woman whom Thou gavest to be with me, she gave me of the tree, and I did eat." And the LORD God said unto the woman: "What is this thou hast done?" And the woman said: "The serpent beguiled me, and I did eat." And the LORD God said unto the serpent: "Because thou hast done this, cursed art thou

from among all cattle, and from among all beasts of the field; upon thy belly shalt thou go, and dust shalt thou eat all the days of thy life. And I will put enmity between thee and the woman, and between thy seed and her seed; they shall bruise thy head, and thou shalt bruise their heel." Unto the woman He said: "I will greatly multiply thy pain and thy travail; in pain thou shalt bring forth children; and thy desire shall be to thy husband, and he shall rule over thee."

[...]

And the LORD God said: "Behold, the man is become as one of us, to know good and evil; and now, lest he put forth his hand, and take also of the tree of life, and eat, and live for ever." Therefore the LORD God sent him forth from the garden of Eden [to till the ground from whence he was taken].

[...]

And it came to pass, when men began to multiply on the face of the earth, and daughters were born unto them, that the sons of God saw the daughters of men that they were fair; and they took them wives, whomsoever they chose.

[...]

The Nephilim were in the earth in those days, and also after that, when the sons of God came in unto the daughters of men, and they bore children to them.

[...]

"Neither shall thy name any more be called Abram, but thy name shall be Abraham; for the father of a multitude of nations have I made thee. And I will make thee exceeding fruitful, and I will make nations of thee, and kings shall come out of thee. And I will establish My covenant between Me and thee and thy seed after thee throughout their generations for an everlasting covenant, to be a God unto thee and to thy seed after thee. And I will give unto thee, and to thy seed after thee, the land of thy sojournings, all the land of Canaan, for an everlasting possession; and I will be their God." And God said unto Abraham: "And as for thee, thou shalt keep My covenant, thou, and thy seed after thee throughout their generations. This is My covenant, which ye shall keep, between Me and you and thy seed after thee: every male among you shall be circumcised. And ye shall be circumcised in the flesh of your foreskin; and it shall be a token of a covenant betwixt Me and you. And he that is eight days old shall be circumcised among you, every male throughout your generations, he that is born in the house, or bought with money of any foreigner, that is not of thy seed. He that is born in thy house, and he that is bought with thy money, must needs be circumcised; and My covenant shall be in your flesh for an everlasting covenant. And the uncircumcised male who is not circumcised in the flesh of his foreskin, that soul shall be cut off from his people; he hath broken My covenant."

Bodour read God's words written in the Torah, and wondered how God's covenant could possibly lie in cutting off a piece of flesh from the human body. How could God give the land of Canaan or Palestine to an army of killers in return for a covenant of the flesh? How could He command a woman to desire her husband when he dominated her? Why did He promise her pain in bringing forth her children? And how did the sons of God marry the daughters of men? Why was it that God's children were all male? And how was it that God had children in the Torah, His first book, and was later described as having no children in His third book, the Qur'an?

Bodour opened God's second book, the Bible, and she read similar statements though with minor variations. Here God also preferred males, for the Virgin Mary gave birth to Christ from the spirit of God that was male and not female. Christ was God's son and God warned people against adulterous women.

And there came one of the seven angels which had the seven vials, and talked with me, saying unto me, Come hither; I will shew unto thee the judgment of the great whore that sitteth upon many waters With whom the kings of the earth have committed fornication, and the inhabitants of the earth have been made drunk with the wine of her fornication. So he carried me away in the spirit into the wilderness: and I saw a woman sit upon a scarlet colored beast, full of names of blasphemy, having seven heads and ten horns. And the woman was arrayed in purple and scarlet color, and decked with gold and precious stones and pearls, having a golden cup in her hand full of abominations and filthiness of her fornication And upon her forehead [was] a name written, MYSTERY, BABYLON THE GREAT, THE MOTHER OF HARLOTS AND ABOMINATIONS OF THE EARTH. And I saw the woman drunken with the blood of the saints, and with the blood of the martyrs of Jesus.

[...]

The seven heads are seven mountains, on which the woman sitteth. And there are seven kings: five are fallen, and one is, [and] the other is not yet come; [and when he cometh, he must continue a short space].

[...]

And he saith unto me, The waters which thou sawest, where the whore sitteth, are peoples, and multitudes, and nations, and tongues. And the ten horns which thou sawest upon the beast, these shall hate the whore, and shall make her desolate and naked, and shall eat her flesh, and burn her with fire.

[...]

And he cried mightily with a strong voice, saying, Babylon the great is fallen, is fallen, and is become the habitation of Devils, and the hold of every foul spirit, and a cage of every unclean and hateful bird. For all nations have drunk of the wine of the wrath of her fornication, and the kings of the earth have committed fornication with her, and the merchants of the earth are waxed rich through the abundance of her delicacies.

[...]

How much she hath glorified herself, and lived deliciously, so much torment and sorrow give her: for she saith in her heart, I sit a queen, and am no widow, and shall see no sorrow. Therefore shall her plagues come in one day, death, and mourning, and famine; and she shall be utterly burned with fire: for strong [is] the Lord God who judgeth her. And the kings of the earth, who have committed fornication and lived deliciously with her, shall bewail her, and lament for her, when they shall see the smoke of her burning.

[...]

And I saw heaven opened, and behold a white horse; and he that sat upon him [was] called Faithful and True, and in righteousness he doth judge and make war. His eyes [were] as a flame of fire, and on his head [were] many crowns; and he had a name written, that no man knew, but he himself. And he [was] clothed with a vesture dipped in blood: and his name is called The Word of God. And the armies [which were] in heaven followed him upon white horses, clothed in fine linen, white and clean. And out of his mouth goeth a sharp sword, that with it he should smite the nations: and he shall rule them with a rod of iron: and he treadeth the winepress of the fierceness and wrath of Almighty God. And he hath on [his] vesture and on his thigh a name written, KING OF KINGS, AND LORD OF LORDS.

Bodour felt out of breath as she read God's book, the Bible. She had no idea why there was so much animosity toward the sinful woman whose wine the kings of the earth drank. She didn't understand why a bloody war broke out both in the sky and on earth between the kings in cooperation with the greatly sinful woman and the new king, the King of Kings, the Lord of Lords, on whose thighs and dress his name was written.

Bodour stopped at the verse speaking about Gog and Magog:

And when the thousand years are expired, Satan shall be loosed out of his prison, And shall go out to deceive the nations which are in the four quarters of the earth, Gog and Magog, to gather them together to battle: the number of whom [is] as the sand of the sea. And they went up on the breadth of the earth, and compassed the camp of the saints about, and the beloved city: and fire came down from God out of heaven, and devoured them. And the Devil that deceived them was cast into the lake of fire and brimstone, where the beast and the false prophet [are], and shall be tormented day and night forever and ever.

Bodour trembled from the enormity of the war, the fire and the bloodshed in the three books of God. The Qur'an mentioned the same names, Gog and Magog, Satan and the blazing fires for those who did not worship God. God recognized the presence of men in the Qur'an, but not that of women, whose names were completely absent. He didn't mention the name of Eve but referred to her as Adam's wife. Pharaoh's wife who tempted the prophet Joseph had no name, and neither was Khadiga, Prophet Muhammad's first wife, mentioned in the Qur'an by name. Only the Virgin Mary, Jesus' mother, was referred to by her name and a whole chapter was dedicated to her.

Nessim encouraged her to rebel against God. He wondered how she could believe in a god that did not address her or mention her by name, and made her subservient to her husband. In all three books, women were not treated as the equals of men.

At nineteen Bodour was torn between her love for Nessim and her faith in God and her belief in the truthfulness of the Qur'an, the Bible, and the Torah. Before sleeping, she opened the Qur'an to read:

> And they ask you about menstruation. Say: It is a discomfort; therefore keep aloof from the women during the menstrual discharge and do not go near them until they have become clean

> Your wives are a tilth for you, so go into your tilth when you like

> And the divorced women should keep themselves in waiting for three courses; and it is not lawful for them that they should conceal what Allah has created in their wombs, if they believe in Allah and the last day; and their husbands have a better right to take them back in the meanwhile if they wish for reconciliation; and they have rights similar to those against them in a just manner, and the men are a degree above them

So if he divorces her she shall not be lawful to him
afterwards until she marries another husband

Bodour stopped at this verse. Her aunt was divorced from her
husband three times. When her husband wanted to re-marry her,
the Ma'zoun told him he couldn't until she had married another
man. Only after the temporary man had divorced her might he
re-marry her.

She was ten years old when she saw her aunt cry the whole
night, talking to God: "But where is the justice, God? Why put me
through such misery? My husband divorced me at a whim three
times, and every time he re-married me. After the third time, I have
to sleep with a stranger for a day, two days or even half an hour so
that I can re-marry my husband. But what am I? A doormat to be
trampled on by men? You should punish my husband for divorcing
me three times, and not punish me by making me sleep with a
strange man. Where is the justice in that, God?"

Bodour also read:

Surely your Lord is Allah, Who created the heavens and

the earth in six periods of time

Wasn't this statement uncannily similar to the statement
in the Bible? And why six days? God also addresses the
Prophet saying:

O Prophet! surely We have made lawful to you your
wives whom you have given their dowries, and those
whom your right hand possesses out of those whom
Allah has given to you as prisoners of war, and the
daughters of your paternal uncles and the daughters of
your paternal aunts, and the daughters of your maternal

uncles and the daughters of your maternal aunts who fled with you; and a believing woman if she gave herself to the Prophet, if the Prophet desired to marry her – specially for you, not for the (rest of) believers; We know what We have ordained for them concerning their wives and those whom their right hands possess in order that no blame may attach to you; and Allah is Forgiving, Merciful.

Bodour said to herself, why should the Prophet have all those women? He was supposed to be more chaste than other men, a role model of faithfulness to his life's partner. He stayed faithful to his first wife, Khadiga, for twenty years and never slept with any other woman until she died. Why did his marital fidelity change following the death of Khadiga?

After Bodour became an adult and got married to Zakariah al-Khartiti, she understood why her husband committed adultery. She saw him creep out of her bed to go to other women. When she stopped him, he waved in her face saying, "This is a God-given right. Do you think your husband is going to be better than the Prophet himself?"

After discovering his first infidelity, she couldn't bear him touching her, let alone penetrating her. His naked body made her sick. She left him naked in bed and went to the bathroom to vomit silently, fearing he might hear her. A deep-seated fear was lodged within her heart from childhood and she had no idea where it came from. She felt repelled by her husband and never believed a word he said to her. If he told her he was going to attend a meeting or a conference, she would immediately know that he was going to spend a night of lust with another woman. As far back as she could remember, she heard women repeat the saying, "Trusting a man is like trusting water to stay in a sieve."

Bodour tossed in bed, unable to sleep.

How could she carry on living with a faithless man? How could she sleep next to him in the same bed?

She lied to him only once, while he lied to her every day over the period of twenty, thirty or even a hundred years.

Did he know that she lied to him? That she was in love with Nessim when she was nineteen? That she joined the demonstrations with him? He opened her eyes to injustices on earth and in the heavens, and removed the blindfolds from her mind. He granted her body the forbidden pleasure, and she ate with him from the fruits of the two forbidden trees: the trees of life and knowledge. Like God, she knew good from evil. Good was justice and freedom, as Nessim said, and evil was injustice and chains.

Bodour never broke her chains. She tossed sleeplessly in bed and the baby's eyes were like motes in her own. Since the two closed eyes opened briefly and peered at her, since that moment that seemed to happen outside time and space, Bodour came face to face with her own cowardice. She felt her heart dripping with blood on the pavement as her liver was torn out of her body with a knife.

If the baby hadn't opened her eyes at that moment, it was possible that she might have forgotten her. She might have slept like other mortals and continued her life and her career in literary criticism. Badreya, the heroine of her novel, and Nessim might have left her alone and stopped chasing her. Those two ghosts lived on top of her bed. She saw them in the flesh lying next to her in bed, and when they left it, she saw them walking like shadows on the wall, going to and fro. They didn't leave the bedroom when she slept or the study when she sat at her desk spreading the papers in front of her. She saw Omar al-Khayyam's lines of poetry in front of her. What was the difference then between God and human beings if God repaid evil with evil, nay, even with a more horrific evil? He burned her in hell forever and ever for one moment of pleasure and joy. He deprived her of her child forever just because the police killed the baby's father before he could sign the marriage contract. She was sceptical of God's justice and consequently of His existence. She lost her faith during her sleep and was exhausted by all the buried sorrows in her heart. She chased away the doubts and embraced faith again as soon as she was up, realizing that faith brought joy like alcohol, like Omar al-Khayyam wine.

She hid a bottle in the bottom drawer of her desk together with the novel folder. She drank a glass to drive away her sorrows. After the third glass her mind became open to the wide horizons and she could hear the voices of gods and demons arguing. Her body broke all barriers and soared with her mind and soul in the wide space. She became as tall and graceful as Badreya, and just as courageous. She held the pen and began to write a new chapter of the novel, continuing until she heard the sound of footsteps in the hall or a key turning, or saw the shadow of her husband walking on the walls. It looked like God's shadow moving behind the clouds, or the Devil's phantom moving over her head as she lay in bed, his finger as hard as nails boring through the hole of her left foot while God's finger bored through the sole of her right foot like an iron rod.

When the psychiatrist had listened to her childhood memories, he told her, "You were raped as a child, Bodour, but your fear of God makes you deny it!"

"No, no, doctor. No man ever touched me in reality. I only had sinful dreams. Yes, I confess that I committed many sins while fast asleep."

The psychiatrist's voice streamed through her ear as she tossed and turned in bed. She reached out for the light switch to turn it off, but she trembled when she realized that her husband was not in bed. It was three o'clock in the morning. He had gone out at eight in the evening to attend an editorial meeting at the newspaper.

"Could a meeting possibly continue for seven hours?"

On the bedside table stood a dark bottle on which the word VIAGRA was written. He had forgotten to hide it in the bottom drawer of his desk. His memory was getting worse and he often forgot things. He was a few years older than she was, a fact he often forgot as well. He liked to think that she was his age or even older.

In the mirror, Bodour noticed the white hairs on her head, the slight wrinkles around the eyes and mouth, and on top of the jaws and neck. Her muscles were sagging and flabby. How old was she?

Her mind could not grasp the notion of time passing. She put her feet in her soft slippers. It was for this softness that she had given up her life, the most precious thing of her life. She left the stuffy, dimly lit bedroom filled with her husband's breath, his shaving cream and his expensive eau de cologne. The odor made her sick when she imagined him in the arms of a girl who was fifty or a hundred years younger than he was. He only got an erection when he was with innocent, inexperienced girls or prostitutes pretending to be innocent and inexperienced.

Bodour walked in sleep as she did during her wakeful moments. She went out of the stuffy room into the air and the sun. She walked in the direction of Zeina Bint Zeinat, toward truth and not toward dreams, myths or illusions. She saw herself walking toward her, going through the long strip from her seat to the stage. The passage seemed endless and exposed to the cold air from every direction. The flowers on both sides withered, while the trees died where they stood, their green leaves turning yellow.

Bodour suddenly stopped in her tracks. Looking behind, she saw the emptiness, the darkness, the cold air and the fear. Turning to look in front of her, she saw the lights gleaming and Zeina Bint Zeinat playing music, singing and dancing. But the lights suddenly went out and there were sounds of explosions or gunshots. Everything turned dark, illuminated for a second, then dark again. The power was cut off and she was no longer there. She looked for her in sleep and in wakefulness, on the streets, the alleys and the pavements. She had cleared the pavement of the stones and pebbles, laid out the cover, swaddled her in a blue woollen blanket to keep her warm in the coldness of winter. She left her in the dark, and withdrew her plump fingers from the tiny hand, from the five fingers clutching her index finger, which she held on to even during sleep. She didn't want to open her eyes to see her as she disappeared gradually until she became a star in the distant sky.

How did her body become disconnected from the pavement? How did she develop legs to take her away from her like a phantom?

As Bodour was engrossed in writing, Badreya whispered in her ear, "You're a hopeless coward. Nothing but writing can cure you of cowardice. Only the letters on the page can cure you of your pain and sadness. With black, blue or red ink, shed your blood on paper, Bodour, cut your chest open with the knife and open your heart. Only the knife can cure you. Don't keep your tears locked inside, let them loose the way you scream out in the face of God and the Devil. Don't fear death or hell fire. You've had enough hell on earth."

Bodour tottered in her sleep. Badreya's voice quivered before it disappeared, melting in the night as though she had never been. The ink also melted on the page. The letters vanished and the pages became empty. The whiteness stuck to her eyes and prevented her from seeing anything except the blackness. Sorrow and depression overwhelmed her and she spoke aloud during sleep. No one was there, not even herself.

"Like God, I don't exist."

Speaking to herself, Bodour said, "I'm a literary critic and not a novelist. I'm good at nothing except polishing the shoes of others, for this is the function of literary criticism. In a newspaper interview, I confessed that I felt proud to shine my husband's shoes. I got votes at the university elections but lost my own voice. I lost my ability to write, and my pen was as broken as my heart."

Bodour wasn't speaking to herself, but to her psychiatrist, confusing herself with him. She moved from her bed to the couch in the clinic with slow, careful steps as though sleepwalking. She feared she might fall suddenly if she became conscious again. During the act of writing she got rid of her short plump body and took on Badreya's tall, graceful figure. Her complexion changed color with the intensity of the light. She looked ruthlessly at her image in the mirror, seeing the signs of decline graphically clear in front of her. Nothing could save her from falling, except falling further in the pit of writing.

The ink, however, was white and the letters were invisible on the white page. The whiteness stuck to her open eyes and she slept with her eyes open, like a lidless animal.

"My chronic ailment, doctor, is my life. Nothing except death or writing can cure me."

"Write, then, Bodour. What stops you?"

"God did not create me to write, doctor!"

"Are you embracing faith in God once again?"

"Faith protects me from writing, doctor, because God created me to lie beneath my husband, polish his shoes, rub his feet in warm water, wash his stinking socks with fragrant soap and leave my body to him as a receptacle for his stinking ..."

"You've been saying this ever since you got married, Bodour. How many years now?"

"I don't know, doctor, perhaps a hundred years."

"Twenty years?"

"Longer, doctor. Each day I ask myself why I still live with him. I can't make a serious decision, doctor. My friend Safi is much more courageous, for she got rid of her husbands and is now free. Badreya is also more courageous ..."

"Badreya?"

"She was with me in primary school. We called her a child of sin and wrote her name on toilet walls."

Bodour struggled to open her eyes. The images and names were confused in her mind. She couldn't distinguish between reality and fiction. She lay on the couch and the psychiatrist looked at her with sympathy. On the same couch her husband Zakariah al-Khartiti complained of his sins and sorrows, and their daughter Mageeda opened her heart to the same psychiatrist. Safi, Bodour's friend, did the same as well. Even the emir himself, Ahmed al-Damhiri, lay on the couch and told the doctor of the agony of unrequited love and the infernal desire for revenge. He didn't mention the name Zeina Bint Zeinat for he feared the psychiatrist might tell the police.

They all came and lay on the psychiatrist's couch. They wanted to unburden themselves of the heavy loads weighing down like mountains on their hearts. They relieved themselves of the loads by speaking to the psychiatrist, whose ears were as large as those of God in his heavens or the priest sitting behind the curtain, receiving confessions from guilt-ridden, tortured men and women believers.

"You carry the secrets of the whole country, doctor, from top to bottom, old and young. All the secrets, stories, and weird tales on the couch."

"What a lovely title for a new novel, Bodour!"

"Yes, doctor, you must write a novel with the title 'On the Couch'."

"I'm only a psychiatrist, not a novelist. I can listen well but I can't write a one-page letter. Writing is a gift from God, a gift granted to whomever He pleases."

"Writing is a curse, doctor. It is suffering, pain, tears, and blood. Writing is endless patience and work, day and night. It is a chronic disease, doctor, which can only be cured by writing, real writing, writing a novel and not literary criticism, which is a parasitic activity, a profession akin to tapeworms living off the blood of others."

"You are the greatest literary critic in the country, professor."

"I should have presented my resignation to the university. Every day, I tell myself I must make up my mind to resign and must take the step of leaving my husband. Every morning I tell myself, 'Bodour, enough is enough. You've got to decide to get a divorce from your husband and literary criticism. You have to free yourself from the two things that have choked you, the two things that have ruined your life.'"

"You are the most successful woman in the country, Bodour. You're a well-known celebrity."

"I'm a failure, doctor. I've failed in the most important thing in life."

"And what is the most important thing in your life, Bodour?"

"I don't really know, but I feel I've given up the most important thing in life in return for trivial things."

"Trivial such as what?"

"Like a chair at the university, for example, my name in large font in the paper, a photograph inside a frame, the honor of the family, a greatly respected husband, the large villa in Garden City, the luxury and wealth and all this rubbish."

"And the most precious thing in your life?"

"My daughter, doctor."

"Your daughter Mageeda, God bless her, is a great writer."

For a long time Bodour was silent, hesitant, perplexed. Could she possibly tell him the most serious secret of her life? She had told him everything except that. Would he keep it secret? Would she have the courage to tell? She longed to shake off the load that was weighing down on her heart, to cure herself of this chronic disease. She wanted to walk with Zeina Bint Zeinat, to take her in her arms, to confess to her that she was her mother, and to ask her for forgiveness. She would tell her, "Have mercy on your tortured mother who was paralyzed with fear: the fear of God, of people's tongues and of the tongues of flames in hell. Forgive me for having abandoned you on the pavement, on a bed of dust, your back to the railings of the Nile front. I swaddled you in a woollen cloth and covered you with the bigger blanket of darkness. I abandoned you to the dew and the croaking of frogs. I called you Zeina, and walked away in the night's darkness before the break of dawn."

Bodour woke up to find herself sitting at her desk. In front of her was the yellow folder on which the words *The Stolen Novel* were written.

How many times had the novel been stolen from her? How many times had she retrieved it, rewritten it and lost it again?

Her husband Zakariah al-Khartiti was probably the culprit, for he believed that a wife's proper place was underneath him in bed. Even if she moved up in the world and became a professor, a doctor, a minister, a prime minister or a president, her natural place would still be beneath her husband in bed and never on top of him. Should she climb momentarily to the top, she must be returned to her place again.

Zakariah al-Khartiti wrote in his column about women's liberation and was awarded first prize on International Women's Day. In Egypt, he received accolades and was called the champion of the Egyptian woman's liberation. Journalists asked him, "Behind every great man there's a great woman, so who's the woman behind you, Mr Khartiti?"

"My mother. She was the one who encouraged me to tell the truth and respect women."

They turned to his wife, Professor Bodour, to ask her, "Behind every great woman there's a great man, so who's the man behind you, Professor Bodour?"

"My husband was the man who encouraged me to write. Without him I would have written nothing."

Bodour skulked away into a dark corner, shrinking inside her short, plump body, slapping herself several times, admonishing, insulting, castigating herself.

"You're nothing but a lying, cowardly hypocrite. Lies, cowardice and hypocrisy are the three causes of depression. They are the source of your sadness and sterility, your inability to write or to face the truth. You're beyond redemption and your impotence and sterility have no cure except death."

Badreya woke up when Bodour went to sleep. Bodour lay curled up in bed beside her husband like a porcupine, visited by the youthful dreams when she joined the demonstrators and shouted "Down with injustice and long live freedom, long live love." She surrendered to love and freedom. The idea of the novel came to her and she became pregnant with it at night. But she dumped it on the pavement and ran away. She was now being chased by ghosts and phantoms, by Satan's finger which was as hard as an iron rod, by God's unsleeping eye, by her husband's half open eye pretending to be asleep in spite of being awake, or pretending to be awake although he was sound asleep.

Badreya whispered in her ear, "The price of freedom is high, Bodour, and there is no writing without freedom. Break your chains, Bodour, break free of your prison and reach out for the forbidden tree. If you eat from it, you will not die, for knowledge leads you to life and not to death. You will live forever."

Badreya's voice sounded like that of the serpent luring Eve. Although the name Eve meant throbbing with life, it became connected in the minds with the serpent and death. Bodour quivered in her reveries, and her hot breath came out of her mouth like intermittent waves of light. The words that came from her lips were truncated and filled with fear:

"But God, Badreya, told me I would die if I ate from the tree."

"That was the voice of the Devil, Bodour, and not God. If it was God's voice, it wouldn't be any different from the Devil's. I ate from the tree, Bodour, and so did all the creative men and women in all the areas of knowledge, from philosophy and art to science. Human civilization was built on their ideas. We've never tasted anything better than the fruit of this tree. We enjoyed the pleasure of knowledge and the exuberance of life, and not a fake dead life. If God stopped you from enjoying life, then He was not God but the Devil. Satan's pointed finger stole your life and your novel, Bodour."

Bodour trembled in her sleep. She tried to move her lips to say something, but they were as heavy as lead. Her body was a rock glued to the earth, curled in on itself like a porcupine. It was a ball of lead rolling from bed and falling on the floor with a thud like an explosion or a gunshot.

Her husband woke up when he heard the thud. His eyeballs protruded with fear, for his wife Bodour wasn't really herself. Her body, which joined them, was now setting them apart, and her writing, which connected them, created a wedge between them. Badreya, the Devilish woman occupying her body, was pushing her toward vice. There was also her illegitimate daughter, born in sin, Zeina Bint Zeinat, who was in fact the fruit of countless sins. There was also the novel she wrote at night, filled with ghosts, phantoms, shadows walking on the walls, and the finger tickling the sole of her left foot. Was it Satan's finger? Or God's? And the iron rod that tickled her right foot? But how dare she write all this rubbish about me? How could she write this about me, Zakariah al-Khartiti, her husband, a man of faith and virtue, who had never known another woman, who had won the prize of science and faith, as well as ethical conduct medals at primary and secondary schools, the university, the higher academy and the Supreme Council for Literature and Culture? I, Zakariah al-Khartiti, had a daily column in the paper, read by millions of men, women and young people, and had been awarded the golden cup on International Women's Day. How could she paint such a disgusting image of me? She described me as a man who looked like an iron rod penetrating any hole in the wall or any human body, whether of a man, woman or child. Even the lame illegitimate street boy wasn't spared the viciousness of her pen.

Zakariah al-Khartiti read her novel while she slept. Badreya saw him creeping in the darkness while his wife slept. He took her key from under her pillow, tiptoed to her study, opened the bottom drawer, got out the yellow folder, drew the lamp closer to him, read the blank pages besmirched with black, blue and red ink, and saw the drops of blue and black blood. Rivers of yellow tears streamed between the lines and underneath the hidden illegible words and those not yet written. There were rivers of streaming sweat, real sweat, on the pages. He knew the distinctive, unmistakable smell of his wife's sweat. It was a smell that contained no perfume or eau de cologne, but the smell of an exhausted body, a body tired of sinfulness, guilt, and grief. It was ridden with fear and scandal, a short plump body that seemed to have no bones at all.

Badreya whispered in his ears as he read, "Why should your wife wear any perfume for you when you betray her every night? Why should she wear perfume when you hate perfume? You're only attracted to stinking bodies that never wash with soap and water, bodies oozing sweat, tiredness, wretchedness, and misery, the bodies of oppressed housemaids or secretaries who close their eyes when they lie beneath your weight, unable to open them or look you in the eye. They are unable to shy away from your kisses or obscenities, for you desire nothing but obscenities. Your ears have become attuned to them."

Zakariah al-Khartiti waved his hand in Badreya's face as though to drive away the Devil, "Get lost, you wretched serpent. You've driven Adam out of heaven."

But Badreya was not his wife, Bodour, and did not have a body that he could subjugate in bed when he failed to subdue her in the novel. Badreya exposed his innermost secrets, which his own wife didn't know about. And he hadn't told those secrets to anybody, not even his psychiatrist. He invented clean secrets and childhood memories that happened only in his imagination. He wrote these memories in his daily column under the titles "Science and Faith", "Trusted Words", "Truth", "Honoring the Pledge", or "Loyalty to God, the Nation and the President".

Zakariah al-Khartiti dried his tears with the palm of his hand. His profuse sweat fell on the pages of the novel, mingled with his tears. His sweat merged with his wife's on the papers as it did in bed during the temporary moments of pleasure and the longer-lasting moments of pain. He whispered in Badreya's ear as though she was his innocent, uncouth lover, the secretary or the housemaid, "My wife, darling, gave me nothing but misery, for I'm a wretched husband who never had any joy in the marital bed. My wife is so frigid that not a single hair moves on her body."

He whispered obscenities in the ears of the maid/secretary: "You bitch, you're the most beautiful woman on earth and in heaven. You're a nymph in paradise, the virgin who never loses her virginity, even if she's lost it a thousand times. You're my refuge and my salvation from grief. You're my happiness and my paradise. Take me in your arms, between your legs, and make me taste your honey. Raise me high to the heavens of love and faith and bring me down to the earth of profanity. Pour in my ears the words of God and the Devil, speak to me, bitch, daughter of a bitch, and fill my ears with obscenities until I come to the height of pleasure."

Badreya's hearing was sharp and her ears were as open as

God's unsleeping eyes. She picked up the words before they were produced. The reason was perhaps that Badreya was an ethereal presence, without a body, like the spirit of God or the Devil or the other unseen entities. Badreya was an idea in the head of the sleeping Bodour, and she came to her during sleep. But when the light was on, she vanished. The novel and all its characters disappeared under the effect of the bright lights, except for Zeina Bint Zeinat, who came to life in the light. This was because she was perhaps the only one who possessed a body, a body that housed the spirits of gods and Devils together. She resembled ancient goddesses: the goddess of life and death, the goddess of vice and virtue, the whore, the saint and the virgin all rolled into one. She rose above the laws of earth and sky and had no god but herself.

On the stage Zeina Bint Zeinat stood graceful and upright, her large sparkling eyes filled with light. The hall was full of men, women, young people, and children. There were the children of good families and the children of the streets. Her eyes roamed, looking for the face of Zeinat, her mother. She found her sitting in the back rows with housemaids and illegitimate children. She descended the platform and walked toward her mother, held her hand and led her to the front row, where she placed her next to the ministers, the heads, the men and women of letters, the winners of literature, science and faith prizes. She placed her mother in the front row, where her head towered above the rest. Mariam's band of street children, led by Miss Mariam on stage, stood around Zeina Bint Zeinat, who danced and sang her new song which she had written before dawn.

Music had flowed in her blood with poetry since her childhood on the street. In the open air and under the rays of the sun she sang and danced to the music, and the children born on the pavements sang along with her. From birth the dew dropped on them, and the sun and the fresh air dried them. Those children were never confined within four walls or controlled by a mother or father. They knew nothing about hell fires or the gardens of Eden. They tapped with their little bare feet to the music she played. She sang for them until they fell asleep. They called her Mama Zeina Bint Zeinat. The word mama was like music to her ears. She called her mother Mama Zeinat. Her mother held her in her arms at night. In the morning she walked to school with the other girls who wrote her name, Zeina Bint Zeinat, on the toilet walls. But Miss Mariam held her fingers high for all the other girls to see, speaking in a resounding voice, "Zeina Bint Zeinat has fingers that have been created for music. She's talented and unique, born to be a musician."

Her wide eyes gleamed in the light. The other girls gazed at her enviously, admiringly, especially Mageeda al-Khartiti, her only friend from among the girls. Mageeda was attracted to her by the power of admiration and envy, as well as by a mysterious force like blood, for her features were like hers and her mother's when she looked in the mirror.

Mageeda inherited her mother's short stocky build, the squat chubby fingers that writhed on the piano keys like pieces of dough, as though they were boneless. She inherited from her father the strong drive toward success. Like him, she wanted to achieve glory through writing although she had no desire to write.

The two distinguished families, al-Khartiti and al-Damhiri, never missed a performance by Zeina Bint Zeinat, for she had become the artist of the oppressed masses in Cairo, the city stretching from the eastern to the western desert, and from the green delta to the yellow sands of the desert. The deserts were creeping and devouring the green areas, and concrete constructions were rising on fields and agricultural lands while the asphalt streets were invading the farms, meadows and cornfields. Police cars and equipment trampled on the white cotton buds, and the children stopped singing "You've come to bring us light, oh Nile cotton, how lovely you are!" Maize stalks for animal feed replaced cotton shrubs. Steel constructions sprouted along the banks of the Nile, turning the great river into a sickly, ailing crocodile, imprisoned between tall walls and buildings. Houses and flats were as tiny as match-boxes, and mosques and churches multiplied like rabbits. Victory arches carried the names of God, Christ, Prophet Muhammad, and the president, while the alleys and cul-de-sacs were filled with rubbish. Sewage water ran like rivers on the streets after the real rivers had become dry. The stools of stray dogs and cats littered the streets, and there were three million boys and girls living without families and fending for themselves on the pavements.

Zeina Bint Zeinat tapped on the stage with her foot, dancing, singing, and reciting poetry. She cut the air with her tall, robust figure, walking the fine line between earth and sky, breaking the barriers with her feet, opening for herself a pathway never trodden before. She opened and closed the windows to her soul with her own will, which was as strong as her powerful figure. By facing hardships, she had become as hard as a rock.

Her gleaming eyes seemed to be ageless, for they could be the eyes of a young woman of twenty or an old woman of more than a hundred. Their charm was deceptively alluring, for men regarded them as inviting love although they were only reflecting the sunlight. Journalists described her as a fiery woman, while critics thought of her as hot-blooded. She responded with the lyric of a song, saying that they were cold-blooded. The head of the department of literary criticism described her as the worst thing that had happened to the country, using "thing" and "worst" to refer to her, as though to deny her being a woman and an artist in a single stroke.

When she was on stage, people forgot what critics wrote about her, for she had a presence that obliterated books, articles, and critical studies. On stage, her beauty became her special virtue. People's eyes moved toward her as if driven by a spell. They gazed at her eyes, the two windows open to the sky and reflecting the depths of the sea. They didn't just look at her eyes, but dived deep into them to discover and to remain, not wanting to leave them even after the lights were out at the end of the performance.

Badreya wrote a secret letter to her mother, Bodour, saying, "Did you give birth to so much beauty, Bodour? How can you possibly produce so much beauty and be unable to describe it in your novel? Can your womb be more creative than your pen? Such beauty does not only crush us with pleasure, but it also fills us with pain and uncertainty. We feel frustrated and incompetent before the power of this beauty and this charm, for we cannot give it up. It pushes us toward knowledge. The unknown makes us feel anxious, and drives us to resistance and revenge. This beauty makes us lose our delusions of grandeur. Although we are the gods of literature, art, and culture, our inherited language is incapable of describing this beauty, as it is incapable of defining love, life, God, Satan, and all the other mysterious notions."

Zeina Bint Zeinat never paid any attention to refined, sophisticated language, for she hadn't obtained a university degree. She didn't wear high heels, or a scarf on her head. She wore no make-up, no bracelets on the wrists, and no ornaments on her feet. She didn't apply paints to her lips or eyelids, no reds, greens, or blues.

Zeina Bint Zeinat wasn't conscious of her own beauty, her greatness or her talent. It was all natural to her, nothing to boast about. It was like freedom and health. Only those deprived of them were aware of them.

At school Zeina Bint Zeinat wore a uniform made of cheap cotton, with irregular collars and a loose belt. Her hair was dishevelled and her shoelaces untied. Zeina Bint Zeinat never looked at herself in the mirror, for she didn't have a mirror at home. She didn't in fact have a home. The principal would draw her out of the morning congregation to give her a wrap across the fingers. She would punish her by making her stand for an hour or two with her face to the wall and her arms raised. The only crime perpetrated by Zeina Bint Zeinat was that she ran faster than the other girls during physical training classes. The other girls' legs were short and plump. They could not run. Or she might have been punished because she received the highest marks in music or poetry reading.

The girls' stubby fingers couldn't move quickly over the piano. Girls from good families had no bones in their fingers, and their tongues slurred when they read Arabic poetry, for Arabic wasn't respected in good aristocratic homes. It was spoken only by housemaids, chauffeurs, cooks, gardeners, make-up women, and fortune tellers. It was the language used by housemaids and prostitutes, who were indispensable for masturbating males from distinguished aristocratic families.

Mageeda al-Khartiti cried all night, asking God why He created her with such short fingers and narrow eyes lacking sparkle. Why did He give all the talent to the child of sin? Did He prefer the girls born in sin to the daughters of decent families?

During the music lesson Miss Mariam would say, "In music, talent alone is not enough, and neither are the fingers. You're lazy, Mageeda, because you want everything to come to you easily. God has given you numerous gifts and blessings, and therefore you have no motivation for creativity and no ambitions. Zeina Bint Zeinat sleeps and dreams of music and never stops playing music or singing. She trains three hours a day, at school or in my house. I welcome her into my home because she loves music and singing. This love is her secret and her motivation to live. In music she has found the love she has been deprived of in her life. Music, like writing and all other arts, loves those who love it and dedicate themselves to it. Zeina Bint Zeinat has no other love in her life. And you, Mageeda, what is the love of your life? What is the dream of your childhood? What would you like to be?"

This question haunted Mageeda at night as she slept: what do I want to be? What do I want to be?

She didn't know the answer. All she knew was that she wasn't interested in the workings of the language or its letters. She preferred figures.

"One plus one equals two, exactly two. Not three."

Figures were simple and clear, while language was complex. A word could have several meanings, often contradictory meanings. Sometimes, if you added a letter or a punctuation mark, the whole meaning changed. One instant might be worth thousands, or even a whole lifetime.

Mageeda didn't like this ambivalence. She preferred figures because they were definite, clear, straightforward, and unambiguous. But more than anything, Mageeda loved sleeping, because during sleep she was transported away from reality, from the voices of her parents quarrelling, from the voice of God threatening eternal damnation in hell, from the voice of Satan tempting her. Before she was ten, she had committed many sins, one of which was that she hated her parents instead of loving them as she should have done. There were times when she drank a few drops of water before breaking her fast in Ramadan. Sometimes she didn't perform ablution before praying. At other times, she farted during prayers but didn't break her prayers to go and wash. She didn't cover her hair while praying and sometimes urinated in bed out of sheer terror. In the dream, she saw herself walking on a tightrope on Doomsday to test the righteous, her small feet bleeding from its razor-sharp thinness. But she swerved and fell into hell. She woke up drenched in sweat and crushed by shame.

The gravest sin she committed after the age of ten was obeying her father, Zakariah Al-Khartiti, and joining the Department of Journalism. Her father had always looked up to journalists who had their own columns in the distinguished *Sphinx* newspaper. He had his photograph placed within a frame at the top of his long column, on the front page on the left. His head in the picture was titled toward the left side, like Satan. Then he changed to the right side, after he got his column about science and faith in God. His head in the photograph had a triangular shape, with a sharp apex resembling the Pyramid of Cheops. His eyes stared vacantly into space, like the great thinkers: Plato, Aristotle, Newton, Freud, Marx, Avicenna, and Averroes. Despite this, his features didn't hint at any great intellect. There was only the reflection of light on the bald spot as the photograph was taken. Cigar smoke concealed part of his face, particularly the nose, whose bone changed shape with the changes of the light falling on the face and the movement of the earth around the sun.

Mageeda al-Khartiti became a distinguished writer at the *Renaissance* magazine, earning the highest salary possible. Her parents helped her write her articles. On Journalism Day, she was awarded the Literature Prize for an article she had written entitled "The First Lady's Achievements on Women's Day".

The magazine building was shaped like a white pyramid. It towered high above the low, dark buildings around it and the slum behind it, which was inhabited by new immigrants from the countryside coming to seek a livelihood in the city. They lived alongside old immigrants without work, ex-convicts, pimps, whores, and the sellers of salted fish, sardines, canned beef, rosaries, charms, censers, and Ramadan time schedules.

The editor-in-chief was one of the aides of the first lady. An opposition paper published some facts about his embezzlement of a couple of million pounds from the magazine funds. People, mostly unemployed young men and women, went out to protest, calling for his indictment. Police forces dispersed them using water hoses and tear gas, and a few shots were fired. Blood flowed on the pavements and merged with sewage water when the pipes burst. In a few hours, peace returned to the city and people forgot all about the case. The editor-in-chief's photograph shone once again within its frame on top of his daily or weekly column. It was a more youthful photograph, where the bald spot had disappeared underneath the black wig, and the wrinkles had been ironed out during cosmetic surgery in New York. His eyes, which were fashioned anew, sparkled with ecstasy. His lips smiled triumphantly.

Mageeda al-Khartiti had a large office on the top floor, next to that of the editor-in-chief. On her door was installed a red lamp. No one was allowed to enter her office except through the office manager and the private secretary. As soon as they heard the voice of a young upcoming writer, male or female, asking to meet her, they would say, "Oh, the great lady is at a conference abroad with the first lady", "She's at an important meeting with the minister", "She's busy writing her column and isn't answering calls. I swear to God she has locked herself in to write her article. She's now writing and nobody can interrupt her work. This is Thursday, a sacred day for her because she is writing the article, which the printing department is clamouring for. Can you call her next week? I apologize for the inconvenience."

Mageeda al-Khartiti didn't write her article on Thursday, and she didn't go to the office that day either. Thursday was the day she went to the club to play golf with her father. The golf course was the place where great writers and intellectuals met. They were mostly men and a few well-known women writers and critics. Golf or croquet was their new passion. They would walk in the heat of the sun and the open air, followed by a pale, sunburnt boy with a face filled with white spots and black freckles, looking like a street child and dragging a bag full of clubs and balls. The woman would hold the club in her plump hand. Her nails would be painted red, violet or orange, according to the dictates of fashion. She would bend with her stocky figure over the ball and hit it with ultra feminine tenderness. The ball would fly over the distance of one or two meters then fall on the green, which looked as carefully trimmed as Zakariah al-Khartiti's well-shaved face.

The editor-in-chief was playing golf one day when he told Mageeda, "Listen, Mageeda. I want you to write an article on the achievements of the first lady for the upcoming Women's Day."

Whenever the magazine was preparing a new issue for International Women's Day, or perhaps the birthday of the president or the first lady, the editor-in-chief would take this opportunity to renew his allegiance and declare his loyalty to the powers that be. Editors competed with one another to curry favour with those powers, and their imagination soared to great heights to create projects that never materialized and achievements hitherto unknown. They would congregate in their tens or hundreds in the large editorial hall on the first floor, exchanging seats as though they were playing musical chairs. Although they were usually referred to as junior editors, some of them were already past their prime. They were appointed as temporary workers or unpaid interns, because they had no connections in the higher echelons of power to raise them from lowly to senior positions, a promotion needing a written or spoken presidential ruling or ministerial decree.

Mageeda al-Khartiti hired one of those junior editors to write her article for her. She paid him a hundred and sixty pounds a month in return for four articles, at forty each. She received a monthly salary of eight thousand pounds, at the rate of two thousand pounds per article.

On her desk were four telephone lines: the red one for the president, the green for her office manager, the white for her private secretary, and the black for the editorial hall on the first floor.

Mageeda reached with her chubby white hand for the black telephone and called the young poverty-stricken writer of the article.

"Please come to my office right away, Mohamed."

She didn't address him as Mr Mohamed, as she did with senior editors, and nor did she ask him whether he was free to come up to her office right away or not. She knew that he would come to her as soon as she asked him, for he was at her beck and call all the time. She gave him a monthly salary of a hundred and sixty pounds, which he badly needed to feed his children and his sick mother, and to buy some new books and novels.

With his lean figure and pale face, Mohamed went up to the top floor, using the the senior editors' fancy elevator, which moved up as softly as the morning breeze. Mohamed walked with his dusty shoes on the Persian carpets covering the corridor floors. The walls were decorated with artistic paintings and photographs of ministers, kings and presidents. The picture of the editor-in-chief looked out from a golden frame next to the pictures of al-Manfalouti, Taha Hussein, William Shakespeare, and Bernard Shaw. He probably hoped that his presence in this distinguished company might confer greatness on him.

Mohamed was out of breath when he stood in front of the door. A shining gold plate on the door carried the engraved name of Mageeda al-Khartiti in letters taking the shape of a sun disc. Mageeda was not in the habit of coming to her office very often, sometimes only once a month to collect her salary. But she never missed a meeting with the president and the first lady, a presidential event or a cultural or literary festival sponsored by the editor-in-chief.

Before going into her office, Mohamed was stopped by her

office manager, who asked him his name and the purpose of the meeting. The manager told him that she was not available because she was at an important meeting with the editor-in-chief.

"But she called me just a minute ago about an urgent matter concerning her article, sir!"

"I apologize! She has just come back from the meeting. Please go in, Mr Mohamed."

Mohamed entered the lavish office, the heels of his worn shoes sinking in the thick Persian carpet, which felt as soft as flesh. Behind the huge desk sat Mageeda al-Khartiti, diminutive and plump. Her head hardly showed above the glass surface of her desk. On the wall behind her were the pictures of the head of state and the first lady in large gold frames. The president's half smile, which revealed his teeth, was a cross between a cordial beam and a military grin. The first lady's wide feminine smile revealed her full teeth. Underneath the two pictures stood a smaller picture of the minister, and underneath it, still smaller, was the picture of the editor-in-chief. As the eyes looking at the collection moved downward, the picture sizes decreased and the gold frames became thinner and turned into other metals like silver, copper, or tin.

Mageeda al-Khartiti didn't offer Mohamed a drink, although she was drinking her coffee in a gilt cup and had a full glass of water filled with ice cubes. The air conditioner produced a soft noise resembling the faint rustling of wind. Between her thick red lips was an expensive black Havana cigar of the type smoked by her father, as well as by the editor-in-chief, and the great authors and journalists who had their own daily or weekly columns. As soon as any of them was awarded a title or appointed to a prominent position, the black cigar was sure to appear between his lips, the prayer mark on his forehead and the yellow rosary in his hand. If he believed in Christ and the Bible, the prayer mark would still appear, even though he didn't prostrate in prayers. Holding the rosary in his hand, he would move it with his fingers without mentioning God's name or reciting verses of the Qur'an. He would declare that he was a Coptic Christian but that his culture was Islamic. He would go to the mosque on Friday without performing ablution to pray behind the president or the minister, mentioning God's name and reading the Islamic testimony or the Opening while moving his lips only slightly. He would close his eyes, muttering and mumbling without producing any sounds except for the hot breath coming from his radiant lips.

Mageeda's little head appeared from behind her fancy desk, with her chubby face, her sagging skin, and her sallow complexion. It was this pallor that distinguished great writers, whether men or women, young or old. The pen in her hand was as grey and colorless as the dusty, ashen words writers like her used in their articles and columns. Those writers seemed to write with an invisible ink that no one could read, for no one understood whether they were supporters or opponents of the regime. They concealed themselves behind a film of cigar smoke like a god disappearing behind the clouds.

She wore a green suit made of pure natural silk. Around her neck she wore a transparent red scarf tied like a flower underneath her pointed chin. Her little white fingers were childlike, but the look in her eyes was sad and old. The white skin of her hands was covered in red spots. Noticing him staring at them, she hid her hands in her pockets.

"I have inflammation of the skin, Mohamed, a type of allergy to the newspaper print. One of the hazards of the writing profession. You are an excellent journalist, Mohamed. Your pen can help in the issue dedicated to the achievements of the first lady, and of the president of course. You surely know that the whole country cannot do without his guidance. Shall I order a cup of coffee for you, Mohamed?"

"No, thank you very much, ma'am."

"Why are you standing, Mohamed? Please have a seat."

"Thank you, ma'am."

"Shall I order you a lemonade?"

"Thank you, ma'am, but the fact is I have a stomach ulcer and cannot drink anything outside my home."

"What ulcer, Mohamed? We all suffer from ulcers in various parts of our bodies, and not just the stomach. This is one of the hazards of our profession as journalists and literary men and women ..."

She emphasized "literary men and women" as though forcing herself into their congregation. Her father had dreamed that she would become a literary figure of the stature of the eminent writer May Ziada. Early in her career she wrote a short story that nobody read except her father and mother.

The red telephone line rang and she was busy talking for a long time. Throughout the conversation, she produced soft intermittent laughs. She sighed and gasped, and her body shook ecstatically behind the desk. Mohamed was still standing in front of her, not wishing to sit down. He wanted to apologize for not agreeing to write the article and leave. He wanted to break the glass surface of the desk with his fist. Boiling inside him was an anger that had been suppressed since childhood, now emerging in the form of an ulcer.

When the phone call was over, she turned to him as if just noticing his presence for the first time.

He said to her in a low voice, "Please excuse me, ma'am, I have a doctor's appointment to have my stomach x-rayed."

"Have a seat, Mohamed. I need the article very soon. I want it to appear in the achievements issue. You realize, of course, that her achievements are numerous in every field. Choose whatever you like. You have free reign. But you have to deliver the article before the end of the week. Now, come on, write something nice for us like you did before. What ulcer are you talking about, Mohamed? It's just a psychological disorder resulting from an ulcer in the brain."

Mageeda gave a sharp, high-pitched laugh that sounded like her father's. She moved her head backward as she chuckled, the way her father did with younger writers.

"I'm just joking, Mohamed. I know you have a good head on your shoulders."

After Mohamed was gone, Mageeda pursed her lips and fell into a long silence. She heard a voice coming from deep in her soul whispering, "The ulcer is in your brain and in the brains of your father, the editor-in-chief, the minister, the president and the first lady."

She looked at her watch and jumped to her feet.

"Oh my God! I almost forgot the doctor's appointment!"

In a few minutes, Mageeda al-Khartiti was driving her white Mercedes to the psychiatrist's, where she would stretch on the couch.

Ahmed al-Damhiri stared at Zeina Bint Zeinat, who was radiant on stage, playing music, singing, and dancing. He sat in the back row, hiding behind dark glasses. He wore a large white turban on his head and a kaftan with a wide, gold sash underneath a loose velvet overcoat. Around him were his armed guards in civilian clothes, each carrying a silent gun. From the first time he heard her singing, he couldn't stop listening to her. Her voice had the power to traverse the distance between his mind and his heart in seconds. It penetrated his soul in the twinkling of an eye, breaking the barriers standing between his body and mind and making him whole once again. As he sat looking at her, he became a foetus inside the womb of his mother. Opening his eyes from a deep slumber, he found himself surrounded by darkness, his heart beating regularly in his ears and a melody coming from far off. He rubbed his eyes, which were wavering between sleep and wakefulness, unable to decide where the sound was coming from.

"Whose voice was it? Where did it come from?"

He had no idea how long he was in this state. Was it a minute, an hour, a year or a life time? He couldn't really tell. Then the voice came once again, deliciously familiar to his ears, like heartbeats that were so close that he could feel their rhythm from his head to the soles of his feet. The voice rose and fell, then rose and fell again. It rose to a high pitch with the rhythm once more, then disappeared. It tickled his ears with a softness that was similar to his mother's breasts. He seemed to have heard the tune a thousand or a million times since he was in the womb, surrounded by warm water, listening to his mother's heartbeats which came at a regular, expected pace or at a fast, disturbed rate. The heartbeats followed the cadence of the music, nonetheless, and carried the fragrance of his mother's hair and her voice whispering "Ahmed, darling".

The large hall was full to overflowing with men, women, youngsters, and children. Next to him sat a young mother holding her baby. The baby stopped crying when Zeina began to sing, his eyes fixed on her face, his ears attentive to her voice. He followed her closely as she moved across the stage. His head shook with the rhythm of the music and his little body swam in his mother's embrace as he had done in her womb.

Research has shown that the foetus can hear sounds inside the womb and outside it. As soon as it is a hundred and forty days old, it is able to recognize the voice of its mother when she sings and when she cries. It hears her heartbeats, her breaths and the pulse of the blood inside her veins. It hears conversations between its father and mother, though without understanding their meaning. It can, however, distinguish between beautiful melodies and off-key tunes. Its ears become trained to listening either to music and the tunes of love and happiness, or to the sound of slapping, kicking and moaning.

Ahmed al-Damhiri didn't know what exactly attracted him to Zeina, or what shook his entire being when he listened to her voice. He had no idea why her eyes restored his lost and buried memories, or where all the recollections came back from. With the music came his mother's voice when she sang to him before he slept, and the smell of her milk filling his nostrils. At the end of the show, after the lights had dimmed and the audience had left, he remained in his seat, staring at the darkness and the emptiness.

Zeina Bint Zeinat became a phantom chasing him day and night. Her voice streamed into his ears in his sleep like the voice of God or the Devil. He began to believe that music came from the Devil and not from God. Her music took away his equilibrium and his faith in God. His body became as light as a feather, a body without flesh or bone, a body of pure spirit. He flew as freely and happily as pure spirits unshackled by the body. It was as if he was dying and his soul was rising to heaven. Then he woke up to find himself among the living. Death and resurrection, then death and resurrection, ad infinitum ...

Miss Mariam called her the Egyptian Mozart. She introduced her before every show saying, "This is Zeina Bint Zeinat. She's our Egyptian Mozart. But Mozart lived with his father, the great composer, who trained him to play music three hours a day from the age of two. When Mozart was eight years old, he composed his first symphony. His genius wasn't just talent or inherited genes, but long arduous hours of training amounting to ten thousand hours between the ages of two and eight. Genius requires long hours of hard work. But when industry is combined with natural talent, it becomes extraordinary, unstoppable."

From the moment Miss Mariam saw Zeina for the first time at primary school, she was certain that this girl had an extraordinary talent. Zeina learned tunes by heart on first hearing them. She was self-confident to the degree of vanity, as though she was the daughter of a god in heaven and not a child born on the street.

Zeina Bint Zeinat sang her song, which began with the following lines:

I came from this earth and to it I return.
I have not descended from space.
I am not the daughter of gods or Devils,
I am Zeina, and my mother is Zeinat,
My mother is dearer to me than the sky.

Her words were simple and spontaneous, like breathing in and breathing out. It had no rhyme or meter, but only the cadence of her voice which resounded in the large hall, strange to the point of familiarity and familiar to the point of strangeness, like the dusk born out of darkness and the sun falling into the night.

Ahmed al-Damhiri came out of the coma of ecstasy. The word "sky" struck a jarring note in his ears and his hypnotized mind was alerted.

"Why does this woman challenge heaven? What does she mean by her poor servant mother is dearer to her than the sky?"

But the moment of epiphany soon vanished when Zeina Bint Zeinat began to sing:

I am neither Mozart nor Umm Kulthum.
I am the daughter of the earth and the street,
I am the offspring of error and sin,
I am the child of honor and virtue.
Since childhood I've had countless blows,
Since childhood I've had countless falls,

But every time
I manage to get up again and sing again,
And play music and play and play,
And dance and dance and dance,
Get up and dance and dance,
Then write a love song with a new cadence.

All eyes in the hall stared at her, and the ears were attentive to her simple words that were as free of embellishment as a face without make-up. Her unique face knew no compromises and did not solicit admiration. It didn't consciously draw attention to itself, and yet it attracted eyes with its mysterious power.

Her face seemed empty except for the two large eyes, the black eyes that burned with a blue light and blazed like a piece of the sun. Her eyes penetrated barriers and masks. They penetrated the surface and plumbed the depths, seeing what others could not see.

Ahmed al-Damhiri fidgeted in his seat, his short plump body moving from one side to the other. He stretched his short legs under the chair in front of him and his foot hit the foot of the man sitting in front of him.

The man turned to him whispering, "Yes, dear sir. Do you need anything?"

"Nothing, Mahmoud. Lower your voice."

It was the driver sitting in front of him, the chauffeur of his black stretch limousine with blue curtains and tinted glass which made it possible for passengers to see out but kept them invisible inside. Ahmed al-Damhiri relaxed on the back seat of this luxurious car, his tired flabby backside sinking into its soft plush upholstery.

Zeina wasn't singing at one of the state theaters, nor at either of the auditoriums at the elegant opera house. She was in fact performing at a rundown theater in an old slum neighborhood. The theater was a tent made of some thick cheap fabric which looked like linen or gabardine, and the seats were made of wood, bamboo or braided palm leaves. Their backs were straight and hard. They were painful for people with weak backs and for people used to softer seats. The show continued for two or three hours, and every time Zeina Bint Zeinat stopped singing, there was cheering in the large hall, "Encore, Zeina, encore ..."

Mahmoud, the chauffeur, was also one of the emir's bodyguards. He carried a gun which was licensed by state security authorities. He walked behind the emir wherever he went, and sat in the seat right in front of him during public events. The emir's personal bodyguard sat right behind him. This was the way the emir was protected from the front and the back. On his left, a third guard was stationed, and a fourth on his right. Three able-bodied guards surrounding the emir with his diminutive figure were like four pillars around the short mausoleum of a sheikh who was buried a thousand years ago, or of a priest buried underneath an old cloister. They called the emir "the Eminent Sheikh", "his highness the Prince", or "the Pasha".

The title of pasha had been abolished following the overthrow of the king. It came back, however, with the open-door policy, the multi-national corporations, the turban, the prayer marks on foreheads, the rosaries, the loudspeakers attached to mosques, the church and school bells, the police sirens on the streets, the water hoses, the tear gas, the proliferation of illegitimate children on pavements and in slums, the death lists, the religious rulings accusing thinkers of apostasy, the burning of cinemas, theaters and churches, the practise of women following funerals wailing and striking their faces, adolescent girls covering their heads and revealing their bellies and their bottoms in tight American jeans, the hamburger and cola shops, the red nights along the Nile Corniche and the black cloud overhanging the city day and night.

Ahmed al-Damhiri was elated to hear the driver address him as "Your Greatness, al-Damhiri Pasha". He remembered that when he was eight, he was immensely proud of the greatness of his father, the eminent Sheikh al-Damhiri, and his uncle, the celebrated general. At school he was proud to write his name in full: Ahmed Mohamed al-Damhiri.

He descended from a long line of men stretching back to his great grandfather, who were all educated at the religious establishment al-Azhar or at the army and police academies. Gold stars and medals shone bright on the chests of some of them and on their wide shoulders padded with straw or cotton. Others had large turbans wrapped around their small heads and velvet sashes around the waists of their kaftans. In their hands they either held the rosary and the stick, or carried batons, guns and pistols, according to their distinguished position in the hierarchy of the state or religion.

Mahmoud the chauffeur turned, pursing his lips. He knew, like the other guards, that his greatness the pasha would not leave his seat until Zeina Bint Zeinat's singing and dancing came to an end.

"Yes, dancing, by God. It's the most hateful of arts for God and the Prophet, as his eminence the sheikh in charge of the cultural section of the group has asserted. Dancing means moving the body with the aim of arousing lust. Singing comes second on the list of abhorrent activities after dancing, because a woman's voice, like her naked body, is forbidden and must be concealed, even if we have to use the force of arms if necessary, or the power of words. Keeping our objections in our hearts would indicate a weak faith."

The driver remembered one of the sayings of the Prophet: "Whoever of you sees an evil, he should change it with his hand; and if he cannot do that [he should change it] with his tongue; and if he cannot do that [he should change it] with his heart and that is the weakest of faith."

Was it possible that the faith of his greatness, the emir, was weak? The question vexed the driver, who didn't have the courage to move his head either to the left or to the right because the emir's head was right behind him.

The driver preferred sitting behind his master to sitting in front of him. But the head of the military wing decided where each one of the guards should sit. The most experienced among them sat behind the emir to protect his back from any gunshots, since they usually came from behind. Stabs, on the other hand, rarely came from the front. But if they did, they would be intercepted by the driver's head, no doubt.

The driver drove the question out of his mind without moving his head, lest the emir should realize what was going on inside it, for the emir was in constant touch with God. And God knew what went on inside human minds, hearts and bellies. But the question persisted in the driver's mind and almost flowed with his blood. He felt certain that his master, the emir, was enthralled by this whore, who was herself the daughter of a whore.

"Women's cunning is great," as God has said. This whore has sullied the clean reputation of the emir, because a good, pious man can only be tainted by a woman. Cleanliness is godly and dirtiness is womanly. If he had his way, he would bring out his gun and shoot her. But it was all in the hands of the emir, who was, after all, a man like any other. When aroused, he lost two thirds of his mind.

The head of the cultural section of the group was unhappy about the emir's conduct. He warned him against attending public events related to politics or religion, let alone theater and opera performances.

But the emir's rank was higher than that of the head of the cultural section, for he was responsible for the military wing. He was in charge of arms and money. The head of the cultural section controlled nothing more than words, spoken or written. Only the words of God had weight. And the words of God followed the military wing and not the cultural section. The logo of the group contained the images of the Book and the sword. Every follower of the emir hung a tiny golden Qur'an on his chest, and in the back pocket perched on his right buttock he kept a black revolver. It was to keep up with advances made in the field of weaponry at the hands of the infidels that the revolver came to replace the sword. Each of the emir's followers fiddled with the yellow beads of the rosary, and on his forehead the black prayer mark appeared. He wore a thick beard and a thick moustache that concealed his face like a black veil. The tiny black pupils of the eyes rolled inside two empty, bottomless holes.

The emblem of the group changed from the Book and the sword to God's Law and the revolver, for religion always needed military might to protect it. No religion in history had become stronger without the support of military power, while military might always needed a god or a religion to protect it. The emir walked among his soldiers strutting like a peacock, calling them God's army. He was God's deputy, chosen for the sacred mission of upholding God's words above human words, and of applying God's rules and laws gently or violently as necessary.

Ahmed al-Damhiri inherited his faith in God from his father, the eminent Sheikh. From his uncle, the army general, he inherited faith in arms and the police. From both of them, he inherited the short stature, the fear of rats and cockroaches and the weakness in the face of lust and whims, slave girls and concubines.

The emir had as many women as he wanted. He had the virtuous, chaste ones as well as the whores and prostitutes. He had the inexperienced virgin as well as the woman with extensive experience of men and the games of sex. At his beck and call he had an assortment of divorced women, ripe women, adolescent girls, and pre-menstrual female children. If he fancied a married woman, her husband would voluntarily give her up for the sake of God so that she might be free to offer herself to the emir. God, after all, had made it lawful for the emir to have all the women he desired, for the emir stood one degree higher than other men. By the same token, men were placed one degree higher than women. God created people according to a hierarchical system, at the top of which stood the Prophet, followed by the emir. For this reason, the emir had the right to have his fill of women.

Bodour al-Damhiri jumped out of bed terrified. She saw her cousin, Ahmed al-Damhiri, sitting transfixed in his wooden seat, staring in front of him at the moving circle of light on stage. She knew him well from childhood. If he wanted one of her dolls, he would grab it. If he couldn't, he would steal it. But if stealing wasn't possible, he would break it. One day he fancied one of her little dolls, a doll with large blue eyes made of two sparkling blue beads set in her fair, round face. Her mother had sewn for the doll a lovely lace dress, a silk petticoat and transparent rose-colored pants revealing her soft belly. She placed the doll's small feet in a pair of green velvet shoes. Bodour hid her doll underneath the clothes in her cupboard to keep her from the eyes of other children, particularly those of Ahmed al-Damhiri. She turned the spring mechanism found on the left side of the doll three times. Music came out of the doll's belly and the doll began to move its arms and legs with the rhythm. It danced and sang "Dance, little bride. Dance, lovely bride ..."

The doll shook and moved with the rhythm. With the movement of the spring mechanism on its side, it rolled and tumbled in the air, opening its arms and legs in successive somersaults.

During one of these jumps, Ahmed al-Damhiri glimpsed the transparent rose-colored pants as the doll opened its legs. His eyes penetrated the transparent fabric but couldn't see beyond the belly. Moving his eyes down to the pubic area, he found no slit and no aperture of any kind. He was shocked to see the blocked body of the doll. It was very different from the bodies of Bodour and the girls of the family.

As soon as Bodour left her room, Ahmed al-Damhiri pounced on her doll. With his short, effeminate white fingers, he dragged it under the bed. There he took off the lace dress and tore the rose-colored pants to pieces as he pulled them down to look for the slit between the thighs. But his fingers didn't find any aperture and found only a blocked road that was impossible to penetrate.

He grew angry imagining that the doll was stubbornly challenging him with her blocked thighs. He flung it to the ground in a rage and removed its arms, legs, and the spring mechanism on its side. He wrapped the torn pieces in a newspaper and buried it in the back garden, without Bodour or any of the children seeing him.

Bodour sat in the first row of the large hall, together with the intellectual elite, the great writers and critics. Next to her sat her life-long friend Safi, Mageeda and her husband, magazine columnists, screen and media stars, and the leaders of political parties, groups and societies. After the great defeat and the opening of trade links with America, the creation and establishment of religious groups became legal. The easing of restrictions was intended as a blow against the enemies of capitalism and free markets, and was also meant to show support for the values of freedom of trade, freedom of faith, and democracy. Mosques and churches proliferated, with the aim of spreading the word of God in cities and villages, and in alleys and narrow lanes. At the foot of the Moqattam Mountain, the cemeteries were transformed into homes for the poor immigrants deserting the countryside. The living and the dead competed for dominance over the cemeteries. But the dead were defeated, for they didn't have a political party to defend their rights or a religious group to speak in their name. And nor did they have any members to represent them at the People's Assembly or at the Consultative Council.

Ashamed of their impotence, the dead shrank in their graves. Concrete walls and minarets were built above them and loudspeakers were attached to them. Before and after dawn, as well as throughout the day and night, blasting noises resounded out of those loudspeakers.

The loudspeakers blared out, "God is great, God is great, prayers are better than sleeping. Make haste toward success. Make haste toward prayers. There is no deity but God, and Mohamed is His messenger. Oh worshippers of God, have faith in God's mercy. Be patient when you suffer the miseries of life. Do not seek life's pleasures and lusts, for life is ephemeral. The hereafter is more lasting and permanent. Paradise awaits you and God's generous face."

At the end of the show, there was thunderous applause from all and sundry: from front and back rows, from believers and unbelievers, from people in love with music, poetry, singing and dancing, and others who were disdainful of the arts. The emir's group belonged to that latter category, for they believed that the sound of music banished God from the hearts of believers. The emir had issued a fatwa prohibiting these sinful arts which were inspired by the Devil. Their hands clapped nonetheless. They followed the emir with their eyes as he sat in his seat. If he clapped, they would do the same, and if he fidgeted from right to left in his seat, they followed his example. If he sighed audibly, they sighed as well, and if he growled under his breath, they produced the same sound. If his hand reached for his pocket, their hands reached for theirs. Even Mahmoud, the chauffeur, observed him closely from the corner of his left eye, his ears wide open trying to spot any slowing or acceleration of his breath, and any irregularity of his heartbeats or of the movement of his blood through his veins.

The chauffeur was the closest aide to the emir and the one who knew most about his secrets and his private life, for he was at his beck and call day and night. On Friday he took him to the mosque for congregational prayers, and on Saturday to the headquarters of the group to attend the Executive Council. On Sunday he drove him to the club to play golf with members of the two blessed families, or on a trip with the family to the Pyramids, Fayyoum or the northern coast to the west of Alexandria. There, away from the polluted beaches of the cities, he had an elegant villa in one of the fancy resorts such as Marina, Marabella, Badr, al-Huda or al-Madina al-Munawwara lying on the route between Alexandria and Marsa Matrouh. There the emir took off his clothes and swam in the sky-blue waters under the golden sun. His wife hidden behind a black cloak covering her whole body eyed him enviously. Her husband, the emir, splayed his arms and legs in the refreshing waters of the sea, diving, tumbling and later sunbathing, while his wife sat swimming in her sweat, saliva and tears, all pouring from her nose, mouth and eyes. Within a stone's throw of the wall, a beach was set aside for servants, cooks, drivers, and gardeners, as well as for the summer camp for young believers. Mahmoud, the driver, walked on the sand wearing bright bathing trunks colored red, green, blue, yellow, and purple. It was the Islamic bathing outfit which covered men's thighs down to their knees. But the esteemed masculine member often stood out from underneath the colorful rubber trunks. However, it was no shame for a man to have a rebellious member that had no piety or fear of God. It was no disgrace for a man to swim in the sea. It was forbidden for women to show their faces, let alone their thighs, legs or arms. The emir issued a ruling that women's voices were a source of shame. Every part of their bodies, in fact, was a shame, including the head, the seat of thought and intellect.

Mahmoud the chauffeur stroked the few hairs on his chest

under the rays of the sun. Then he threw himself into the sea, splaying his arms and legs to the air and sky like his master. He dived and tumbled and danced and sunbathed, thanking God that He created him male and not female like the emir's wife and the other women soaking in their sweat under the umbrellas on the beach. God created him poor and not rich like his master, the emir. But God created him a man and not a woman, and for this, praise was due. As he saw the emir's wife wrapped inside her black cloak, fumes almost coming out of her eyes and ears, he talked to God saying, "Thank you, Lord, for your blessings. It's no shame to be poor, for you have distributed wealth and blessings among people, and have created the rich and the poor, the good and the evil. But women are the worst of all creatures."

He heard his father and grandfather say that women were the Devil's allies. Cleanliness was godly while dirtiness was womanly, they often asserted. The driver knew more about the emir's life than the emir's own wife. The emir doubled his bonuses to make sure that he kept his secrets. The driver knew the addresses of brothels and prostitutes, and the homes of his slave girls and concubines. He kept their addresses and telephone numbers in a small notepad. He wrote their names in a childlike scrawl similar to the handwriting of primary school children, for the driver never attended school. The emir taught him the fundamentals of reading and writing, and trained him to drive and to read the Latin figures on the car gauges. He taught him to recite the Qur'an, carry arms, aim and fire accurately in a training camp, note down women's phone numbers in his notepad, and carry out basic counting operations to be able to calculate expenses, gas charges, bonuses, and secret gifts. The driver was closer to the emir than his wife, because unlike the wife who could easily be replaced, the driver had no substitute. He was the emir's confidant and his personal guard who accompanied him everywhere, day and night. If it hadn't been so embarrassing, he might have accompanied him to the toilet too. But he stood totally alert in front of the closed bathroom door until the emir had finished. The emir urinated like all other mortals and the chauffeur heard the sound of the urine as it dropped into the luxurious ceramic toilet bowl imported from Europe, the land of infidels and unbelievers. The chauffeur often drove the thoughts that Satan whispered in his ears out of his mind. But when he heard the sound of the emir urinating, he couldn't help noticing that it was peculiarly similar to his own. Princes and common folk were equal when it came to urinating, for God in His infinite wisdom didn't discriminate between a poor man and a prince.

At the end of the show, the emir slipped a folded piece of paper into his driver's hand. The driver knew his cue inside out. He immediately understood the gesture, got up from his seat, and walked toward the stage. He made his way to Zeina Bint Zeinat, who was surrounded by her fans, both men and women, old and young. They shook hands with her and asked her to sign a copy of her new poetry collection or one of her songs or musical pieces. Around her were the street children that she admitted into the theater without tickets. Each one of them carried a card with his name and photograph. There was no space on the card for the unknown father. Children, in fact, could write their mothers' names, which were accorded full respect in Mariam's band. The religion field was also absent from the card, for the band didn't discriminate between one religion and the next. Policemen chased children on the streets, confiscating their cards by force and disposing of them in the sewers. They put children in armored vehicles and transported them to prison or detention. There they were kicked and slapped and punched, and their young ears were assailed by nasty insults, from bastards to sons of bitches. The children lay down on the floor along with hardened criminals, drug dealers, pimps and addicts. Male adults raped young boys in the silence of the night. Childish screams were drowned by men snoring, blocked noses and open mouths. All eyes were closed except God's open eye, which stayed as large as a teacup, seeing and witnessing what was happening to these children, but not interfering in a scene that was of no great concern. When the children were released from detention, they didn't look out for God's banquet in heaven but gazed on the ground under their feet and scavenged the rubbish bins along with stray cats and dogs. Zeina Bint Zeinat held them in her arms and registered their names in Mariam's band. They tapped the earth with their little bare feet, the music flowing warm in their veins like blood, or like a mother's milk. Their souls and bodies danced to the tune, and they sang and reeled and jumped up in the air, their heads hitting the dome of the sky, then coming down again, up and down again, dancing and singing and turning ceaselessly like the earth turning around the sun.

Mahmoud the chauffeur extended his long arm toward Zeina and handed her the folded piece of paper, then disappeared between the rows of seats. Zeina Bint Zeinat put the paper inside her pocket without opening it. She was busy talking to people, laughing and throwing her head back. Her laugh was as melodious as music, and it was loud and hearty. She did everything passionately, ardently, with every atom of her being and every particle of her soul, body and mind. Her voice had never been heard in the whole universe before. Hers was the laugh of a woman who was in full possession of herself and wasn't the plaything of anybody or anything else, a woman who was free of fate and destiny, a woman who stood outside earth and sky, outside time and space. Her laugh sounded strange and unfamiliar, like the dream of happiness or the impossible hope of love. It was like the mystery of life throbbing with sinfulness and virtue.

Ahmed al-Damhiri's body quivered in his seat when he heard her laugh. It rescued him from the sorrows buried deep in his heart since childhood. It saved him from the pain that had dwelled in his soul since primary school, when children hit him on the nape of his neck and wrote his name in chalk on toilet walls. "Ahmed al-Damhiri has a whistle."

Her laughter flowed into his ears as warmly as his mother's milk. It lifted him high in the sky and allowed him to catch a piece of the sun and forget his pains and sorrows. He almost laughed aloud with her. He had almost forgotten how to laugh, until he heard her laughter. Her joy was contagious and he heard himself laugh as though for the first time in his life, except that his voice remained silent.

In one of his moments of black despair, he wrote to her another message. How many messages did he write? How many times did his driver, Mahmoud, approach her, extending his long arm to her with the folded paper? It might have been twenty, thirty, fifty, a hundred or a thousand times!

Zeina Bint Zeinat didn't open those messages. If she did, she only glanced over it quickly then threw it in the bin. She was familiar with this type of man. They thought they could possess her, that she was a whore, a slave girl or a concubine. They believed that no sooner did they beckon to her than she would rush to them, for they were men who possessed everything in this life and in the next. But she only had her voice, her songs and her music. All she wanted was to play music, and to sing and dance, until she died on stage.

Zeina Bint Zeinat was not strikingly beautiful. It was not beauty that attracted people's eyes to her, but something else, something mysterious, something that radiated around her like waves of light, or rather waves of existence. She had a presence that was unique, and a charisma that filled space and time, obliterating everything else.

Ahmed al-Damhiri saw her presence in the eyes of others. Her image was reflected in them in such a way that they saw nobody else. In her presence, the whole place became vibrant and almost turned into a living organism. Waves of life moved in the air in what seemed like electric or magnetic waves. The magnetism of her eyes and voice was transmitted to everything around her. The stage was no longer a stage, but a piece of life itself, as she tapped rhythmically on it with her feet.

Zeina Bint Zeinat didn't dress up for the evening. She didn't wear shimmering outfits or sparkling jewellery. She wore a soft white dress made of Egyptian cotton. Her shoes, made of soft leather, were flat. Nothing about her appearance was extraordinary, but her plainness itself was extraordinary. It had the simplicity of the sun as it shone or set. Ahmed al-Damhiri's eyes couldn't stop staring at her, wanting to discover her secret, to unravel her mystery, and to tear her apart as he did that doll as a child.

In comparison, women around her seemed like dolls made of wax or clay, painted white, red, green or what have you, and decorated with rings, bracelets, and gold necklaces. They looked like marionettes whose strings were manipulated by other people holding them by the neck, the arm or the leg, and moving them in any direction they pleased.

In the dead of night, as Ahmed al-Damhiri lay sound asleep, he swallowed his dark desires and imagined Zeina sleeping with him in bed. She was completely naked and submissive to his desires, moaning with pleasure and pain, and screaming just like other women underneath his whistle.

He wasn't overcome with sinful desires except while praying to God after eating and smoking something to alleviate his depression, or after swallowing the pill of happiness prescribed by the psychiatrist. As he prayed on the mat, the sinful desires slithered up to him like a snake, or like the serpent that lured Adam and Eve. It crept until it touched his full belly. It flowed with the blood that escaped from his head following a large meal and descended across the neck to the chest and then to the belly, and from thence it crept toward the pubic hair which used to be thicker in his youth. He continued to shave it off until it began to fall out of its own accord with age. The little member became engorged under the hair and stood erect after sniffing femaleness in the air. His brain turned cold and bloodless while his body blazed with sinfulness. As his forehead touched the ground, he implored God to keep the Devil and temptation away from him, but he only heard a hissing sound resembling Satan's voice saying, "Come off it, man! She's just a woman like any other, deficient in mind and religion, weak before her lusts. If aroused by a man, she would no doubt surrender. And God has made it permissible for you to have as many women as you wish, for you are the emir, God's deputy on earth. Go to her tonight and empty the Devilish gland inside her so that you are free to devote yourself in the morning to your serious work. Tomorrow you will give the inaugural speech at the International Religious Dialogue Conference, in which you will lash out against unbelievers and renegades and all those who have no faith in God or the three divine books, the Qur'an, the Bible and the Torah, which have been sent to guide humanity and illuminate their paths. Go to her, man, and don't hesitate or worry, for God is with you every step of the way. God will give you victory and no one but God can do that, for He is love and beauty. God is beautiful and loves everything that is beautiful, like beautiful music. A beautiful voice is a God-given gift, so why do you prohibit music, dancing and singing, man? Why do you blindly follow that blind Sheikh who cannot see beauty with his eyes? For this reason he bans statues and says whoever listens to music will never come within a hair's breadth of paradise. He also says that a woman's lovely voice will lead a man's mind away from the worship of God, and her uncovered face will banish God from his heart. The problem then lies in the man's mind and not in the woman's voice. Lift your head high, man, and go to her. She's a pious Muslim woman, very different from the frivolous Coptic woman who lured a young Muslim man and sparked off sectarian tensions between Muslims and Copts in Alexandria. These women ruin the country and cause poverty and religious conflict. Their cunning is great, as God points out in His glorious Book. But if they use cunning, God is much more cunning, man, and He will protect you from the cunning of any woman. God will make you victorious over your enemies and keep you on the right path, so don't despair of God's mercy. Take heart, man, and go to her. Take your personal body guard and your revolver in your pocket. Don't go out of your house without the bodyguard and the revolver, for God tells us to take all necessary precautions. If you help yourself, God will help you. God will change nothing in the life of the community until they change it themselves."

The Devil then whispered in his ear, "But what is God's role then, if He does nothing until you have done it yourself, Ahmed al-Damhiri?"

As Ahmed al-Damhiri prayed to God, he tried to banish the Devil crouching on his left and whispering in his ear. The Devil kept arguing with him, saying that if God protected him, there would be no point then in having guards and revolvers. If the Qur'an, the Bible and the Torah came from God, why were there so many massacres among the followers of these religions? And ...

Ahmed al-Damhiri shook his fist in the face of the Devil, lifted his body from the prayer mat, went into the bathroom and peered at himself in the mirror above the sink. The more he examined his face, the less self-confident he became. He didn't like this face, least of all his nose and chin. The two lips stood idiotically apart. Could he possibly kiss her with those lips? He also had large yellowing teeth, and his mouth reeked of salted fish and garlic. He brushed his teeth with the new mint-flavoured toothpaste. He rinsed his mouth and gargled with a blue antiseptic mouthwash. He took a warm shower and rubbed his hairless chest, his hand descending to his belly to rub his muscles, and further down to the little shrivelled mouse between his thighs.

His wife saw him as she passed in front of the bathroom, because he never closed the door behind him, even when he was sitting on the toilet. He walked naked in front of her, belched loudly in her face, fiddled with his nose, and scratched his thighs in full view of her eyes. Embarrassment decreased as the years of marriage went by, until it disappeared completely along with desire. Touching his wife or seeing her naked didn't produce a single tingle in his body. Her large and sagging breasts reached down to her belly and reminded him of his mother's.

The smell of his expensive eau de cologne hit her nose as it wafted through the open bathroom door. She realized that he must be on his way to a night of passion with a new woman, and not to an Executive Council meeting at the headquarters of the group. But he had enough compassion for his wife not to tell her the truth, for he followed the great principle laid out in the verse telling believers to display their good sides to others. God alone knew what was lodged in the heart and could see one's hidden intentions.

Bodour al-Damhiri tossed sleeplessly in bed, chased by the phantoms of her novel, particularly Badreya, the heroine. She was a strong, stubborn woman that had no god, superior or husband. She vowed never to have any relations with men after her first love, Naim, had been killed in prison following the great demonstrations. They killed him after he had deposited the seed of life inside her. Badreya was not a real woman of flesh and blood, but a spectre walking on the wall and penetrating closed doors and shut windows. She was a spirit that could soar high in the sky and descend to the bottom of the earth, penetrating surfaces and barriers to uncover concealed feelings and emotions. Her eyes stayed open like God's eye, reading the unknown.

Badreya realized that Ahmed al-Damhiri was on his way to Zeina Bint Zeinat and was intent on raping her, or killing her if she resisted him. Badreya knew his track record since childhood and how religious faith came to him after doubts. She knew he swung between doubt and faith, between left and right, between the Devil and God. He was a Marxist atheist first, before turning into an obsessed Islamist. She had no idea, though, how he became a member of a secret, communist cell or how he later joined the underground religious group. She didn't know how the prayer mark appeared on his forehead, or the rosary between his fingers. She didn't know how much money he'd embezzled, how many women he'd raped, or how many people he'd killed. Badreya knew that he sought the protection of God and the Prophet. He shook the Qur'an and the guns in the face of those who disobeyed him. She heard him cry and moan on the couch of the psychiatrist, and his accelerating heartbeats reached her when his eyes fell on Zeina Bint Zeinat.

Badreya whispered in the ears of the sleeping Bodour, "Your cousin, Ahmed, will kill your daughter Zeina. Watch out, Bodour. Get out of bed and kill him before he kills her."

Bodour tossed and turned in the wide bed, unable to sleep. She saw her husband lying asleep beside her, the sound of his snoring as regular and continuous as a ticking clock. His face was as pale as the faces of other columnists. It also had the ashen color of the smoke coming out of his nostrils when he puffed his cigar with his head lifted toward the sky. He reproached God for giving him less talent than others, particularly Mahmoud al-Feqqi. His wife read Mahmoud al-Feqqi's column before she read his. She thought of him as a gifted writer and secretly stared at him as she strolled around the golf course. He was tall and graceful, and held the club with sturdy fingers. The fingers had the same strength as his words and the muscles of his phallus. He hit the ball with the power of forty horses, sending it high in the sky to fall far away where no eye could see it. His wife, Bodour, clapped for him, saying, "Bravo, Mahmoud. Bravo!"

She called him by his first name Mahmoud without any embarrassment, and he did the same with her. He read his column aloud to her before it was published, and she read a few pages of her secret novel aloud to him. She concealed the novel from her husband as though it were her last will and testament.

Zakariah al-Khartiti's father died of testicular cancer. At the funeral, he sat beside his mother listening to the Qur'an. He was eight at the time. His mother, mourning his father, wept silently and uncontrollably. Death became connected in his mind with the recitation of the Qur'an, the huge number of visitors, the plates filled with food and the smell of smoke coming from roasted meat. The verses of the Qur'an recited in a soft melodious voice streamed into his ears with the mouth-watering smell of roast, whetting his appetite in the same way as during the fasting of Ramadan when he waited for the canon shot announcing the end of fasting. He felt guilty when he took a sip of water before the end of fasting or when he broke wind as he kneeled to pray.

His father's will was a scandal that was more aggravating than his death itself, for it revealed that he had a secret wife, and two children by this marriage. Part of his inheritance went to the two of them, while the new wife shared the house with his mother. So his mother took off her mourning clothes and black scarf, and wore a colorful dress and put a red flower in her hair. She produced a hearty ululation celebrating his death. Although he loved his father when he was a child, this love decreased with the passage of years and with the increased knowledge of his father, whose true character became apparent only after his death. He started to hate his father the way his mother did. But he turned out to be a carbon copy of his father, both in appearance and character, in outward and secret behaviour, in political and sexual activities.

Zakariah al-Khartiti was fast asleep when Bodour crept out of bed and tiptoed to her study. The events of the novel were swarming in her head. A shiver ran through her body as though she had been infected with malaria. The muscles of her face contracted as if she was a psychiatric patient undergoing electric shock treatment, or a person being executed by the electric chair. The pen froze in her hand and would not move on the paper. Her mind had stopped functioning since she married Zakariah al-Khartiti. She married a man she did not love, and loved a dead man who lived only in her imagination or her dreams. Love did not exist except in the mind. It came in the shape of fragments of a dream or pages of a novel. From these scattered pages her imagination created another man who filled the blanks between the letters on the page. On the page the man she loved took shape and his features were drawn in ink, although those features belonged to a man she did not know. The less she knew the man, the more she loved him.

Her husband, Zakariah al-Khartiti, gave her a good morning kiss every day. They had their breakfast, lunch and dinner sitting at the same table every day. He talked to her in the insolently courteous manner characteristic of the upper classes.

"Could you possibly pass me the bread, please?"

She handed him the plate filled with toasted bread and he smiled at her saying "Thank you."

She returned the smile, saying with the politeness of well-bred wives from good families, "You're most welcome."

He gave her a soft, polite glance that had the appearance of love. She returned his glance and her moving head looked like the head of a marionette, pulled by unseen strings from the top of the stage.

Her head was heavy with sleep as she sat holding her pen

and writing her novel. She loved sleeping better than writing. Deep in her heart, she hated writing as much as she hated her husband, although she couldn't tell this secret to anybody. She was awarded the state prize for writing and she carried the title of Distinguished Writer like her husband and her daughter, Mageeda al-Khartiti. She received the Model Mother Award on Mother's Day, the Model Wife Award on Marriage Day, and the First Lady Companion on International Women's Day. Her head fell like a log on the desk, producing a heavy thud, and her body was seized by successive shivers. She reached for the switch on the wall to cut off the electrical power. She whispered in a choking voice, "Please, doctor, I've had enough electric shocks. My brain has melted from the electricity, doctor, and my memory's gone. I can't remember a thing about my life."

"This is what you need, Bodour. You've got to forget. Forgetfulness is the target of the treatment."

"But forgetfulness is dangerous, doctor. The novel is now gone from my head. I can't remember anything. Without my memory I can't write a novel."

"Your health, Bodour, is more important than your novel. To hell with the novel, Bodour."

"The novel is more important than my life, doctor. To hell with my life."

"To hell with everything except your health, Bodour."

The doctor's voice came to her while she was asleep or absorbed in writing. It was pain, she realized, that drove her to write. But it was also pain that stopped her from writing.

She opened her eyes with great difficulty and saw her husband sleeping beside her, his snoring as regular as a ticking clock. She extended her hand from under the cover, hit the clock and threw it off the bedside table to the floor. Her husband, woken by the sound, screamed at her, "What did you break the clock for?"

"Because I can't break your neck."

This last statement didn't come out of her mouth as an audible sound but was expressed in silent letters written in black ink on the blank page. Badreya's angry eyes peered at her from the pages. But the anger concealed disdain, for Badreya couldn't understand this woman called Bodour al-Damhiri. She couldn't comprehend the fear lurking in her heart since childhood, the terror that she lived with throughout her youth and maturity. Terror paralyzed her mind and made her unable to write. But why was she so terrified? Was it God or the Devil? Or was it her husband, their deputy on earth?

From her primary school days, Badreya was more courageous than Bodour and never hesitated to speak her mind.

"Why did God create Muslims and Copts? Why do Copts confess their sins to the priest if God already knows everything that goes on in their hearts? Why do women stand behind men in church? Why is silence imposed on them? Why do Muslims pray five times a day and not three or four? Why does a man marry four wives and a woman marries only one husband? Why do men get female nymphs in paradise, while women do not get male nymphs? Why is having a father's name an honor and having a mother's name a disgrace?"

Badreya read in the Qur'an that paradise lay at the feet of mothers. She wondered, how can paradise lie at the feet of mothers when their names bring disgrace to their children?

Badreya was more intelligent than Bodour, and her writing was more beautiful. She also learned poetry much faster and solved mathematical problems more efficiently. But Bodour was always awarded the prize of excellence, while she never received any. Badreya was angry with the teacher and argued with him aloud, providing evidence to prove that her marks were higher than Bodour's.

The teacher lost patience and said to Badreya, "I'll give you the prize when hell freezes over! Or perhaps when you bring me the dust of paradise."

He was being funny, knowing she couldn't perform miracles.

The next day Badreya brought him a plastic box filled with dust and told him, "Here's the dust of paradise."

The teacher opened the box and saw the dust inside it.

"Where did you get the dust from?"

"After my mother walked on the ground, I collected the dust with my hands and put it in the box."

"Who said that it was the dust of paradise?"

"You did, Mr Mohamed. You told us in class that paradise lay at the feet of mothers."

Despite her obvious intelligence, Badreya didn't get the prize. The teacher accused her of using God's words disdainfully. School prizes like those awarded by the state in literature and science were not given on account of intelligence or efficiency, but on account of family connections.

Zeina Bint Zeinat heard this story from Miss Mariam, who told the girls that the most important thing was excellence and not family connections. She told them that a mother's name was a source of honor for girls and boys because paradise lay at the feet of mothers.

"God stands for justice, beauty, love, and freedom. There's no difference between a boy and a girl, a Muslim and a Copt, a poor and a rich person. Truth is a virtue and lying is a vice. Those who lie to others only lie to themselves. Nobody kills another without killing a part of himself."

Zeina Bint Zeinat went to Miss Mariam's home to practise music and singing for three hours every day. She had her dinner with Miss Mariam before she went back home to her mother Zeinat.

Miss Mariam filled her bag with sweets, music books, poetry collections and novels, telling her, "Listen, Zeina. You're talented and you have the patience to practise for long hours to boot. Genius is patience. You're a lucky girl because you've known pain and you've known happiness, and one can't achieve happiness without having experienced pain. Be proud of your mother and your name Zeina Bint Zeinat. There's more honor in a mother's name than in a father's, because a father often gives up his children for a passing sexual whim, but a mother never abandons her children unless she is psychologically ill or mentally deranged."

The pen quivered in Bodour's fingers and she stopped writing. Was she psychologically ill? Did she lose her mind? How did she abandon her newborn baby on the pavement and go home to sleep in her bed? Was it more motherly to kill a child to avoid scandal or leave it alive on the pavement? What would Zeina Bint Zeinat say if she confessed to her that she was her daughter? What would people say?

Bodour turned around perplexed, Badreya's voice talking to her from the depths of her being.

"Go to her! Confess to her! Take her in your arms and hold her close to you. Weep hot tears on her chest and ask her for forgiveness. Say to her 'Forgive me, my child, forgive me!' and Zeina Bint Zeinat will forgive you, because she has a warm heart. Instead of having one mother she will have two, in addition to the third, Miss Mariam."

Bodour chased that phantom. She drove away Badreya's voice and image when the stifled voice inside said to her, "Death is better than scandal, Badreya. What's the point of confessing the truth after all these years? Zeina Bint Zeinat no longer needs this confession. Zeina doesn't need you, Bodour, in her life, but you, Bodour, need her now. You're trying to compensate for your failures, both in writing and in life. You're trying to cure yourself of sadness and depression. But it's pointless, utterly pointless. You should have done it a long time ago. The time is past and you can't turn the clock back."

Badreya's voice came to her: "It is never too late, Bodour. The clock can go back. Read a little in the new science of cosmology and you realize that time will go back with the change of the movement of the planets and the earth around the sun. You will become youthful once again, Bodour. This will be possible in the future. The universe wasn't created in six days, and woman wasn't created out of Adam's rib, for Adam was born from a woman's womb. The future lies in the human mind and not in superstition."

On his way to Zeina, Ahmed al-Damhiri was in a state of deep anxiety, trepidation, elation, lust, caution, and fear. He wanted to go forward but at the same time something held him back. He was moving toward paradise and all its nymphs, but at the same time he was trying to keep away from the flames of hell fire. With his hand he touched the killing machine in his back pocket, above the right buttock, and the contact with the hard metal gave him some confidence and courage. But when his hand slipped further and touched the little piece of flesh underneath the pubic area, his confidence and courage vanished. Since his childhood, this piece of soft flesh afforded him nothing but humiliation, and always let him down at the important moments when his heart was ablaze with desire. At those moments, his body became limp, and his little masculine machine didn't get an erection except in the company of a woman he neither loved nor respected, a woman he never dreamed about, a slave girl or a prostitute, who would lie underneath him in total submission, offering him her body like a piece of flesh without a mind. Deep in his heart, he feared a woman's mind. He wanted a woman who offered him her body in return for a sum of money, or a car or a flat he'd bought for her. He would take her under the covers and enter through her as through an open hole, without any effort, anxiety, or fear of the consequences, whether they were worldly or otherworldly consequences. But he feared Zeina Bint Zeinat. The more he looked into her eyes, the more fearful of her he became. The more he feared her, the stronger his desires grew. He feared those two wide eyes, reddish in color, and those two bluish black pupils looking out of a mysterious well inside her soul.

As he sat on the plush seats of the black limousine driven by Mahmoud, the chauffeur, heading for her house in a distant slum, a voice emerging from the depths of his soul spoke to him. The driver's narrow sunken eyes peered at him through the front mirror of the car. But Ahmed al-Damhiri turned his eyes away. With his eyes closed and his body relaxed, he listened to the voice whispering to him, which sounded like the voice of God that spoke to him in his sleep: "You, Ahmed al-Damhiri, are never satisfied or contented. I've given you everything, in this world and the next. A huge palace is reserved for you in heaven and all the nymphs you can wish for. In this world you have all the good things of life: money, children, positions, women, palaces, servants, guards ..."

"Yes, God, it's true. I've got all that and I'm truly thankful for your many gifts, but ..."

"But what, Ahmed al-Damhiri? What more can you possibly want?"

"I want her, oh Lord! I want that woman, Zeina Bint Zeinat! I want those eyes blazing with the blue black flame, burning with the desire to challenge and violate your laws, oh Lord, and the laws of nature, and the laws of private property, and the laws of the free market. This woman is depriving me of my freedom to possess her. Something in her is beyond possession and therefore beyond your will. How did you create her with such extraordinary beauty that violates all rules? I'm about to go out of my mind. I've lost my ability to distinguish between virtue and vice, between good and evil!

"Her powerful femininity, oh Lord, is almost masculine, paradoxical, elusive. It entices me to possess what I cannot possibly have. All my attempts at possessing her have produced the opposite results, exposing my weakness and my failure. Why did you create her like this, oh Lord? She would not succumb to me even if I offered her all I had. I've written many messages to her, but she answered none. I confessed to her that I was in love with her, a pure spiritual love. I told her that I would give her myself and everything I owned. But she never answered me. What should I do, oh God, Lord of the world? You bear witness to my torment. Your unsleeping eyes can see me sleepless in bed and on the psychiatrist's couch. You can see me cry and stifle my moans all night."

Ahmed al-Damhiri looked up toward the sky, his eyes penetrating the tinted glass of the car window, which revealed to him everything outside but kept him invisible to prying eyes. He saw God hiding behind a black cloud. But the heavenly eyes couldn't penetrate the tinted glass, the bullet-proof glass imported from the lands of the infidels. It was proof against the eyes of foes and friends, proof against all the prying eyes on earth or in heaven, hiding behind masks. Even God's eyes couldn't penetrate it because it was made in the lands of infidels, the allies of the Devil. Nobody challenged God's will except the Devil.

He relaxed on the soft seat, imagining that God's eyes would not see him, that they couldn't pierce through the bullet-proof glass. But he soon remembered that he was only fooling himself, because God's eyes were stronger than bullets and infidels. They could penetrate steel, for God was almighty and omnipotent. Whatever He willed He did. So why did He not order this woman to submit to him, the emir, the man God had chosen and no one else? Why wasn't God with him on this mission as He was on all the previous missions with other women?

Zeina Bint Zeinat waved to him as she danced and sang.

Her voice and image took hold of his mind which whispered, "Nobody owns this woman, but on the contrary she's the one who possesses others."

He closed his eyes, surrendering himself to sleep, to being possessed by her. He felt a strange kind of pleasure in surrendering to something more powerful than himself. He wanted to be rid of suffering and pain, the pain of resistance, the burden of leading others, the load on the shoulders of rulers and emirs. He saw himself in her arms, feeling out of breath and whispering voicelessly in her ear, "Come on top of me, take me, and possess me, my adored love!"

He shuddered, opening his eyes. The word "adored" escaped with his hot breath. He did not hear it with his own ears but felt it as a pang in his throat. It was like a huge non-human hand blocking his nose and mouth. It was God's hand suffocating him, and His voice shaking his whole being.

"You unbelieving infidel! Don't you know that I forgive all sins except the sin of worshipping other deities than me? I forgive you all your crimes and your acts of embezzlement and rape of women and children, but I cannot forgive you when you worship another than me, let alone a female!"

Ahmed al-Damhiri almost shouted to Mahmoud the driver, "Take me back home. Don't take me to her."

But his voice didn't come out. He fidgeted on the seat, moving from one buttock to the other. This woman deserves to die because her existence threatens mine. It threatens my faith in the one and only God. I mustn't go to her. I must finish her off. Yes, this should be the only goal of my visit, before she destroys me and all the other believing men. My sacred mission is to kill her before she gets the chance to destroy God's religion.

He smiled to himself, comforted by the thought of the nobility of his mission. The car found its way to her house in the distant slum, which was located at the borderline between the homeland and the land of the homeless, between reason and insanity, between God and Satan. The car went along dusty roads, alleys and pathways that were blocked with rubbish and sewage water. It passed by children playing in the mud with cats and dogs, cemeteries inhabited by the living, and dead people walking with sad, pallid faces. There were the sounds of drumbeats, lutes, tamborines, and finger cymbals clacking in the hands of belly dancers at weddings. The dancers' soft bodies reeled and turned in dancing costumes that revealed their bellies and thighs. Their voices rose high in song, and colored beads vibrated on their wobbly breasts. Bullets were fired in the air in celebration of the bride and groom. Smoke drifted from censers reproducing the shape of Satan burning. Supplications rose from minarets, calling "God is great! May He keep and preserve us from the evil eye!" Ululations came out of women's throats sounding like the wailing and howling at funerals.

Children surrounded the black Mercedes, their bottoms bare. One child produced a healthy fountain from his little penis directed at the car. A girl threw a ball of mud at the back window. A flock of children, cats, and dogs ran after the car, shouting and screaming, flinging rubbish at it.

"Where's Zeina Bint Zeinat's house, kids?"

This was the voice of Mahmoud the chauffeur, his head sticking out of the window.

The children answered him all in the same breath, "Zeina Bint Zeinat is at the theater. She has a big, big concert. It's her mother's birthday and we're all invited. But who are you? And who's the man sitting behind you? He looks like a big minister, a big, big thief ..."

The children laughed, chanted and danced, shouting, "This is the idiot, the idiot, the idiot ..."

"Shut up, bastards, sons of bitches. This is his Excellency the Emir ..."

Insults poured out of the driver's mouth. He cursed their whoring, fornicating mothers and drove his car amid their bodies that were blocking the alley, almost running them over. But they were the offspring of the street and they had been run over time and again. If they were raped and trampled by adults, they would still get up and go. Although their bones and bodies were as hard as steel, their spirits were as ethereal and tender as those of other children, and they laughed and cried almost at anything.

It was the birthday of her mother, Zeinat. Decorations were placed on houses and cemeteries, and lights were placed around the theater. The large hall was filled with men, women and children, all clapping and cheering "Encore, Zeina, encore!"

How many times did they ask for an encore? Countless times, for she didn't stop singing, dancing and playing music, and they kept clapping and cheering, while she continued to stand on stage and take only brief breaks. All the time her eyes looked ahead at the faces in the auditorium. There were men in elegant suits and women wearing heavy make-up, colors and jewellery. The pupils of her eyes looked as black as the night, surrounded by a blue circle that gleamed in the sunlight. Her eyes had the power to penetrate masks and see beyond the medals and decorations on the chest. No barriers or fears stopped her eyes from getting straight to the heart of things. Perhaps that was the secret of their magnetic power, for they produced an electric current. Her voice was both joyous and sad, and so were her songs. When she talked to people she dissipated their tedium and their deep sorrows. They laughed with her when she cracked sarcastic jokes about things. Her words and music were biting, uncovering phoniness and exposing inconsistencies. Nobody could predict what she might say or do next. But people sought her, nonetheless, because without her the whole universe would fall into silence and darkness, in spite of the glaring lights and blaring sounds.

He saw her sitting with some women and men at the end of the show. Ahmed al-Damhiri took a cautious, hesitant step toward them. He joined the group and sat with them, listening to her, staring at her, looking her straight in the eye. But it was all useless. Zeina Bint Zeinat did not see him. His face was featureless, indistinguishable from the others. Her eyes moved around but never noticed him. It was as if he didn't exist. He wanted to draw her attention and remembered a statement he had read in a book which said, "Speak so that I may see you."

He started his talk as usual by saying, "In the name of God ..."

"When somebody speaks in the name of God I feel he means the opposite."

That was her voice, simple and natural. It came as a response to his statement.

There was absolute silence. Pursing his lips, Ahmed al-Damhiri looked rather embarrassed and a little angry. But God inspired him to continue.

"You're absolutely right, ma'am. Many people use the name of God in vain, but I can assure you I'm not one of them."

His personal guard stood not very far from him. He wished to introduce him to those present.

"This is his Excellency the Emir, Ahmed al-Damhiri Pasha."

"Yes, yes, we all know him. His picture is everywhere."

Those were the voices of some of the people standing nearby. A young man gave out a choked laugh. A woman mumbled some incomprehensible words and gave a scornful smile. Zeina Bint Zeinat knew who he was, for she had met him a couple of times at the house of her friend Mageeda al-Khartiti. He used to nod in greeting whenever he met her, and she reciprocated likewise. It was a simple, spontaneous nod, as she used with anybody who greeted her. He stared at her tall graceful stature as she walked and did not take his eyes off her. Her body seemed to him to be made of something other than flesh and bone. An overwhelming kind of light emanated from her, blinding him. He kept staring at her back until she disappeared and the lights went out.

Her image came back to him at night, invading his sleep, waking him up mercilessly, rudely. The two large eyes blazed with life, radiating a magical beauty, a beauty that was self-sufficient, marching on its infinite route toward the horizon.

He said to himself, the nature of magical beauty, like the nature of God the Creator, cannot admit of reciprocation or equality with other human beings. This is divine justice for you, Ahmed al-Damhiri, which is based on injustice and inequality!

Before falling asleep, he heard her voice chanting on stage:

Because I love to sing and dance,
And because music and poetry are my romance,
I'm not impressed by praise,
And blame cannot ruin my days.

He whispered to himself as he tossed in bed sleeplessly, "What arrogance! What insolent pride! It's almost like Satan's pride in challenging the authority of God."

He imagined her bleeding after being shot in the chest. The bullet would tear through the wall of her heart and into her soul, which would go up to heaven to be punished and tortured, for God's will was uppermost. He felt defeated by her and beseeched God to help him. God couldn't possibly let him down in front of a female, an arrogant, insolently proud female at that. She committed sins on a daily basis, defied God's prohibitions and fomented trouble. She banished God from the hearts of men with her dancing, singing and poetry, because she was possessed by the Devil of art. This woman must bleed to death and be tortured in the grave before she received eternal torment. In the grave she would hang from her hair, and in hell she would hang by the neck so that her lower half would burn first. The fire would then move to the upper part of her body until it reached the two eyes with their two pupils that had tormented him day and night.

In the darkness his imagination transported him far away. His body quivered with pleasure when he imagined her in pain. His soul rejoiced to see her blood streaming on the ground, just as the god of the Torah was elated to see the blood flowing from the cut off piece of flesh from the masculine member. His heart exulted in the sight of killing and violence. Ahmed al-Damhiri used to shoot little birds with his sling. As the bird fell bleeding, his eyes sparkled with joy. He ran toward it and held it between his fingers. He severed the head from the body, tore it apart and scattered the pieces in the air. He watched the little soft feathers as they flew into the horizon and disappeared.

Since childhood, his father taught him to be violent in order to make a man of him. His mother, like his father, told him, "You're a man like your father and grandfather and great-grandfather."

His mother was intensely proud of him. She thanked God for giving her the gift of a male child, for males were superior to females by one degree, as God in his Glorious Book had pointed out. Men were the maintainers of women, for they spent out of their own property. God preferred men to women because women were deficient in reason and religion. This was His wisdom and His will. Women were born of a crooked rib that could never be straightened. If one tried, it might break. A crooked rib was beyond redemption or repair.

His mother was awarded the Model Mother Prize. The more keenly aware a woman was of her deficiencies, the more pious she became and the closer she got to receiving state awards. The more a man enjoyed the sight of blood, the closer he became to the Torah god whose anger disappeared when he smelled the blood flowing from the piece of flesh cut off with the knife or the razor, even when it belonged to an eight-day-old baby. God's covenant with the children of Israel was that they should cut off this piece of flesh in return for the Promised Land, the land of Canaan or Palestine. As soon as Moses' mother saw anger in the eyes of God, she held the knife and spilled blood. The god was never so pleased as when he smelled roasted flesh.

Ahmed al-Damhiri closed his eyes and soared with his imagination, opening his nostrils to the smell of roasting. He was God's deputy on earth and his heart was filled with faith and acceptance of God's commandments as they were laid down in his three Holy Books:

And the LORD said unto Moses, When thou goest to return into Egypt, see that thou do all those wonders before Pharaoh, which I have put in thine hand …

And it came to pass by the way in the inn, that the LORD met him, and sought to kill him. Then Zipporah took a sharp stone, and cut off the foreskin of her son, and cast it at his feet, and said, Surely a bloody husband art thou to me. So he let him go: then she said, A bloody husband thou art, because of the circumcision.

[…]

And the LORD spake unto Moses, Say unto Aaron, Take thy rod, and stretch out thine hand upon the waters of Egypt, upon their streams, upon their rivers, and upon their ponds, and upon all their pools of water, that they may become blood; and that there may be blood throughout all the land of Egypt, both in vessels of wood, and in vessels of stone. And Moses and Aaron did so, as the LORD commanded; and he lifted up the rod, and smote the waters that were in the river, in the sight of Pharaoh, and in the sight of his servants; and all the waters that were in the river were turned to blood.

[...]

And the LORD spake unto Moses, Say unto Aaron, Stretch forth thine hand with thy rod over the streams, over the rivers, and over the ponds, and cause frogs to come up upon the land of Egypt.

[...]

And the LORD said unto Moses, Say unto Aaron, Stretch out thy rod, and smite the dust of the land, that it may become lice throughout all the land of Egypt. And they did so; for Aaron stretched out his hand with his rod, and smote the dust of the earth, and it became lice in man, and in beast; all the dust of the land became lice throughout all the land of Egypt. [...] Then the magicians said unto Pharaoh, This is the finger of God: [...] Else, if thou wilt not let my people go, behold, I will send swarms of flies upon thee, and upon thy servants, and upon thy people, and into thy houses: and the houses of the Egyptians shall be full of swarms of flies, and also the ground whereon they are. [...] thou mayest know that I am the LORD in the midst of the earth. [...]And the LORD did so; and there came a grievous swarm of flies into the house of Pharaoh, and into his servants' houses, and into all the land of Egypt: the land was corrupted by reason of the swarm of flies.

[...]

And the LORD did that thing on the morrow, and all the cattle of Egypt died: but of the cattle of the children of Israel died not one.

[...]

And it shall become small dust in all the land of Egypt, and shall be a boil breaking forth with blains upon man, and upon beast, throughout all the land of Egypt.

[...]

For now I will stretch out my hand, that I may smite thee and thy people with pestilence; and thou shalt be cut off from the earth.

And in very deed for this cause have I raised thee up, for to shew in thee my power; and that my name may be declared throughout all the earth.

[...]

Behold, tomorrow about this time I will cause it to rain a very grievous hail, such as hath not been in Egypt since the foundation thereof even until now.

Send therefore now, and gather thy cattle, and all that thou hast in the field; for upon every man and beast which shall be found in the field, and shall not be brought home, the hail shall come down upon them, and they shall die.

[...]

And Moses stretched forth his rod toward heaven: and the LORD sent thunder and hail, and the fire ran along upon the ground; and the LORD rained hail upon the land of Egypt. So there was hail, and fire mingled with the hail, very grievous, such as there was none like it in all the land of Egypt since it became a nation. And the hail smote throughout all the land of Egypt all that was in the field, both man and beast; and the hail smote every herb of the field, and brake every tree of the field. Only in the land of Goshen, where the children of Israel were, was there no hail.

[...]

And the LORD said unto Moses, Stretch out thine hand over the land of Egypt for the locusts, that they may come up upon the land of Egypt, and eat every herb of the land, even all that the hail hath left.

[...]

And the LORD said unto Moses, Stretch out thine hand toward heaven, that there may be darkness over the land of Egypt, even darkness which may be felt. And Moses stretched forth his hand toward heaven; and there was a thick darkness in all the land of Egypt three days: They saw not one another, neither rose any from his place for three days: but all the children of Israel had light in their dwellings.

[...]

And Moses said, Thus saith the LORD, About midnight will I go out into the midst of Egypt: And all the first-born in the land of Egypt shall die, from the firstborn of Pharaoh that sitteth upon his throne, even unto the firstborn of the maidservant that is behind the mill; and all the firstborn of beasts. And there shall be a great cry throughout all the land of Egypt, such as there was none like it, nor shall be like it any more. But against any of the children of Israel shall not a dog move his tongue, against man or beast: that ye may know how that the LORD doth put a difference between the Egyptians and Israel.

[...]

For I will pass through the land of Egypt this night, and will smite all the firstborn in the land of Egypt, both man and beast; and against all the gods of Egypt I will execute judgment: I am the LORD.

And the blood shall be to you for a token upon the houses where ye are: and when I see the blood, I will pass over you, and the plague shall not be upon you to destroy you, when I smite the land of Egypt.

[...]

And it came to pass, that at midnight the LORD smote all the firstborn in the land of Egypt, from the firstborn of Pharaoh that sat on his throne unto the firstborn of the captive that was in the dungeon; and all the firstborn of cattle.

[...]

And God spake all these words, saying, I am the LORD thy God, which have brought thee out of the land of Egypt, out of the house of bondage. Thou shalt have no other gods before me. Thou shalt not make unto thee any graven image, or any likeness of any thing that is in heaven above, or that is in the earth beneath, or that is in the water under the earth: Thou shalt not bow down thyself to them, nor serve them: for I the LORD thy God am a jealous God, visiting the iniquity of the fathers upon the children unto the third and fourth generation of them that hate me;

[...]

Ye shall not make with me gods of silver, neither shall ye make unto you gods of gold. An altar of earth thou shalt make unto me, and shalt sacrifice thereon thy burnt offerings, and thy peace offerings, thy sheep, and thine oxen.

Ahmed al-Damhiri woke in the middle of the night to read the three Holy Books, starting with the Torah, the Bible, and then the Qur'an. His conscience was uneasy, for he hated the image of the god and his voice. It was a god who revelled in scenes of destruction and war, and in the sight of bloodshed all over the earth, a god who took revenge for the sins of the fathers on innocent children. Ahmed al-Damhiri shivered to think that God might crush him as He crushed Pharaoh and his slaves. His bed might be attacked by lice, locusts, frogs, cockroaches, and beetles. Since his childhood, he had been afraid of insects. He couldn't sleep in the same room as a cockroach or a mosquito. He heard his mother scream when she saw a cockroach running on the floor or a mosquito coming from the window to hover around her head. She screamed out so loudly that he quivered and fell off the bed. She carried him in her arms and rocked him in order to calm him down.

"Don't worry, my darling, I'm here with you. I don't know why God has sent us all these cockroaches? All these mosquitoes? Although I've sprayed the whole house with insecticides."

Ahmed al-Damhiri fell asleep. He saw the people of Egypt win the battle of the locusts, the cockroaches, and mosquitoes over God.

God hadn't discovered insecticides yet, but the people of Egypt had an old civilization. They built the pyramids and the obelisks. They discovered the sciences of medicine, astronomy, and engineering. The children of Israel worked as servants and slaves in our homes. The Torah was full of lies.

When he was a child, he heard his father say, "The Torah had been altered, my son. The words of God got confused with the words of human beings. But the Qur'an is a hundred per cent God's words, no changes and no distortions. The state of Israel was built on lies, deceit, killing, and bloodshed. The Palestinian people are being exterminated, son. Israel is a country of killers and therefore deserves extermination, not us Egyptians. We could have thrown Israel into the sea had it not been supported by imperialism, son."

"Is imperialism stronger than God, then, Dad?"

"No, son. God is stronger than all. But God is angry with us, son."

"Why is He angry with us, Dad?"

Ahmed al-Damhiri arose from sleep, having forgotten his dreams and his childish questions. He forgot the faces of his father and mother. Nothing remained in his memory but the face of Zeina Bint Zeinat. If her face appeared from behind the clouds, all the other faces would disappear, including that of God. The black clouds crouching over the city would vanish as though her face were a piece of the sun and her eyes two stars sparkling in the horizon. Her eyes energized him and inspired joy and hope in his heart. He quickly jumped out of bed and stood under the shower, vigorously rubbing his chest and belly. Warm blood rushed to his heart and he felt the accelerating heartbeats pulsing in the palm of his hand. He repeated her name with the pulse, "Zeina Bint Zeinat, Zeina Bint Zeinat". He put on his elegant new suit and shaved his moustache and beard.

"But what's the connection between body hair and faith in our heart?" Satan whispered to him.

He shaved his pubic hair, sprayed eau de cologne under his shaved armpits, and gargled some mouthwash. He placed a mint or cinnamon tablet under his tongue to refresh his soul and dispel his hesitation and despair. He filled his chest with the smell of mint and cloves as he imagined her in his arms, smelling his fresh breath as he bit her lower lip with his teeth. He encircled her slim waist with his arms, descending to her firm, recalcitrant buttocks. They were the buttocks of a wild mare that would not be mounted or subdued. She united masculine strength with feminine gentleness, and danced like an unruly horse without an owner or a bridle. The earth shook under her feet. Her voice flowed softly and gently like the whisper of a heart, and strongly and angrily like the rumbling of waves. Contradictions existed in strange harmony in her heart, in a balance which came close to imbalance, in a kind of self-love that amounted to self-denial.

He drove the car to her house, hoping to be alone with her without his driver or his guards. Darkness fell while he was still on the way. The sun set early and a cold breeze crept into his body and under his clothes. He trembled with a vague kind of fear, and a tremor overtook him in anticipation of pleasure. Fear and pleasure coexisted in his heart. The moon appeared from behind the clouds. It was connected in his mind with love and dreams. He stopped the car, uncertain whether he should go forward or retreat. Going forward implied the anticipation of those pleasures that had been suppressed from childhood, while retreating implied going back to safety and peace. His car moved forward with more determination toward happiness. He wished to melt in a bigger presence than his own, a larger spirit, a better body. He wanted to shed hot tears in her arms, the tears of dying at the height of pleasure, and the tears of regret because he hadn't known anything in his life except his own misery.

He opened her door and tiptoed inside, fearing that any noise might take him out of his state of ecstasy. A faint light shone and a dreamy melody filtered from her bedroom. Everything was ready for the descent into the bottomless pit of pleasure. The door of the bedroom stood ajar. Bookshelves lined the walls up to the ceiling, and the dark book covers gave a kind of solemnity to the prospect of love-making. She sat playing the piano. He lifted her with his arms from the chair until their lips touched. Then he descended with her and, after placing her on the bed, he removed her white cotton dress. When he looked at her naked breasts, he saw that they were neither dark nor fair, but a transparent color that almost revealed her soul. As in his dreams, she didn't give in to him but resisted him as a strong fort, a fort that nobody had invaded before him. He went into the battle with her in complete silence except for the noise of his hot breaths. His hands reached down to the center of lust in the folds of her flesh. He restricted her movement on the bed, like a trainer stopping a ferocious bull with a single gesture or an angry look. But the bull jumped up in one instant and dug its teeth into the flesh of his naked shoulder.

Ahmed al-Damhiri sprang out of bed drenched in sweat, feeling the pain in his left shoulder. A stubborn mosquito had bitten him. It had buzzed around his head before he fell asleep. He tried in vain to kill it but it evaded him and eluded his swatter, before disappearing into some corner beyond his reach.

He sprayed it with insecticide, which had no effect. Insecticides had become inadequate in dealing with the new species of mosquitoes, which acquired heightened characteristics and challenged the will of God, like the new generation of loose girls. At the underground meeting of the group, the decision was taken to carry out God's commandment without argument or question. The name of Zeina Bint Zeinat was added to the death list, which included other names violating religious principles and threatening public order. These were women and men poets who wrote against the regime and called for love, justice, and freedom. There were young students and workers who went on demonstrations, calling for the eradication of corruption, bribery, and neo-imperialism. They shouted against poverty, war, and the abuse of religion. More names were added to the death list with the rise of unemployment, the growth of slums, and the spread of drugs and rape crimes. There were three million children living on the streets. Fathers refused to acknowledge their children born after they had raped young girls on the pavement.

Bodour al-Damhiri sipped her black coffee as she always did before getting ready to write. She took a warm shower, washed her hair and head from the residues of literary criticism, and brushed her teeth with a refreshing toothpaste. For Bodour al-Damhiri, writing was a ritual which was akin to love or prayers. She looked up to the sky with her eyes half open, receiving inspiration, smacking her lips, enjoying the taste of the black coffee. Its bitterness felt strong and refreshing in her stomach, banishing the remnants of sadness and chronic depression. On her desk were the pages of her novel, smudged with stains of black and blue ink, yellowing drops of tears and red blood turning dark brown. There was the odor of sweat between the lines and beneath them. But she was prevented from writing by tiredness, intense sorrow, and a more intense kind of fear. She couldn't tell the difference between truth and lies, fact and fiction. She stared at the dissolving lines between things, for faith melted into apostasy, ugliness and insolence into beauty and civility. Honesty and integrity had turned into theft, treason, and disgrace.

Faces looked at her from between the pages. She couldn't distinguish her father's face from the faces of her grandfather, uncle, and cousin, for all male faces became one, a double-sided face with a devil and a god on each side. The faces of women also merged into one: the tender-hearted and the killer, the pious and the atheist, the sincere and the unfaithful, the woman wrapping her head but at the same time baring her belly and wearing tight jeans around her taut buttocks like a tiger's. Her hips shook as she took long strides. Her walk seemed rather crude and indecent to women of good families, and her voice rang high among their muffled, repressed voices.

She whispered in her ear as she stared scornfully at her novel, "You're too mediocre to be a novelist, for you're clean and innocent and virginal and incapable of creativity. You can't write a novel, Bodour, until you have known evil and until you have drunk the cup of pleasures dry. You need to forget first of all about this world and the afterworld, about punishment and reward, about hell and heaven. Honesty and disgrace will become identical after you remove the mask from your face and see yourself naked. Only then will you realize that loneliness is far better than an obnoxious companion. Divorce, Bodour, is the solution. You need to free yourself from this abhorrent marriage.

"When injustice reigns, loneliness becomes the only civilized option, the warm motherly breasts. Lust and virtue are as inseparable as day and night. Virtuous women like you, Bodour, are obsessed with their desires, while lustful women only dream of chastity.

"Why did you leave your newborn baby on the pavement?

Was it for Zakariah al-Khartiti, your husband, the man obsessed with his mutilated phallus which he uses to rape orphan children? The man obsessed with his column that nobody reads? How many years have you shared your bed with him and lain helplessly underneath him? Can you still dream of writing a novel? Are you dreaming of writing a novel without having to pay the price? The price of creativity? Freedom comes at a price, and so does courage. But when we pay the price, Bodour, our lives change for the better. Our souls soar high and become cleansed. The woman novelist never finds the man who deserves her. There is no tender heart to soothe her except her own. Her only companion is her pen. But the woman literary critic like you enjoys all the privileges of this life and the next, including having a great writer for a husband, the honor of belonging to a distinguished family, state prizes, a palace on earth and another in heaven. A woman novelist, Bodour, doesn't taste happiness. And if she does, happiness will come from within her, from her writings. A woman novelist has no country, family, religion, native city, or tribe. Her homeland is the street, the open road without four walls. Her life is a journey into the unknown. You've inherited writing as you've inherited your religion. You're driven by the desire to receive accolades and not by the desire to write. That's why your novel has been as evasive and as slippery as an eel. A novel, Bodour, is like living fish swimming against the current, and is very different from the dead fish floating on the surface and moving with the current. A chaste woman like you, Bodour, is a dead fish floating with the current. And you still want to write a novel?"

Bodour shook her soft white hand in Badreya's face, chasing her terrifying black spectre, raising her pen to gouge her eyes out and stop her voice. But Badreya had no eyes and no tongue. She was a roaming spirit, appearing at night on the walls like a phantom, peering like Satan's finger from between the pages of the novel, like God's finger, and as real as God and Satan. She was the great truth of her life. Bodour might doubt the existence of Satan or God, but Badreya was the only irrefutable truth in her life. She was authenticity itself, and everything else was untrue, unimportant, unnecessary, and unreal.

Bodour's fingers quivered as she held the pen. It moved uncertainly on the blank page, and her scrawl was like a child's. A question persisted in Bodour's head: why should the most truthful things in our lives remain hidden? And if they happen to come out, they are stolen by those closest to us.

She lifted her head from the desk. Her husband, Zakariah al-Khartiti, was standing right in front of her in his white silk pyjamas, fiddling with the sparse white hairs on his chest and under his belly, and rubbing his eyes. His mouth reeked of dead fish as he opened it wide and yawned aloud.

Before he could ask her anything, she burst out, "Why do you swim with the dead fish, Zakariah?"

Their daughter, Mageeda al-Khartiti, was sound asleep in her room far away. Their loud voices pierced her ears as they quarrelled. She had been hearing their squabbles since childhood. The noise was faint at the beginning, then the volume rose gradually and she heard the sounds of slapping and smacking and kicking. She had no idea who dealt the blows or who received them. In the morning, they sat at the breakfast table, reading the papers and talking as if nothing had happened the night before. They exchanged talk, smiles, tea pots, the salt, the toasted bread basket, and the plates of butter, honey, and white cheese with olive oil.

Mageeda slammed the door shut behind her. She drove her car to her office at the *Renaissance* magazine. She ordered a cup of coffee and called the unknown writer, Mohamed, in the editorial hall.

"Where's the article, Mohamed?"

"I wrote another article, about Zeina Bint Zeinat."

"But censorship will never allow the publication of this article."

"Why not, Miss Mageeda? She's the greatest artist in the country, ma'am."

"True, but censorship has forbidden anything to be written about her."

"But this isn't fair, ma'am."

"Of course it's not fair. Life is full of people suffering from unfairness, and they have God to protect them."

"God doesn't protect anybody, ma'am. If God protected those suffering from unfairness, there would be no injustice."

"What kind of talk is this? Have you gone out of your mind to speak so heretically?"

"May God forgive me for all my trespasses, ma'am."

"That's better."

"But this is unfair, ma'am. God cannot approve of unfairness."

"God approves of unfairness every day of the week. If He didn't, we wouldn't have three million children living on the streets, fifty per cent of the Egyptian population living under the poverty line, or thousands and millions of people dying in Palestine, Iraq, Afghanistan, Somalia, and Sudan, let alone the injustices everywhere in the world. God approves of unfairness!"

"Are you being sacrilegious here, ma'am?"

"Yes, Mohamed, I am. All this is enough to drive you to heresy. I can't imagine how Zeina Bint Zeinat's name came to be on the death list! She's an honest soul who's never harmed anyone. She was my schoolmate and friend from primary school. I know her well, a good girl like no other."

"I must write about her then, ma'am. I have the article with me."

"Publish it in one of the opposition papers, Mohamed.

This magazine is a government publication, and, as you know, the government works with the emir and those groups. And everybody works for America and its allies. As journalists, we all want to earn our living, and the biggest liars are those with columns in that great government paper. My father, Zakariah al-Khartiti, is at the top of that list."

Her voice quivered through the telephone, and the receiver shook in her plump white hand. Her facial muscles contracted nervously and her voice turned into a hoarse, stifled blubber.

It wasn't the first time she'd had an outburst of this kind. Though still an unknown journalist, Mohamed was the closest person to Mageeda at the magazine. He wrote her articles and she confided in him, told him some of her miseries and gave vent to her pent-up feelings. They had a special friendship. She might have fallen in love with him had he not been poor and unknown. She might have considered him if he had some of Zeina Bint Zeinat's pride and refused to hire his pen. Since childhood, Mageeda al-Khartiti had looked up to Zeina Bint Zeinat, comparing herself to her, wishing she possessed that proud head, the tall, graceful stature and the long, elegant fingers moving with the speed of lightning over the keys of the piano. She wished she didn't have a father who scolded her if she was late, or slapped her on the face if she made a mistake. Sometimes he slapped her for no fault of her own but only as an outlet for his rage. Deep in her heart, she hated her father. She heard people speak ill of him. Her colleagues whispered among themselves about his corruptions and his conquests of girls and whores. She buried the secret deep in her soul and noted in her secret diary: the fiercest of men turn into tame animals in brothels.

A few days later, Mohamed, the unknown journalist, published an article about Zeina Bint Zeinat in the *Thawra*, the opposition paper.

The voice of her mother's friend, Safaa al-Dhabi, came to her across the telephone line saying, "Great article, Mageeda.

You must read it. And tell your mum to read it. But who's this Mohamed Ahmed? He's excellent. He also has courage and experience in literary criticism. Do you know him, Mageeda?"

"Yes, Auntie Safi. He's my colleague at the magazine."

"Give him my best regards, Mageeda. He deserves encouragement, and Zeina Bint Zeinat deserves a hundred articles like this. Write about her in your magazine, Mageeda. If I had a page or a column in any paper, I'd write about her. But you know that I'm banned from writing since the day I published my article on the first lady in an opposition paper."

"Yes, Auntie Safi. But you know of course that censorship forbids articles on Zeina."

"To hell with censorship! Don't worry about it and never fear the government. It's a corrupt government and it collaborates with imperialism. People are now fed up with everything, and revolution is on the way. It's coming for sure. The hungry and the starving will go on the rampage inside, and invasion will come from outside. Those groups will then seize the reins of power. But the hungry will surely revolt ..."

The framed photograph of Zeina Bint Zeinat was published on the front page of the *Thawra* newspaper. The article by Mohamed Ahmed appeared on the third page. Eyes stopped at the photograph before the hands turned the pages. They stared for a long time at the magnetic light radiating from the pupils of her eyes. Even on paper she had an overpowering presence. Innocence and experience were united in those eyes, and wisdom and madness. The whole face was radiant, and her wild hair fell down as though it had never been combed before. Her face was free of make-up and color, and her elongated neck was swan-like and proud. The collar of her white dress was creased, as though she had dressed in a hurry and left without looking again in the mirror.

The article occupied half a page and was signed by Mohamed Ahmed:

Zeina Bint Zeinat is an exceptional artist *par excellence*. Her genius is revealed in the simplest movement she makes. As soon as she enters the auditorium or appears on stage, her presence annihilates everything else around her. Eyes never tire of looking at her. Her spirit lifts our souls to the high heavens. Her ingenious voice assumes a palpable shape in our ears. We can touch it and taste it like red wine, because it can remove distances between hearts. Her tunes throw light on the dark corners of our minds. We become intoxicated with the joy of knowledge and overwhelmed with an unparalleled kind of ecstasy.

Zeina Bint Zeinat has created her destiny with her own hand, for she does not admit of the presence of any other will than her own. Adverse conditions have not defeated her, for she creates her circumstances and not the other way around. She has said of herself, "I am the daughter of the streets and I am proud of my mother, Zeinat, the servant who took me from the pavement and nourished me with pride and confidence. Miss Mariam, my second mother, surrounded me with music, poetry and song. She filled my heart with joy, rhythm and harmony."

What drove me to write about Zeina Bint Zeinat? It was her beauty, her voice, her rhythm, songs, and conversation. She exudes a magic that has no name. Because she is natural, she is in possession of the miracle of nature. She moves in a harmony that is akin to the movement of the earth around the sun, a movement in tune with the rebellions of slaves in history. She has emerged from the bottom and risen to the top, transforming an atrocious tragedy into a rich, joyful victory. She plays the right tune at the right time in this age of mediocrity. She uncovers veiled faces, exposes lies and falsehood, and discloses inconsistencies and disgraceful acts.

Was it to get rid of her that they put her name on the death list? Zeina Bint Zeinat, however, cannot be killed with gunshots, because her body is not made of flesh and bone, but of an ethereal substance that is not susceptible to bullets. Even when she dies, she will not disappear. Her star will rise higher in the firmament because true art challenges death. True artists do not die, because their hands have reached the tree of life after eating from the tree of knowledge. They have tasted the forbidden fruit and have become immortal like the gods.

Umm Kulthum, our great singer, had a tremendous sense of humour and irony. When she cracked a joke, she made the most important men laugh. Presidents, ministers, princes, as well as the person who was the target of her humour, laughed at her jokes. She sometimes even laughed at herself. Laughter takes off the edge and the venom of the criticism, because it purifies the spirit and invites tolerance and forgiveness.

Zeina Bint Zeinat is not just a star. She is a whole constellation. When I heard her laugh, my buried sorrows suddenly vanished. Her laugh rings in the air, revitalizing bodies and minds and saving souls from stagnancy. She is like the secret potion of happiness or love, well known yet mysterious, natural and unnatural at the same time.

When Zeina Bint Zeinat dances, everybody dances with her, men, women, youngsters, and children. The whole universe dances with her, the trees, the sun, the moon, and the stars in the sky. Zeina Bint Zeinat possesses nothing except her art. She fears nothing, wants for nothing, and hopes for nothing. She is a free spirit. She has freed herself with her own hands. She has led a life harder than death and is no longer afraid of dying.

By Mohamed Ahmed

The journalist Mohamed Ahmed used to live in a basement room in one of the buildings. His name was known to no one. Suddenly his name was in circulation among people, and his friends and neighbors congratulated him on his article. His mother got up from her sick bed and hugged him. When he was eight years of age, his father died in prison following his participation in demonstrations. Mohamed therefore avoided protests. He had no regular salary or income, but worked in the editorial hall as an unsalaried intern. Mageeda al-Khartiti paid him a small salary in return for the articles he wrote for her. With this small sum, he bought medications and food for his mother, paid the rent for the room and bought himself the occasional shirt, pair of shoes, or book. He dreamed of being liberated from poverty and humiliation. He dreamed of reclaiming his pen and not hiring it to Mageeda al-Khartiti. After publishing his article on Zeina Bint Zeinat, her pride seemed to seep into his soul. When he saw her on stage, his soul was touched, and the voice of his father returned to him, saying, "Death is easier to bear than humiliation. Lift your head high, my son, and don't be ashamed of poverty. Don't let the difficulties of life beat you. Those who persist can never be vanquished. To struggle is to be free, even if the result is imprisonment."

Her pride stirred the memory of his father in his mind, so he stopped going to the editorial hall of the *Renaissance* magazine and stopped ghostwriting for Mageeda al-Khartiti. He continued writing for the *Thawra* newspaper. His name became known and people were keen to read his articles. In a short while he was placed in charge of the artistic page in the newspaper.

Zakariah al-Khartiti sat in his usual chair at the breakfast table, his right hand holding the coffee cup and his left holding the paper. He stared hard at his new photograph inside the frame at the top of his column. It stretched on the page from top to bottom. His signature at the end came as an illegible scrawl next to his email address with his name @yahoo.com. During the time he was a member of a leftist party, his column was placed to the left of the page. When he was awarded the official state prize, it moved to the center. But with the rise of free market forces, religious men, and businessmen, it moved to the right. Many establishments carried his name, including a mosque, a charity organization for the prevention of cruelty to animals, and another for the care of orphaned children, an international publishing and printing company, and a satellite channel broadcasting movies and interviews about science and religion, as well as about religious dialogue.

In front of him sat his wife, Bodour, in her usual chair, sipping her tea and glancing briefly at his column. Reading his column was boring, for she knew his written and unwritten words, the words appearing on the page and those lurking behind the lines. For how many years had she read his column every day? Twenty? Thirty? A hundred? She couldn't distinguish one day from another since her wedding. She knew his column as intimately as she knew his phallus. As soon as she looked at either, she felt sick in the stomach. She wished to reach for the scissors in order to cut off his column and pin it on the wall next to all the other columns by Mahmoud al-Feqqi, the editor-in-chief, and other writers, and next to the photographs of the head of state and the first lady.

Her husband was jealous of Mahmoud al-Feqqi's column. He noticed her reaction when she read al-Feqqi's column and read his own. Although Mahmoud al-Feqqi was nothing but a colleague, practically a stranger to her, she read his column before she read her husband's. It was possible for a woman to have several colleagues, but she had just the one husband, and a husband was like God Almighty, who would not allow the presence of a partner. If a woman took two husbands, she would be arrested and placed in solitary confinement. She would earn the title of whore, fornicator, or fallen woman.

As he read his column aloud to her as usual, he was overtaken by a great sense of joy. His voice streamed to her hearing in spite of the cotton swabs she used to stop her ears. Her eyelids stood half open, and she fell into a coma-like state:

Our country is going through a very dangerous phase. The city of Cairo, dear readers, is no longer the city we have known. Every day we hear of new events referred to as regrettable. These are serious events predicting an imminent explosion. We fear the outbreak of riots by the rabble and the hungry street children. We anticipate a rebellion by the women aping Western women in flagrant defiance of our deep-rooted ethical values, our age-old traditions, and God's laws laid down in our great religion. God has given men the right to have four wives, according to the true verses of the Qur'an, which state that a man may have two, three or four wives. This is God's law and human beings have no right to object to this ruling. God also ordained that children be named after their fathers, which makes it clear that a child's affiliation must be to his father. This is God's command. Only infidels, unbelievers and renegades will challenge His commands. A new feminist organization is now calling for giving the mother's name to the child with an unknown father. This organization defies the precepts of religion. It is paid by the West, dear readers, for the purpose of destroying Islam. This organization calls for moral disintegration, and for the same kind of sexual freedom enjoyed by women in the West, where diseases abound such as AIDS, gonorrhoea, illegitimate children, communism, prostitution and atheism.

Islam, my dear readers, is the true religion and it suits humanity everywhere and at any time. Its perfection leads us to uphold its precepts everywhere and throughout all ages. We have no right as human beings to change any of the rulings laid down in the Qur'an or in the teachings of the Prophet, may God's peace be upon him. In the Qur'an God says: "This day have I perfected for you your religion and completed my favour on you and chosen for you Islam as a religion." The Qur'an explains everything. We have to keep our religion and hold on to its precepts. We have to keep our faith in God, in the hereafter, in God's messengers and prophets, and in the three divine religions. We have to perform prayers, fasting, and pilgrimage to the holy places. These are the basic principles that protect our social texture and save us from wrongdoing and delinquency. They will control our excesses and prevent instincts, lusts and Devilish temptations from superseding the word of God and from violating Qur'anic and ethical laws.

I therefore call for the banning of this dangerous organization, because it is made up of women of dubious character who encourage apostasy and the violation of Islamic principles. This organization threatens the peace of our country, which regards Islamic law as the only source of legislation. And Islamic law does not allow sexual freedom for women, for morality and virtue are far more important than freedom.

Signed: Zakariah al-Khartiti

Zakariah al-Khartiti finished reading his long column. His wife was struggling to open her half-closed eyelids. She stared at him slyly, wishing to scream in his face and shower him with insults: "You corrupt, degraded child rapist, you're defending morality?"

Bodour held the tea cup in her left hand, and in her right she had the white cheese knife with which she was cutting a cucumber. The knife in her hand reached for her husband's column in the paper as though to tear it to pieces. But it retreated a little, then came forward a step or two, aiming to cut into her husband's chest covered with a few grey hairs. The knife descended little by little from the chest to the belly, and from thence to the pubic area with its sparse hairs. It quivered in her short white fingers, almost reaching the tip of his small, shrunken phallus. She wished to cut off both his column and his phallus at one stroke, for the two seemed to her to be one and the same thing. They were like the hazy finger appearing from beyond the clouds, belonging to either God or Satan, which came to her in her dreams when she was a child of eight. It crept over her neck and belly as she lay in bed. It moved like a hard nail from her head to the sole of her left foot. She knew it was Satan's finger because it came from the left side. God's finger, in contrast, came from the right side. The knife recoiled in her quivering hand, hesitating between going forward and retreating. The tea cup fell from her fingers and crashed loudly on the floor. Her husband lifted his eyes from the newspaper and glared at her angrily.

"That's a very expensive cup. I paid a hundred and twenty pounds for that."

He stared at her short, trembling fingers. They were incapable of holding the pen or writing a worthwhile article. She dreamed of writing a novel, but she slept most of the time. She did absolutely nothing except go to the psychiatrist and swallow Valium.

Bodour moved her heavy body from the seat. She stood on her bare feet and walked like a sleepwalker. A splinter of the broken cup cut through the skin of her left foot. She extended her right foot so that another splinter might cut through its skin.

She experienced a mysterious kind of painful pleasure as she watched her blood flow on the white tiles of the floor. Something in the bright red color of the blood woke her from her slumber and brought her back to reality. She stepped with her two feet on the splinters on the floor. They felt like nails, so she walked and walked on them, feeling a mixture of pleasure and pain. The pain merged with pleasure, the fantasy with fact, the present with the past and the future. She saw Nessim's face as he walked beside her during the great demonstration, his large eyes sparkling.

He wrapped his arms around her and whispered in her ear, "If we have a girl, we will call her Zeina, and if it's a boy, we'll call him Zein. Our child will change this world and the next, and will put an end to injustice, poverty, and disease."

She bent down with her short, plump body and touched the blood spots on the tiled floor. She stared hard at the drops of spilt blood and felt a burning in her finger when she touched it. It seemed to her to be a hot tongue of flame that was teeming with life and energy. Its color changed with the movement of the earth around the sun and turned into a bluish black flame burning in the darkness of the night. It was like the eyes of cats staring at you, or the gazing eyes of newborn babies left in the open air without any cover except the sky. A child was born on the pavement with large, bluish black pupils that had the light of day and the darkness of the night. She might have gone away without seeing the baby's eyes. But the eyelids opened suddenly and the two gleaming pupils looked at her, piercing her heart like darts, cutting through the flesh and the bone, and reaching the grooves of her soul inside her heart of hearts.

Bodour took her car and went to see her psychiatrist who had become her only friend. She paid him a hundred and fifty pounds for half an hour, at the rate of five pounds a minute. If she stayed with him for ten minutes, she would pay fifty pounds. If he took her in his arms and the visit continued for an hour or an hour and a half, the payment would be larger because he would be working harder. He would be using not only his body and heart, but his words and conversation as well. The minute of conversation was worth five pounds, but the minute of platonic love was worth seven and a half. One minute of un-platonic love, in contrast, was worth ten. The psychiatrist didn't feel any embarrassment when she placed a stack of banknotes in his hands.

"This is my profession, Bodour, like your literary criticism. Do you feel embarrassed to receive your salary every month? Do you feel embarrassed to be paid five hundred pounds for an article? I ease people's suffering and alleviate the pains of the body, the heart, the mind, and the soul. There's no difference between physical and spiritual pain. And why is spiritual love more sublime than bodily love? This is my profession and this is how I earn my living in a legitimate manner that God has made permissible for me."

"He has made it permissible for you to have four wives, doctor, hasn't He?"

"No, Bodour. I'm not one of those men. I have just one wife and I love her and am faithful to her. When I do these things in the clinic, I'm not being unfaithful to her. It's just part of my job."

"I don't understand you, doctor."

"Any profession follows a code of honor. And all professions are honorable as long as you don't harm others. When I take you in my arms, I harm no one. At the same time I'm easing your pain and curing you of your sadness."

"What is the difference, then, between psychiatry and prostitution?"

"Nothing. I have more respect for prostitutes than for husbands and wives who lie to one another. Lying is the only shameful act, in my view. My wife knows everything about me and I about her."

"Don't you believe in God, doctor?"

"God for me is sincerity and nothing else."

"Don't you believe that God has already decided our fate and has written it on our foreheads?"

The psychiatrist raised his palm to wipe his forehead and laughed. "If anything has been written on my forehead, I can wipe it clean and write what I want."

"May God forgive us all, doctor. This is heresy."

"Have you joined your cousin Ahmed al-Damhiri's group then?"

"No, doctor. I don't agree with his views. But I need God."

"What do you need Him for?"

"Because He helps me stand up to those who oppress me and treat me unfairly."

"Who's treating you unfairly?"

"Everyone who has control over me, starting from the Dean of the Faculty at the university to my husband at home."

"And what should God do to them?"

"It's nothing, doctor. But ... But ..."

"But what, Doctor Bodour?"

"But God will burn them in hell in the next world."

"No, no, Bodour. I think your psychological state is getting worse and not better. You were better a month ago. You need new electric shock sessions."

"No, no, doctor, anything but electric shock therapy. I'm ready for anything, including apostasy, but don't apply electricity to my brain, doctor."

"Do you know what your problem is, Bodour?"

"Yes, doctor?"

"Your life has been too easy. Your parents deprived you of challenge."

"Yes, I had everything. My parents deprived me of deprivation."

"It's not fair. God will never forgive them."

"You mean you now believe in God?"

"It's a slip of the tongue, Bodour. Excuse me, but your time is up. I have to close the clinic and go back to my wife and kids."

The black cloud hung over the city from north to south, making the day indistinguishable from the night. Bodour al-Damhiri lay in bed, a faint ray of light falling on her closed eyelids. It crept over her face and neck, entered underneath her nightgown, and reached her upper abdomen. Hearing the sound of thunder, she awoke with a start. She had no idea what time it was. She called Nanny Zeinat, who came into the bedroom carrying a silver tray with a silver teapot and a silver spoon. Bodour smelled the tea and took a bite from the mouth-watering cake coated with sugar and a piece of jam with butter.

"Is it thunder or canon shots celebrating the feast, Zeinat?"

"No, Miss Bodour, these are the sounds of demonstrations."

Bodour jumped to her small, fleshy feet. She placed them in her blue slippers topped with balls of white fur. She tottered to the window, followed by Zeinat wearing her white rubber shoes. Zeinat reached with her thin, dark hand to the window and opened it. The sound rushed inside the room along with the powerful winds, shaking the whole house. Thousands, millions of people, women, men, youngsters, children marched in lines, carrying placards, their cheers reaching the high heavens: "Down with the regime. Down with the king and the English".

Bodour closed her eyes and her body was all a-tremble as the memories came back.

"Was it only a dream? Was it something that happened to another woman?"

Bodour was nineteen, marching steadily and strongly toward love and freedom. Love and freedom were embodied in one person who walked by her side during demonstrations. His name was Nessim, or Naim, or something else, for names changed with the passage of time. The cheers also changed. Instead of "Down with the king and the English", the slogans became "Down with America and the president", "Freedom or death" and "Long live free Egypt".

The cheers rose higher and came closer to her. The voices of thousands of people on the street were shouting the slogans:

The cost of bread is higher,
Our homes are on fire.
Sugar and oil are dearer
And we've become cheaper.

The cheers thundered, rising and falling like the cascading rumble of a waterfall. Bodies fell on the ground, rose up again, and fell once more. She walked among them, kicking the earth, carried by the human stream that seemed to pour into the sea. A huge wave lifted her from the ground. The closer she was to the center, the more tightly squeezed she felt. She merged with the crowd and disappeared completely, only to be born again. She had become just a part of the whole and her voice melted into the voices of the crowd. She was overtaken by a strong sensation of pleasure akin to sex. Although she walked and walked and walked, she didn't feel tired in the least. Her body was no longer short or plump, but tall and graceful, dancing with agility to the rhythm. Then silence descended as suddenly as the outbreak of thunder, and the streets were emptied of people. Police cars moved hurriedly everywhere, but she stood still, her back against the wall. He stood in front of her, his long, strong arms stretched toward her. They stretched from his wide chest covered with a white vest made of cotton, and a red liquid the color of blood flowed toward her. She reached for his hand, but the distance grew larger and larger. He smiled to her from a distance before disappearing. She saw his back as he walked with his head held high. Children came to him from the alleys and narrow streets, surrounding him in a circle and chanting, "You've come to bring us light, oh Nile cotton, how lovely you are! Come on, girls of the Nile, collect the matchless cotton, God's gift!"

Bodour woke from her reveries to hear the voice of Zeinat offering her a cup of tea.

"Have your tea, Miss Bodour, before it gets cold."

"I don't feel like it, Nanny. I have no appetite."

"Why do you look so pale, Miss Bodour?"

"I have a cold."

"You must have gone on the demonstrations. This is too dangerous, Miss Bodour."

"Please don't tell Mum and Dad."

"I would never do that."

"Please don't tell them, Nanny."

"I would never tell, Miss Bodour. You're very precious to me. But demonstrations are dangerous for you, Miss Bodour. The police took my son, Nessim. They took him in his underwear. They took a lot of youngsters, all poor people who have nobody to speak for them. They shot them dead."

Zeinat swallowed her tears.

"Oh, son, are you dead or alive? Are they torturing you, like people say? If God existed, Miss Bodour, would this have happened? May God forgive me for my transgressions! Forgive me, oh Lord, for my torment is great, and have mercy on my son."

Zeinat wiped her eyes with the sleeve of her wide gown. Bodour put her arms around her and cried. They consoled one another.

"I wish I could die, Nanny Zeinat."

"May God keep you from all harm, Miss Bodour."

"Death is better than this kind of life, Nanny."

"You're still young, Miss Bodour. You're hardly nineteen and God has given you plenty. You will graduate from university and become a great professor, the great Dr Bodour al-Damhiri."

"It's all dark in front of my eyes, Nanny. I'm afraid ..."

"Afraid of what, Miss Bodour?"

"Afraid my mum and dad might find out what happened."

"What happened, Miss Bodour?"

"Nothing happened, Nanny. Nothing."

"If nothing happened, why are you afraid?"

"I'm afraid they might find out I went on a demonstration."

"Many people go on demonstrations, Miss Bodour."

"But I went with one of my colleagues on the demonstration."

"You walked together? There's nothing to it! Demonstrations are not shameful. On the contrary, they are an honor. I went on many demonstrations with workers and farmers."

"Yes, Nanny, but after the demonstration, I went with my colleague ..."

"Where did you go, Miss Bodour?"

"To his home."

"His home?"

"Yes, Nanny ..."

"And did anything happen in his home?"

"Yes, Nanny ..."

Bodour wept on her nanny's chest as she told her the story, her body shaking violently and Nanny rocking her like a mother, embracing her, stroking her hair.

"Tell me, child, what happened."

"Promise you won't tell anyone? Not Mum or Dad?"

"May God strike me dead if I do, Miss Bodour! You're very precious to me, as precious as my son, Nessim. Oh, my dear son, are you dead or alive?"

It was midday on Friday many years later. Horns and loudspeakers were as wide open as the mouth of hell. Though hidden behind the black cloud, the sun radiated scorching heat and sweat. A woman hiding behind her black cloak walked in her pointed shoes on the melting asphalt of the street, panting and hissing. As she walked, she created holes in the sticky mud. She feared slipping on the sticky ground because if she did, everyone would be upon her, tearing her apart. The children would shout at her, "The bull is down, out with the knife."

The world around her shouted through the loudspeakers, "God is great. God is great ..."

Even stray cats meowed, reiterating the words "God is great". Every day, from dawn till dusk, she heard all the sounds coming from the loudspeakers as she kneeled in supplication on the ground with others.

She wondered as she walked: can the whole world, with its men, women and cats, be mad, and I'm the only one who's sane?

On a high wall the words "God guides whom He wills and leaves astray whom He wills" were written.

This principle was her only refuge, for if going astray was God's will, then she was innocent.

The streets were swarming with people, all dressed up for celebration, for the Great Feast which happened to coincide with Christmas. The Great Feast celebrated the sacrifice of a lamb instead of Ismail or Isaac. Their father, the Prophet Ibrahim, respecting the wishes of his wife Sara, Isaac's mother, abandoned his other wife Hagar, Ismail's mother, in the desert. He received God's command to slaughter his son. The son to be offered for slaughter is Ismail, according to the story in the Qur'an, and Isaac, according to the Bible. Nobody really knows which one of the two he was supposed to slaughter. Ibrahim himself probably didn't know, for the Qur'an hadn't been revealed when Prophet Ibrahim was alive. Otherwise, he might have had to kill the two sons in obedience to the two Holy Books, which, together with the Torah, were sent to guide and enlighten people.

It was a dark, overcast morning, the black cloud covering the Cairo sky as usual. Church bells competed with mosque loudspeakers for the dominance of the acoustic airspace. Children played with firecrackers and paraded in their new clothes in front of their peers. With their sturdy leather shoes they kicked the asphalt of the street, made fun of the lame child, and showered him with stones. He ran to escape them, but they chased him until he fell on the ground. They chanted and danced around him, "The bull is down, out with the knife."

A veiled girl happened to be walking by at this particular moment. In the congestion, she collided with a Coptic boy. He apologized and went on his way. But a Muslim man stopped him and slapped him on the face. The boy retaliated with a slap. A row ensued and turned into a full-blown massacre. The church in the neighborhood was burned and many young Muslim and Coptic people died.

The police were ordered not to interfere until the two factions had finished off each other. Then the armored vehicles and the fire brigade arrived. They surrounded the church and the mosque. Many people were arrested and shoved into police vehicles like sardines in cans. They were transported to God only knew where.

Before going out in the morning, Bodour prepared her suitcase. It was greyish blue and moved on wheels. She put in it all she needed for a long trip. But before that, she sat on the edge of the bed thinking about what she should take with her. Her eyes roamed around the bedroom, looking at the large beechwood wardrobe with decorative patterns, the light blue silk curtains on the window, the wide bed she'd shared with her husband since her wedding day, one night after another, one year following another, for thirty, forty, perhaps a hundred years. More than a hundred years passed from birth to death. How many times had she been born and died, been born again and died? She noticed the grey silk pyjamas on a hanger beside the wardrobe. Her husband had taken them off before he went to his office at the newspaper. The pyjamas took the shape of his sagging and flabby body and shook a little with the breeze. The upper part of the suspended bottoms was unbuttoned, revealing the shrunken piece of flesh which was as small as a little mouse ...

Her eyes were wide with astonishment. It was beyond her comprehension why this small piece of flesh had such devastating power and importance. States and religions were built on it. History carried it as a banner and marched with it since time immemorial. It was this piece of flesh that placed women in the jail of serfdom and humiliated men. It led elderly men to rape little girls, and pious men to lose two thirds of their minds when it was aroused. This piece of flesh deprived three million children in a single country of their human rights. Born on the streets, they lived and died there. The little shrunken mouse between the thighs pronounced the verdict of untimely death on millions of girls. It took away their joy and their smile and their hope and the dreams of their childhood. This little mouse swallowed Viagra in the darkness of the night in the hope of being resurrected and reborn once again.

There was a yellow stain that smelled of urine or blood on the silk pyjama bottoms. It might have been the result of a testectomy or the pale colored liquid filled with sperm, which males called the elixir of life. It smelled of death, or the pungent putrid stink of sulphuric acid. Women head over heels in love or dreaming of illusory happiness didn't find this smell offensive.

Bodour accepted the love and the smell, hoping for freedom. She lived and died in one passing instant. Then the blindfolds were removed and she opened her eyes to confront the sadness and the truth.

In the open suitcase she placed the old cotton dress she had worn on the day of the great demonstration. There was an old blood stain on the back of the dress, which was the result of the brief moment of love, the fleeting moment that was worth her whole life. It was a real moment that destroyed all reality and transported her to her death. On the front there was another stain, which happened when he reached out for her with his bleeding arm and the blood spilled on his white vest. She reached for her baby on the pavement and placed her inside the suitcase, beside her cotton dress. She took the yellow folder containing her novel and the stacks of written and blank pages from the desk and put them in the suitcase. She didn't know how many pages there were, but they were all drenched in her sweat, exhaustion, and sleeplessness. The tears had dried and hardened into the shape of a black scrawl similar to the handwriting of primary school children. A tremor passed from the papers to her fingers, her arms, her whole body. The smell of ink in her nostrils was like the smell of death or the smell of the marital bed.

"Does a person feel death coming before dying?"

Badreya peered inquisitively from the pages, looking her straight in the eyes. Badreya spoke to her all the time, her voice filling the house and her presence filling the universe. She comforted her, eased her pain, and dispelled the solitude and the silence. They quarrelled and made up, then quarrelled and made up again. They couldn't live without one another. Bodour noticed some of the lines written by Badreya. They were written in a large, straight, adult hand.

"Sorrows come, Bodour, we don't know where from or when. They hit us unexpectedly and we feel the pain in our chest, under our ribs, and in our head. We blame ourselves for sins we haven't committed, words we haven't written, sounds we haven't produced, or a heartbeat we haven't realized existed. Sorrows are harder than death. After a funeral, even when it is the funeral of a parent or somebody dearer, we wake up the next day, drink our tea and eat our breakfast as usual. We read the papers and the magazines, go to work, and come back home as usual. Dreams return to us at night and we have sex as usual. We do all this with the ease and familiarity of walking on our own two feet, as usual, as usual.

"But sorrows are something else, for they sever us from reality. This is when the wheels of life grind to a halt. Food loses its taste and falls in the stomach like a piece of rock. The taste of the water changes also, as does the smell of the air. Our faces look so different in the mirror that we hardly recognize ourselves. Sorrows don't come at once, but in waves and intermittent currents. Sorrow is a sudden realization of death and a sudden rejection of life. The knees shake, the eyes become blurred, the rituals of everyday life become absurd and the brain cells tremble. The waves of sorrow are like fleeting waves of light that make the body as light as a feather. They enable the body to soar in the sky of happiness before it grows heavier and heavier with sorrow and finally falls down like a log."

Bodour al-Damhiri sat on the edge of the bed, her suitcase open beside her. Her facial muscles contracted imperceptibly. She felt a pang in her throat and her mouth felt dry, although she wasn't thirsty. She was suffocating as though there was no oxygen in the room. She was overtaken by the desire to sob, cry, and scream. But she could neither cry nor scream. There was dryness in her throat and underneath her eyelids, and there was silence and emptiness deep in her heart. She remained motionless for a long time, staring into thin air, drifting asleep with eyes wide open, moving from one dream to another, but never waking, getting up, or crying. Her tears dried up. Her vocal cords became paralyzed and she could no longer speak or scream. The cells of her brain had stopped, and the road to insanity lay open before her. It was a long trip into pre-natal darkness, where she was a foetus in the womb, surrounded by thick, impenetrable black water. Her eyes grew wider with shock. She could see the light and her own shock in the mirror. It was the shock of the naked eye watching itself, the shock of the dead watching their own death. Sorrow disappeared, lighting a dark corner of her brain.

Bodour al-Damhiri no longer feared separation, divorce, or death. She could carry her suitcase and go alone on her unknown and endless way. She withdrew herself from the eye of the universe and God's ever-watchful eye. It wasn't the withdrawal of despair or emptiness, but the acceptance of a rich, newly acquired loneliness. She used to think of loneliness as a punishment or a pain she should avoid, and not as a pleasure she should look forward to. Before leaving she asked Badreya, "Was it through loneliness that I left the world or went deeply into it?"

Seeing her dragging the suitcase behind her, Badreya whispered in a low voice, "Loneliness isn't a pleasure in itself, but it may create new pleasures. You may write a new novel or live a bigger love than your first stunted love. You may write using the first personal pronoun, I, instead of hiding behind another woman and using the third personal pronoun, she. You may abandon literary criticism and stop polishing other people's shoes, including those of your husband. You may begin to polish your own shoes and see your real self on the page. You may banish from your mind the babble of critics and their claim that the use of the first person has less value than the third person, as well as their contention that women's writings are weakened by overly concentrating on the self. Literary critics, Bodour, have lost the self and the truth. Whoever loses the self will lose others as well."

Bodour al-Damhiri opened the door. She dragged her suitcase behind her without looking back, without one word of goodbye to her past life. Her husband saw her walking toward the door, her back straight and her head held high. Gone was the old stoop never to return, for the clock could not move backwards, even if the laws of nature and of planetary movements were to change, even if time were to go backwards as some scientists had proposed. Bodour could not turn back. If fate interfered, she would stop it. She would wipe from her forehead all that had been written and recorded before her birth.

Her husband, Zakariah al-Khartiti, was standing in the hall when she opened the door to leave. Light fell on his face for a brief moment like a slap. The door was closed without a sound, without anger, without sorrow or regret. It was as though the long years they spent sharing the same bed were outside time, as though a hundred years were just a brief, transitory moment. It was as though Bodour al-Damhiri was another woman who was born the moment she opened the door and left. Her eyes were open for the first time in her life. She realized that fear, like inherited faith, was blind. If we opened our eyes, it would vanish like a drop of rain into the waters of the sea.

Her husband stood in the darkness, staring at the closed door. He wore his grey silk pyjamas which had become faded with time. His small, dark, sunken eyes took on the color of a white sheet. They withdrew beneath the lids for fear of confrontation, and tried to escape into sleep. But the sudden slap banished all sleep, although it woke up the other male lurking underneath the pyjamas, which said to him, "You were unfair to this woman. You lied and evaded and manipulated until the door was closed in your face. As men, we never retract unless women compel us to do so, but then it is too late. We never desire a woman we own. Our eyes are always in pursuit of the woman we don't. We don't realize a woman's worth until we've lost her. Something is rotten in the state of manhood, or perhaps in the law of marriage which gives the man the right to hold and control. As soon as he controls a woman, rot sets in. This is the history that was written before we were born, written by the gods, the prophets, the kings, and the pharaohs. We know this history inside out, from birth until death. We take it with our mothers' and fathers' milk, for the father's milk infiltrates into the mother's breasts, disguised by the innocent white color."

Zakariah al-Khartiti shook off the voice. He continued standing in the hall, staring at the door, recalling her image after she had left, remembering the first time he saw her. Although many years had passed, the first encounter remained engraved in his mind. That moment stayed like a piece of real time, as though a human life couldn't be counted with the number of years. He often heard her say, "One brief moment of life may be worth a whole lifetime." He used to laugh at her. He regarded her as a woman who was ignorant of the measurements of time, a woman who was deficient in reason and in faith, as his father and grandfather used to say, and as he read in the books of history and religion. During their first encounter, he told her, "I'm different from my father and grandfather, in fact from all men, for I don't believe in male gods."

But God and Satan had crept into his blood with his mother's breast milk, and had taken up permanent residence in his mind. There was no universe without gods and devils who, like other males, were obsessed with nothing but women.

He tottered barefoot. He hurried a little to get to the bathroom, for the urge to relieve himself had become more urgent with the years. The smell of his urine was more pungent than before and he moved his nose away from the source of the smell. He used not to feel disgusted at the smell of his own urine or sweat, and nor was he repelled by the sight of wrinkles around his own eyes. But his wife's wrinkles and her bodily odors repulsed him. He saw her with his eyes wide open but couldn't see himself at all. His eyes, like those of the gods, saw only worship in people's eyes, and never directed their gaze toward themselves, because they felt that they were above and beyond all human senses.

Zakariah al-Khartiti sat at the breakfast table in his usual chair, drinking his coffee and reading his column in the paper. The column was still there, though a little shorter than before. His name was written in a smaller font size and his photograph didn't appear within the usual frame at the top of the column.

The earth shook underneath his feet. The heavens also trembled as though the pillars in the air holding the sky had collapsed, as God said in his Holy Books, "Could the pillars of heaven collapse and fall on earth? Could the dead rise from their graves on Doomsday? Could the living die on streets and in homes? Could the government fall and the throne move from underneath Pharaoh's buttocks? Could a new ruler and a new god appear, wearing a turban instead of a tie, and carrying the black prayer mark on his forehead and a yellow rosary in his hand? Would he carry the sword in his right hand instead of the gun, and in his left hand God's Holy Book instead of the constitution? Has Egypt become another Afghanistan ruled by the Taliban?"

Zakariah al-Khartiti jumped out of bed. He rubbed his eyes and saw his column in the paper as long and graceful as it used to be and on the right side of the paper. His photograph was inside the old frame. Everything was in order and the heavens still stood on their pillars in the air.

But the seat in front of him was empty. Where had Bodour gone? She might be in the bathroom or in her study writing her novel. She might have gone to the university, to her friend Safi or to her daughter Mageeda. On the cover of the *Renaissance* magazine he saw the picture of his daughter, Mageeda al-Khartiti, with her head wrapped in a white scarf. Her article stood next to the articles of great writers. It had the title "Women in Islam" by the great writer Mageeda al-Khartiti.

His daughter had become an Islamist writer. A presidential decree awarded her a seat at the elected Higher Journalism

Council. It made little difference whether the seat at a higher council was secured by appointment or election. A decree had to ratify both types of seats issued by the one and only authority in the land. The decree was often unwritten, but sometimes it was written in invisible ink, like the death lists, the lists of the righteous destined for paradise, and the lists of infidels and disbelievers who followed in the footsteps of the Devil and Eve and the Serpent. The names on the death list were published in a small font size on the accidents and crimes page. There were forty-four names, including four women and forty men, like Ali Baba and the forty thieves. They were all accused of violating religious and state laws, of making lawful what was prohibited by God, and of prohibiting what was permissible by God. There was little doubt that they deserved death, according to God's canon and the emir's.

His eyes fell by chance on the name of Zeina Bint Zeinat below a photograph showing her as a street child, her black hair dishevelled and in wiry spikes. She was holding her lute as though she were embracing Satan, and was singing and dancing with her mouth wide open, revealing her tonsils. Her bare feet walked steadily on the ground and her face was long and pale like the faces of the dead, or of women of dubious character in brothels and whore houses.

He moved his eyes away from her picture, from the large eyes burning with a bluish black flame. He quivered deep inside to see those eyes, but he banished them with his head, hands, arms, and legs. He wanted to gouge those eyes out, to crush that lean body with his own hands, to dig his nails into the flesh until they reached the bones. In his memory was a nightmare that came to him almost in a dream, an accident that happened outside his conscious mind. The pain crept from the belly to the Devilish gland underneath the pubic hair. In his prayers, he beseeched God for forgiveness. During his visit to the Holy Places, he walked around the Kaaba, kissing the black stone with his lips and hurling stones at Satan with his hands. He came back cleansed of his sins like a newborn babe, for God forgave all transgressions except the sin of worshipping other gods. Zakariah was a strong believer, who had faith in the one and only God. He was not an infidel who worshipped other gods like those who believed that Christ was God, or the son of God, or who went to sleep listening to the sound of music and dancing instead of the recitation of the Qur'an.

At the bottom of the accidents and crimes page, a piece of news was published along with the picture of Mohamed Ahmed. His hair was dishevelled like a madman and his cheek was scarred like hardened criminals. His eyes were half closed and he looked unconscious:

> The journalist Mohamed Ahmed stood before the Public Prosecutor on charges of contempt for religion and violation of public order and God's law. This obscure journalist tried to attract the limelight by joining the opposition. He had suspicious relations with the West. He frequented nightclubs and attended dancing and singing performances. He published articles in the *Thawra* opposition paper, an illegal publication that did not get the approval of the State Higher Council, which issued a ruling to close it and confiscate the last issues. It ruled that its funds be transferred to the Islamic Society for Charity and Piety, to be used in feeding the needy and offering free meals during the month of Ramadan.

Mohamed sat on a small wooden stool in a basement room. He was in his underwear, and the deep cut on his left cheek was bleeding. Around him were men carrying whips that squirmed like snakes. Their eyes were looking in the direction of their boss, who carried the title of investigator, judge, or prince and occupied the position of minister, court deputy, or head. His voice rang high and majestic in contrast with his short, plump body. His soft white hands held a newspaper clipping.

"Your full name?"

"Mohamed Mohamed Ahmed."

"A Muslim?"

"Yes."

"Do you believe in the one and only God?"

"Yes."

"Did you write this article?"

"Yes."

The investigator stared at the face of the young man but did not see the blood on the left cheek. His narrow, sunken eyes were raised to the ceiling, toward God in the sky beyond. His two small pupils trembled within the white eyeballs, and the look in his eyes was cold and hollow. The pupils seemed to be made of glass or plastic. A strong electric light made up of four lamps was directed at the young man sitting on the backless stool. He tried to keep his back straight and his eyes open. He struggled to stay alert by concentrating on the investigator's face.

The investigation continued throughout the day and part of the night, without any intervals except for a few minutes, when the investigator went to the toilet, drank water, or ate lunch or dinner. The young man did not move from his chair. He had to hold his urine and keep the blood inside the wound while being hammered by one question after another.

"Haven't you read the religious ruling that music, dancing, and singing are the works of the Devil? How can you defend an illegitimate, fallen woman from the streets in your article?"

"Zeina Bint Zeinat is a great artist. People love her and feel happy to attend her performances to listen to her. Beautiful art comes from God because God is beauty."

"You know nothing about God, so how can you talk about Him? You're misleading people. You say that building schools and universities is more important than building mosques and churches. Did you say that?"

"Yes."

"Aren't you misinforming people and leading them away from Islam?"

"Islam is based on reason, and everything that builds the mind and knowledge is part of Islam."

"Did you say that washing the dead is an old custom that has nothing to do with religion? Did you say that?"

"Yes."

"Are you against cleanliness, then? Don't you know that cleanliness is godly and dirtiness is womanly?"

"Cleanliness needs soap and clean, running water. Most of the living have neither soap nor water. How can we wash the dead while the living cannot take baths? The dead body will be eaten by worms and dust, so what is the point of washing it?"

"Are you arguing with me? Don't you know that your article is controversial and can incite conflicts and tensions?"

"Arguments lead to knowledge and understanding and not to tensions."

"You're against the veiling of women and you claim that it is not connected with religion or morality. Aren't you going against God's precepts in this way? Don't you know that a woman's face is prohibited because a woman's beauty can lead to temptations and conflicts?"

"Women are not the cause of conflicts. There are other causes, such as religion, injustice, corruption, and lies."

"This is heresy. How can you say this kind of thing? You deserve to die."

"But before I die, I want to express my views. We inherit religion from our fathers and grandfathers. Our ethical conduct depends on awareness and conscience, and not on religion. Some priests and sheikhs rape children and embezzle money. There are women and men who believe in no religion, but they have integrity and fight for truth. They would die defending justice and freedom. Music lifts the spirit and revives the conscience. It never causes rifts or wars. Religions cause sectarian tensions and pogroms. There is no connection between justice and religion, for justice can exist in a world without religion. There is also no connection between morality and religion, for there are people who have no religion but act in a perfectly moral manner. Religion in fact has double or triple standards as far as values and ethics are concerned, a standard for men and another for women, a standard for the ruler and another for the subjects, the slaves, the hired hands, and the poor. I'm tired, really tired ... exhausted. I wish you would end my suffering. Hell is here on this earth and not after death. When I die I will be free from your torture and at peace. There's no hell in death or after it!"

"Do you wish me to record all this heresy in the investigation?"

"Yes."

"This is another document against you to be added to your article. Are you seeking death?"

"Yes. Death is better than living in a world where a person is killed only because he expresses his opinions in an article, because he loves music, poetry, and beauty, or because he exposes injustice, hypocrisy, and corruption, hiding behind the cloak of God's name. I know that you will assassinate me either openly or in secret. You've put my name on the death list. But who are you to pass a death or a life sentence on people? Who are you exactly? You're a group of mercenaries, hired by the governments inside and outside, trained for killing in the wilderness of Afghanistan. You receive money and arms, swap women, slave girls, and concubines. You let your beards grow until they cover your faces, but your heads are empty."

"Shut up!"

"I'll say all I want before I die. You have no conscience, no morality, and no religion ... You are ... the age of darkness and disintegration ..."

Before he finished his sentence, he was shot in the chest. Seven successive bullets were fired at him. Three of them lodged in his chest, one pierced his heart, and another penetrated his forehead and came out through the back of his head. Splinters of his brain were scattered across the floor. They trampled on the pieces with their heels and the butts of their rifles. They wanted to destroy his mind because their world was built on the elimination of human reason.

The following day, demonstrators marched, shouting his name and carrying his picture on placards and slogans over their heads. Among the demonstrators were men, women, youngsters, children, workers, students, low-ranking government officials, children born on the streets, Mohamed's colleagues at the opposition paper, obscure men and women artists, Mariam's music band, men and women thinkers whose names were on the death list, wives, divorced women, deserted lovers, girls raped by elderly men and carrying their little children, peasant women selling watercress and radishes, servants, secretaries, prostitutes, elderly people walking with crutches, lame children and stray limping cats and dogs, meowing and howling and shouting with the people. The cheers rose high and shook the earth and the sky with the slogans:

> We don't need religion,
> Better give us a pigeon.
> Of prayers and fasting we've had enough,
> Better give us some foodstuff.
> We don't want the rosary bead,
> We need bread indeed.
> Enough mosques and churches,
> We need schools and researches.

Police sirens blared out and policemen were ready with rifles, batons, water hoses, and tear gas. People marched side by side like a huge barricade to fend off the attack and ward off the bullets. Loudspeakers and bells were heard together with the whistling and the beating of drums.

Armored vehicles ran over the bodies of children and cats. The children got up from underneath the wheels to receive the bullets with their naked chests. The cats also fought with them, fell down and rose up again. If cats had seven lives, how many did human beings have? Those children lived and died a hundred times over. Life for them was like death, and death resembled life.

Zeina Bint Zeinat walked among the crowds playing her lute. She held it like a baby in its mother's arms. Her long fingers moved over the lute strings with the speed of lightning as they did over the piano keys. The lute was closer to her heart than the piano, for she carried it in her arms and rocked it at night before she went to sleep. She held it beneath her ribs to keep it safe from the thieves and the police. It lay in her arms throughout the night. She wrapped it in a leather case to protect it from the cold, the heat, the little stones and pebbles. Children gathered around her and she trained them to play music. They shared the pavement, the love of music and singing, and the lute. They played music spontaneously, without learning to read notes. They sang when the white cotton buds blossomed and when the golden ears of wheat gleamed in the sun. Without a family to provide for them, they slept on the pavement. Music compensated them a little for the absence of family, eased their pains and sorrows, and lifted their spirits high. It healed their bodies and comforted the pain in their breasts. They slept listening to the sound of music and the voice of Zeina Bint Zeinat singing for them. In their dreams they chanted the songs of the revolution:

"Down with injustice, long live freedom."

"Oh my land, you have all my love."

"You've come to bring us light, oh Nile cotton, how lovely you are!"

"Here's the wheat on its feast, may God bless it!"

She stood in the spotlight on stage before the shots were fired. Her two large eyes were two blue volcanic rocks, two dark blue flames. Their color changed with the movement of the earth around the sun, bluish black like the color of the earth and the sky, surrounded by the transparent whiteness of the waves gleaming in the sun or the high mountaintops beyond the sea.

She looked older than her real age by a hundred years, for she had known life and death, God and Satan, and was no longer afraid of them. Her face shone brightly as she smiled. Her childlike smile dissipated the darkness like the rays of the sun. She hugged her lute, and her long, sturdy fingers moved over the strings with the speed of electricity. They were as strong and hard and pointed as nails. Nobody could attack her or attempt to rape her, for she would dig those nails into the neck of any attacker. She played the rhythmic tune, singing with the children the first song she sang for her mother when she was a child:

I dream of building my mother a house
Made of red brick,
Not of mud,
A house she owns,
A house no one can take away from her.
It has a ceiling to protect her from summer's heat
And winter's cold,
A bathroom with running water
And an electric lamp.

Her mother, Zeinat, wiped her face with a white handkerchief.

She held her tears deep in her eyes. Next to her sat Mageeda al-Khartiti, sobbing silently.

Her mother's friend, Safi, whispered in her ear, "Did you hear the shots?"

"It's the sound of clapping, Auntie Safi."

"It's bullets, Mageeda."

"No, Auntie. Zeina is singing, listen to her."

The sound of clapping drowned the sound of bullets. Zeina Bint Zeinat stood on stage, erect and graceful, hugging her lute. Her eyes met those of her mother, Zeinat, for whom she sang the model mother song when she was a school girl:

> I came from this earth and to it I return.
> I have not descended from space,
> I am not the daughter of gods or devils,
> I am Zeina and my mother is Zeinat.
> My mother is dearer to me than the sky.
> I have known falling and rising,
> I fall and rise, and fall and rise,
> I die and rise again,
> Hugging my lute.

She wore her white dress made of cotton. Blood-red lines started leaking from her chest. Her voice rose higher as she sang and danced to the tune. The audience clapped thunderously and shouted, "Encore, encore, encore ... sing 'I Dream' ... again, Zeina, again."

She started singing again:

> "I dream of building my mother a house ..."

People sang with her, the whole auditorium sang with her, men, women, and children, and they danced to her tune.

"You've come to bring us light, oh Nile cotton, how lovely you are!"

She bled from the chest as she stood singing and playing music, people around her singing and dancing. They carried her over their shoulders, chanting, "Long live Zeina Bint Zeinat, long live Zeina Bint Zeinat, long live freedom, long live freedom, long live love, long live love, long live music, long live music, long live beauty and justice and virtue, long live love and art and beauty and justice and virtue, long live Zeina Bint Zeinat."

Bodour was walking when she heard the sounds of hundreds, thousands, millions cheering and chanting.

Bodour walked, dragging her suitcase behind her. The black cloud covered the whole sky, obscuring the sun and the moon. She couldn't tell whether it was day or night. She walked on and on, following an endless road, until her feet were swollen. She sat on a wooden bench on the Nile front and took off her tight leather shoes with their high pointed heels. She removed the brassiere pressing into her chest and the hairpins and the gold bracelets and the rings studded with stones. She broke the chains that kept her in shackles from head to toe. Her flesh and bones were released from captivity, and the reins restraining her were loosed. She let her body swim freely on the bench which was as long as a boat. She heard a whisper in her heart saying, "I am neither a wife nor a widow and I shall not grieve, like Babylon, the whore in the Bible."

Inside her suitcase, which she placed under the wooden bench, was a yellow folder containing her novel. There was also her old white cotton dress, with the dry blood stain and the tears and the sweat that had never dried. Through her half-closed eyes she glimpsed a phantom dressed in mourning and walking, her back stooped and her white rubber shoes the color of dust. She held a black plastic bag in her hand. Her dark face was pale and she was out of breath. She sat on the pavement, opened the bag and a swarm of street children and newborn kittens, gathered around her, sniffing the bread inside the bag. These were the leftovers from well-to-do families: pieces of meat, bones, and rice. Zeinat collected them from the garbage and put them in a bag every day and walked along the Nile front. If she didn't find a bag, she used a newspaper to wrap the crusts of bread. She recognized the framed photographs published in the paper. The eyes were pierced by a fish bone or a chewed meat bone. On the front page was the picture of the president and the first lady. Their faces were stained with tomato sauce and reeked of onion and garlic and dried *bastourma*. On the second page was the picture of Zakariah al-Khartiti, whom she addressed as sir. His nose was slashed and his long column was soaked in chicken soup. The ink ran on the paper and the words were covered with a black liquid that looked like mercury or tar.

Zeinat sat on the pavement surrounded by stray cats, dogs, and children. Their eyes glimmered as they devoured the leftovers. They chewed the remains of meat and bones with their strong teeth, and munched the dry bones and bread. She called one of the children Nessim, like her son. Her son's eyes twinkled and his large pupils sparkled like the sun when she offered him a glass of fresh milk and an egg fried in butter. The gleam intensified when he smelled the plate. He was eight then, going to school and shouting with other demonstrators, "Down with injustice, long live freedom".

They called her "mother" and carried her name Zeinat. According to religious and secular laws, a mother's name brought disgrace to her children. The little kittens called her Zeinat, and their eyes sparkled when they smiled. A little girl with large kitten eyes filled with wonder and joy was called Zeina Bint Zeinat. Her two black pupils were surrounded by a blue circle and snow whiteness all around. She woke up with the lark singing, "Mum is coming back, coming soon, coming with a gift ..."

Her mother left her on the pavement, withdrew her hands

from the little fingers and whispered, "I'm coming back, dear child, coming back, coming back. Mum is coming back, coming soon ..."

Bodour struggled to open her eyes and arise from sleep. She saw Nanny Zeinat sitting beside her on the wooden bench, singing to her child, "Mum is coming back, coming soon, coming with a gift ..."

The sound of her singing was drowned by the thousands, millions of voices coming from afar, all singing the mother song. The singing rose to shake the earth and sky.

"Is that the sound of thunder, Nanny Zeinat?"

"No, Miss Bodour. It's demonstrations. Get out of bed. Everybody is wide awake, Naim, Nessim, Badreya, Mohamed, Mageeda, Safi, Mariam, and Zeina. Everybody. Even the newborn kittens, Miss Bodour, are demonstrating and saying, 'Long live justice.'"

"Can cats speak, Nanny Zeinat?"

"Yes, child. It's a different world now, and the blind kittens have opened their eyes and can speak."

Bodour stretched her limbs and reached under the bench for her suitcase. It was a sturdy suitcase made of expensive leather. It had been bulging with the pages of the novel, hundreds of papers written with blood, tears, sweat, and exhaustion. Hundreds of evenings and nights were spent writing it. The suitcase had been pregnant with the papers when she placed it under the wooden bench before she fell asleep. She now felt its roundness, pressed on it with her palm, and reached down to the bottom. Between the upper lid and the bottom there was absolutely nothing, only a terrifying emptiness like death. She reached again into the emptiness and almost fainted. She tried to scream out, "My novel has been stolen. Oh my God, it has been stolen while I was asleep!"

Her voice came out raucous, hoarse as though in a dream. People gathered around her asking, "Who has stolen it, ma'am?"

"I don't know. It was in the suitcase. They took the novel from the suitcase while I was sleeping."

"But who stole it, ma'am?"

"I don't know. Perhaps the police. I don't really know. Perhaps the thieves."

"You mean the police are the thieves?"

"Perhaps somebody else other than the police and the thieves."

"Somebody else? Do you know his name? Do you know what he looks like?"

"I don't know. I don't know. My novel is gone, people. My life's work is all gone."

Bodour turned around, completely stupefied. The sun set and the darkness fell while she was still turning, surveying the earth and the sky with her open eyes in the darkness. She crawled on the pavement, searching, reaching with her hand under the wooden bench on the Nile front, feeling the pebbles and the stones, sifting the sand with her hands. The dust leaked through her fingers like water seeping out of a sieve, leaving nothing in her hands. She tripped over a bundle wrapped in a newspaper. She opened the bundle but found nothing but her husband's long column, squirming like a snake, covered with mud and the stools of stray dogs. She wore her glasses and with difficulty managed to read the writing in the faint light:

On behalf of two million illegitimate children, a number of members of parliament who are also mothers presented a new legislation proposal to the People's Assembly and the Consultative Council which will allow children with unknown fathers to carry the names of their mothers. The new legislation also called for the abolition of the words 'illegitimate' and 'children of sin' from dictionaries, and of awarding the mother's name the same honor as that of the father. This proposal, dear readers, was rejected wholly and completely by the two esteemed chambers. It was rejected by women and men alike because it encourages moral disintegration and sexual freedom for women. The women presenting this proposal have been prosecuted on charges of violating the rules of our religion and breaching public order. But out of sympathy for the poor children who number more than two million, the governmental Higher Committee for the Care of Motherhood and Children presented another bill to the two chambers allowing illegitimate children to carry the names of any man. This man will be regarded as a virtual father to the child. The proposal only aims at safeguarding the rights of the poor innocent children. This bill has received the approval of the esteemed al-Azhar and the government. But the members of the two esteemed councils are currently examining the various legislative aspects, in view of the moral dangers involved in this type of legislation.

The committee had earlier presented a bill containing three articles:

1. Prosecuting men when there is proof of infidelity.
2. It is illegal for husbands to demand sexual relations by force.
3. A mother has the right to give her name to her child if the father is unknown.

Al-Azhar, however, refused this bill with its three articles wholesale, indicating that it contravenes the values of our Islamic society and our cultural heritage and traditions. It contradicts science and faith, because science affirms that justice is not absolute but relative and subject to the changing conditions of place and time. Nothing, in fact, is perfect or absolute except our faith in God Almighty.

Signed: Zakariah al-Khartiti
zakariah@yahoo.com

Bodour al-Damhiri was not dead yet. She lived the last days of her life with Nanny Zeinat in her basement room. She started writing a new novel. But her life was hard and didn't make it easy for her to write. She wasn't used to sleeping in an uncomfortable wooden bed and couldn't sit on the ground. She also couldn't sleep in a room swarming with cockroaches. Flies and mosquitoes buzzed around her ears all the time. Her bedroom in Garden City seemed to her like a lost and distant paradise.

She opened the paper one morning and read a news headline: "The new novel by the great writer Zakariah al-Khartiti is now on sale at the bookshop of the great newspaper on Tahrir Street. Reserve your copy now."

Bodour got up and ran to the street. She kept running, only stopping to catch her breath, and then continued running again. She saw the novel carrying the name of her husband. It was the same novel she had written with her own blood, sweat, and sleepless nights. The same novel, every word, every letter, every comma, every full stop, every dash. Her own novel was published everywhere under the name of the great writer, Zakariah al-Khartiti.

Bodour lay on the pavement, her body stretching under the blazing sun and the freezing cold. Her eyelids were half closed and her chest moved neither up nor down. Nothing stirred except her light cotton dress, moved by the breeze which lifted it up a little from the body lying on the pavement. Around her the street children sang, "Mum is coming back, coming soon, coming with a gift ..."

Also Available by **NAWAL EL SAADAWI**

Memoirs of a Woman Doctor

A young Egyptian woman clashes with her traditional family when she chooses a career in medicine. Rather than submit to an arranged marriage and motherhood, she cuts her hair short and works fiercely to realise her dreams. At medical school, she begins to understand the mysteries of the human body. After years of denying her own desires, the doctor begins a series of love affairs that allow her to explore her sexuality – on her own terms.

'El-Saadawi is a superb stylist. This short book, one of her finest achievements, is nakedly inspirational in the impact of its heroine's revolt' *Morning Star*

'This short book is not a gritty account of coping with the macho living as well as the naked, shrivelled dead. It is a powerfully written but simple account of an independent woman's search for identity in a traditional society' *British Medical Journal*

978 0 86356 610 3   £8.99

Love in the Kingdom of Oil

A woman disappears without trace. Nobody, including the police commissioner investigating the case, can understand how a woman could simply walk away, leaving husband and home behind. After all, in the Kingdom of Oil where His Majesty reigns supreme, no woman has ever dared disobey the command of men.

When the woman finally reappears, there is a blurring between the men in her life, as she leaves one to join another, then returns to her first husband who has since taken a new wife. She is trapped in a man-made web, unable to escape from a male figure who continually fills urns that she must carry.

'An intriguing novel about what it means to be unseen and seen.' *Life Lessons on Literature*

'An excellent surrealist mash: visceral, powerful, moving, occasionally very funny' *Goodreads*

978 0 86356 626 4   £8.99

Also Available by **NAWAL EL SAADAWI**

Two Women in One

Bahiah Shaheen is an eighteen-year-old medical student and daughter of a prominent Egyptian public official. She finds the male students in her class rough, coarse and alien. Her father, too, seems to belong to a race apart, and the Bahia has long ceased to be surprised at not being her real self in his presence. But what, she wonders, is this real self?

At an exhibition of some of her paintings, a stranger engages Bahiah in conversation. This proves to be the beginning of Bahiah's road to self-discovery as she abandons the life constructed for her.

Two Women in One tells the story of countless Middle Eastern women, their hopes and ambitions, and their quest for emancipation and dignity.

'These two women live, to some degree, in every thinking woman.' *New York Times Book Review*

'The story represents the lives of thousands of women but here it is also fiercely individual, thanks to Nawal El-Saadawi's spikily stylised treatment ... bitingly to the point' *New Statesman*

978 0 86356 562 5   £7.99

Also Available by **NAWAL EL SAADAWI**

The Fall of the Imam

Bint Allah knows herself only as the Daughter of God. Born in a stifling male-dominated state ruled by the Imam and his coterie of ministers, she dreams of one day reaching the top of a distant hill visible through the bars of the orphanage window.

But nothing escapes the attention of the Imam who is never satisfied no matter what he consumes, and who never feels secure no matter how well he protects himself. When the Imam falsely accuses Bint Allah of adultery and sentences her to death by stoning, he is not prepared for the unexpected repercussions that follow.

This powerful, poetic novel reveals the underlying hypocrisy of male-dominated religious states, and the insufferable predicament of women in a society that must ultimately self-destruct.

'Haunting and mesmerising ... a powerful and moving exposé of the horrors that women and children can be exposed to by the tenets of faith.' *New Humanist*

'A feminist fantasy narrative' *The International Fiction Review*

978 1 84659 062 7   £7.99

SAQI BOOKSHE/F

Saqi has been publishing innovative writers from the Middle East and beyond since 1983. Our new Saqi Bookshelf series brings together a curated list of the most dazzling works from this kaleidoscopic region, from bold, original voices and contemporary bestsellers, to modern classics. Begin collecting your Saqi Bookshelf and discover the world around the corner.

For more reading recommendations, new books and discounts, join the conversation here:

🐦 @SaqiBooks
📷 @SaqiBooks
📘 Saqi Books

www.saqibooks.com